OF DREAMS AND SHADOWS

THE EALDSPELL CYCLE BOOK 1

JESIKAH SUNDIN

FOREST TALES
PUBLISHING

Dystopian Fantasy and Faerie Tales

To all the women who are told they would be prettier if they smiled more. And to the all the men who are our allies.

WELCOME

KINGDOM OF EALDSPELL

Dear Reader,

Welcome to Ealdspell, a kingdom of standalone stories as old as time. A faerie kingdom hidden deep within a Druid's sacred oak tree, on a mere leaf. And welcome to OF DREAMS AND SHADOWS, my Celtic inspired *Sleeping Beauty* story set in a Victorian Industrial Revolution-esque world with high technology and faerie magic.

In case you were curious: the realms within Ealdspell each feature a completely different era in history with dystopian feels and light technology. They're also entirely influenced by Ireland, Scotland, Wales, England, Iceland, Norway, France, and Germany. The faerie tale lands of yore. And why some names and words may seem strange. I love Celtic, Anglo-Saxon, and Norse/Germanic names. *happy sighs*

While reading OF DREAMS AND SHADOWS, if you're unsure of how to pronounce a word or what a word may mean, merrily skip to the end of the book and enjoy the:

Page 240 . . . Glossary of Ealdspell Terms.

Though, here's a quick odd-pronunciation list for this story:

Aroreh – A-roar-uh
Brandu - Brawn-dew
Dalbréath – Dal-bray-ith
Dúnælven – Dune-al-ven
Ealdspell – Awld-spell
Éireanna – Air-ran-uh
Félip – Fay-lip
Líeh – Lee-uh
Rothlín – Roth-leen
Tylluan / Tyllie – Till-shwan / Till-ee

The rest should be easier to figure out. And, if not *gestures to cast of characters link above*

A few other goodies at the end of the book:

Grab your favorite drink and snack, put up your feet, and enjoy this gritty spin on the romantic tale of *Sleeping Beauty,* blending faerie magic and pagan rituals with high technology. Happy reading!

Erin Sea

8

Au

3

Dreglind

9

6

The Wilds

Avenbury

10

Le

9

Perla Tower

Merenna

FALDSPELL

Glensilien

Spired Hills

Ven

Clifstan

Dwarven Mines

Ærin Sea

Ærin Sea

N
W
E
S

HIDDEN LETTER

Day 17 of Fómhar, Year 634 K.E.

I yearn for the days of Éireanna. But I fear I made a grave, irreversible mistake. Dear reader, whomever finds these words, please listen carefully. I am no mere mortal. Nor is this a riddled tale I spin for my amusement.

My True Name is Rònan Ó Conell Macbeatha, a druid from the faerie line of Maebh and the human kings of Éireanna. Perhaps I am reckless in writing down my True Name for anyone to find. But I am already a prisoner of Mælfallyn, the Queen of the Sluagh, Queen of the Malfae, master rune shifter and spell weaver. She alone now determines my fate. A fate to blend my druidic lineage and runic technology with her elemental magic to create a faerie more powerful than she or I. This child will assuredly be weaponize to bend Ealdspell to her will. And since I have refused her hand in marriage—in

Éireanna before our civil war, before she had shadowed, and again a fortnight ago—it is only a matter of time before I am rune spelled to become her king consort.

There is no more of my kind. Before I created the Kingdom of Ealdspell, I was not only a prince but the last druid of Éireanna. Do not forget the land of our ancestors, dear reader. For we still belong to this faerie realm on Earth. Ealdspell is simply a world within this world.

But why, you ask? The land of humans is a polluted wasteland filled with warring machines. Nanotechnology is in everything— the air, the water, the trees, the people. These machines eventually seeped into Éireanna and poisoned faerie minds until many went mad with greed and cruelty. I needed to keep safe those who were not yet infected. I needed to protect what was left of our sacred lands. For if Éireanna falls, then all of Earth will fall too. And we need Earth's magic just as much as Earth needs ours. We are joined strands in an endless knot.

Rather than fight this cursed iron, I wove the language of circuitry and machines with fae elemental magic. Then I used this runic technology to not only create Ealdspell, but to sustain it. I entrusted the magic of Ealdspell with Gedlen Fate Maker and Gellynor Death Talker of the Dúnælven. They alone know where I have hidden the Kingdom of Ealdspell.

Or so I once thought.

I made a terrible mistake. A decision I can never take back. One Mælfallyn will never let me forget nor forgive. And so, I await her vengeance.

Forgive me, dear reader. I tried to protect faerie kind, as a halfling fae prince and human druid. But I have failed.

Burn this note, but do not forget my True Name. Stop Mælfallyn, even if it means you must kill me. I spell wove an Éireannan knot, what those of Earth call Celtic knots, to appear at the nape of Milfae royalty. These are the only faeries you can trust in Ealdspell.

The Malfae found my hidden kingdom, they now live among us, and they introduced their poisons to our land.

Rònan, High Druid and Prince of Éireanna

Any sufficiently advanced technology is
indistinguishable from magic.

Arthur C. Clarke

PROLOGUE

THE BOY AND THE SONGBIRD

The boy sucked in a lungful of dust and steam-drenched air while barreling down an industrial alley. A cough rumbled through his sticks-and-bones frame. Still he ran, past drying clothes and piles of newly spun garments. He tipped over a stack of empty wooden crates dangerously near a row of mineral baths. Factory wash women jumped out of the way and shouted at him with large smiles—programmed smiles. If only one of the older lads behind him would fall into the dye vats. But in Ealdspell, luck was a waste of breath. And breath was a gift.

Since the Cold Winds blew across the realms and dusted crops, livestock, and entire cities, survival demanded greater sacrifices. Food scarcity hollowed out bellies and gritty air sickened lungs. The boy felt hunger powerfully. At eight rotations, remorse didn't crawl across his conscience for stealing food. Others felt justified in taking *his* food. Why shouldn't he take *theirs*?

An apple merrily jostled in his pants pocket—his ill-gotten meal. The three boys behind him would make him pay for snatching their snack too.

Dirt-tinged sunlight blinded the boy as he popped out of the alley and into the town square. Rothlín proper was laid out similar to the spokes and wheel of a spinning machine. Textile factories wedged out from the town square toward the spindle tree orchards—the only tree in the Kingdom of Ealdspell with magical properties strong enough for factory spinning machines and looms. In-between the factories were service and industrial alleys. Outside of the city's wheel were the castle grounds on one side, and on the other, the Castoffs—the disrepaired remains of cottages and crofter gardens. Where his mither awaited his return.

The Temple of Aisling rose in the center of the town square. The boy slowed his escape to take in the white alabaster walls. Compared to the vacantly smiling, dingy factory workers who now congested the streets on their way home, the temple offered a beacon of cleanliness and perfection. It had been ages since the boy stood so near the holy structure. His small brows pushed together before he peered over his shoulder. Then he tucked his head, his left cheek shadowed from sight, and buried himself into the steady current of workers in the streets. But he didn't hide his face well enough.

"Scat, Blight!" A woman shoved at his wiry frame with her basket.

The boy spun on his heel, but a man fisted the back of his tunic, careful to avoid contact with his skin. "Rules are rules, Blight."

"Just heading home," the boy pleaded. "Me mither will be awful worried."

"Rules are rules."

Faces sneered and grimaced in disgust. Several adults spit on him as he was dragged by. It was against the law for blighted children to approach the temple. But he couldn't spend a night in the locks. Terrible things happened to blighted children who did. Tales circulated that their blood filled the temple's ceremonial copper bowls as a sacrifice to the goddess. Though, the boy had only seen cattle and pigs given as an offering.

The older lads elbowed through the crowd. The boy sucked in a terrified breath. They would beat him until the dust drank his blood—forget the temple! And all because they stole his food first. Anger trembled through his limbs. Digging his booted heels into the dirt street, he yanked against the hand that held his clothing. The man paused in a beat of confusion. All the time the boy needed. With a twist, he slid out of his belted tunic and dashed into the thickening crowd opposite of the man and the older lads.

Women gasped as he shouldered past, upper body bare and face blighted. Some even covered their children's eyes. The apple still jangled in his pocket, all he cared about. Freshly dyed garments hung from laundry lines in a service alley—a good cover. The boy slid into the shadows, like the faeries had taught him, and crouched low behind crates and stone partition walls.

And waited.

And waited some more.

As the sun arced toward the horizon behind the factories, the boy ate his apple. He savored each juicy bite, determined to appreciate his hard-earned reward. His stomach grumbled, longing for more. But there was nothing else to be had. The skeleton of a core slipped from his hand and rolled across the dirt path when he slowly rose.

Bit by bit, he crept from his hiding spot and out into the open. The shadows of workers returning home continued to scale the factory walls. No wash women. The alley guard must not have arrived yet either. Satisfied, he skipped down the narrow dirt street and plucked a small green tunic from the line. After a quick search for nearby activity and finding none, he rolled the garment in the thick layers of dust followed by scrubbing the fine weave against the coarse stone wall. He then ripped a small hole near the base hem. Thieving textiles was punishable by death. But this tunic now appeared properly warn and used—hopefully.

Legs tired and belly now partially full, the boy moved with as much stealth as he could muster. A difficult goal as he hadn't been down this spoke before, nor was he sure of where the alley would lead. The spindle tree orchards or toward the Castoffs?

"Yer sister will nae ken," a man whispered nearby.

"I cannae," a woman protested with a giggle. "Anaether night."

The boy stilled and squinted his eyes. Up ahead was the alley guard. A younger man by the looks of it, and one too distracted by a pretty girl with a spell woven face to notice anything else. And so, the boy dodged behind crates and fluttering linens. He almost made it out of the narrow alley when he breathed in a pocket of dusted air and coughed. A wracking cough that shook his entire body.

"Boy!" The alley guard shouted at his shadow. "Ye're trespassing on her Majesty's—"

"He's just a wee laddie," the woman said. "Scurry home to yer mither before her ghost comes a look'n for ye."

The guard feinted in the boy's direction, his club raised. The boy knew it was all a show to scare him away. Still, he didn't need any more encouragement. Perhaps luck did exist in Ealdspell, in the form of a young woman with enough coin to spell weave a pretty face. Her future would remain happy.

Unlike his.

More coughs barked from his lungs. The more he ran, the more he needed to gulp air. The more dust he inhaled. But he did enjoy a large apple and all to himself. The same older lads had stolen his measly lunch yesterday. Other blighted children might submit to their cruel fate. But not him—never him.

Would the older lads still treat him like rubbish to be burned if they knew he was a prince? And that he was the surviving heir to the House of Batten? The Realm he should have inherited was dusted during the Cold Winds, and so was his family. A faerie huntress from the forested Realm of Dúnælven found him as a wee babe, swaddled tight while sleeping in frost-tipped moss. He had survived the Cold Winds, but not without a price.

The boy touched the frostbite scar that ran down the length of this face and across his left cheek. Blighted. Cursed children. Defiled by the goddess. Their kind's punishment wasn't death, but to live with the sins of their dusted ancestors who were believed to have invited the Cold Winds into the Kingdom of Ealdspell. But, really, the realm of Rothlín needed an example of humanity's defectiveness to stitch together Aisling's Dream of beauty and perfection for the New Dawn Era. Even he understood this at his young age.

As a babe, no other Royal House wanted him. Not even the House of Rosen, the royal family in Rothlín—the family he was to marry into when eighteen. The boy screwed up his face in disgust. The faeries had ensured he knew his history, even the marriage contract. But he was to keep quiet and keep a birthmark hidden on his lower neck as much as possible, an apparent family trait among Glenashlen royals. His foster parents were to remain ignorant of his origins as well, for such knowledge could put their lives at risk. Taking in a bedraggled, blighted lad of five rotations from the faeries had been risk enough. The Royal Houses believed him dead, for royals were above blighting, so they believed. A prince without a realm was surely in need of one too. And so dead he would remain.

"Rest, oh great star. Find the moon and kiss her goodnight . . ."

A girl's voice carried on eventide's cool breeze and lulled him from his agitated thoughts. While gathering wool in his head, the boy hadn't noticed how he had wandered close to the castle and the ground's defensive sweet briar thorn bushes. The Castoffs were behind him, in the opposite direction. He swiveled on his feet but didn't take a step forward. Her voice, it was far too beautiful. And kind. His heart wanted to weep with every lilting note. Even though he knew her melodic gift was manufactured by The Dream—a system of holiness created by the goddess Aisling.

Curious, he tip-toed into the wall's shadows until he could squeeze through the brambling limbs of a towering sweet briar bush. A smile tempted the corners of his mouth. His new tunic hadn't hooked onto a single thorn. Approaching the gate was foolish, perhaps more foolish than stepping near the temple. Still, he had to see the girl. Needed to watch her sing. Needed to feel the kindness in her song a little while longer. Slowly, ever so slowly, he moved toward the back gate until he could peek through the bars.

A large, ancient stone circle sat just inside the walls, surrounded by a myriad of brightly colored flowers that dazzled the boy's eyes. But nothing had ever dazzled him quite like the vision the girl made while sitting whimsically on a patch of clover inside the standing stones. White-blonde hair tumbled down her back to her waist. Blue eyes glimmered with the sunset's rosy hue. Her ruffled-lace dress rippled around her in shades of lavender and cream. And a pink- and blue-colored flower chain rested atop her head and graced each wrist. By her size, the boy estimated she was around five or six rotations. A teacher sat patiently before her and offered instruction on how to improve her song. But the boy believed she could already rival any songbird from Dúnælven.

She began another song and the world around her brightened almost immediately. Colors grew more vivid and soft beams of fading sunlight moved toward her. And that is when he knew she was magic, for even the setting sun desired the radiance of her company.

A deep sated sigh left his tightened chest. He desperately wanted to stay until the end of her lesson. The night sky would fully cloak his presence then. Though, the boy needed to find his way home before his mither's ghost haunted Rothlín in search of him. He had never seen anyone die from fright but, after living with the faeries until the age of five, he knew stranger things were possible.

And so, he attempted to creep backward, toward the evening's shadows. Until a thorn snagged his tunic. The boy yanked gently, then yanked again, this time more forcefully. The tunic gave way, but a faerie-enchanted limb tossed him from the brambling sweet briar bush. His knees and palms skidded across the dirt. The girl jumped to her feet with a gasp, her perfect mouth shaped in an O. She blinked prettily and then her sparkling blue gaze traveled to his face and studied his scar.

Shame heated the boy's skin. He couldn't bear the look of horror that surely pinched her lovely face. Nor did he want to shatter the illusion that the kindness in her voice was entirely for him. Scrambling to his feet, he kicked up dust to hide his departing body. And then he ran—hard—even though his legs shook and his lungs pained with coughs, and even though tears made tracts of mud down his cheeks. He ran harder than when the older lads had chased him down various spokes. Harder still than when he escaped the locks.

"Félip!" His mither clutched her chest when he slammed open the front door. "Ye look a sight, lad. Where have ye been?"

He pushed past his foster mither to his bedroom and curled up under the thin covers of his bed. That night, he dreamt of the girl with long blonde hair and her beautiful voice. The next morning, he resolved never to step foot near the castle so long as he lived. Any trilling note from the girl might very well cause his heart to collapse.

It would be ten difficult rotations before the boy would see the songbird again. But unlike last time, he wouldn't miss her smile . . .

The Princess had for her godmothers all the Fairies they could find in the whole kingdom (they found seven), that every one of them might give her a gift, as was the custom of Fairies in those days, and that by this means the Princess might have all the perfections imaginable . . .

. . . The youngest gave her for gift, that she should be the most beautiful person in the world; the next, that she should have the wit of an angel; the third, that she should have a wonderful grace in every thing she did; the fourth, that she should dance perfectly well; the fifth, that she should sing like a nightingale; and the sixth, that she should play upon all kinds of music to the utmost perfection.

"The Sleeping Beauty in the Wood" by Charles Perrault, *Tales of Mother Goose*, 1697

CHAPTER I

AROREH

Every dust-clomped footstep softly echoed in Aroreh's spell-addled head. The sort of dragging rhythmic persistence that sounded more funereal than celebratory to her sensitive ears. Not that she had attended many wakes or death processions. Rather, she had the ability to hear music in just about anything—the clinking water crystals in fog, the zipping peal of laughter in runic machinery, the low hum of a person's shadow. A blessing, she was told endlessly since childhood. For a blessing from the faeries it was, indeed—a sacrament at birth for the temple. And yet, many times the melody of earth and machine grated on her programmed sensibilities.

Such as now.

A zap tingled in her brain and she tensed in anticipation of the full-body flinch.

Aroreh blinked. A kind smile pulled at her rouge-tinted lips.

Complaining about one's blessing—well, complaining about anything, really—was an undesirable trait for a woman. And all undesirable traits were to remain *asleep*, according to the goddess Aisling. Aroreh was a lady, after all. Gentle, agreeable, and eager to please those in her company. Not a nagging ogress from the Spired Hills. For she was created to bring others joy.

A puff of factory smoke wafted by, almost glowing in the predawn shadows. She held her breath until the air cleared—warm smile still in place. Once a year she journeyed from the castle to the Temple of Aisling. Every year, Rothlín proper textured into new images inside her faerie-blessed mind. Strange images that appeared all wrong and yet felt completely right. Without drawing her mother's attention, she allowed her eyes to wander over various sights.

Rats scurried in a dye bin filled with rotting vegetables. Aroreh tilted her head. Did the rot help procure stronger colors? She concluded it must, otherwise the people wouldn't tolerate wasted food. They apparently didn't tolerate wasted time, either. The few bodies she had passed appeared unwashed, their exposed skin covered in sweat-caked dust, many with loose threads in their hair. But they were a happy people, grateful for the goddess's wisdom. Aroreh's body filled with bright giggles of gratitude, the sound like golden rays of sunshine. Those she passed smiled wide at her before falling prostrate onto the alley's street.

The corners of her mouth wavered. Aroreh lowered her focus to the path before her. Something didn't feel right. A slight pull in her middle. A spasm. A knowing ache in her heart. What her eyes took in didn't match what a dark corner of her mind was whispering.

A false dream . . .

Another tingle zapped her head and her back straightened involuntarily.

She needed to speak only of pleasant things. For negativity invited dissension and Ealdspell was still rebuilding after the Cold Winds.

The discomfort in her gut eased and a comfortable warmth trickled out to each limb. The smile tugging on her lips strengthened and she daintily blinked—once more.

The Kingdom of Ealdspell can only rebuild populations if citizens remain loyal to The Dream, the goddess's vision of goodness and order. Aroreh's mind spun round and round until her darker thought threads twisted into yarns of truth. She embraced her role: a faerie blessed female who embodied all that was beautiful and wholesome in a woman for the New Dawn Era, the era that rose from the ashes of the Cold Winds.

The very reason she would sing to the Great Spindle Tree this day.

A cluster of temple maidens currently held the ribboned edges of her tatted lace skirt and crowded her booted steps. Not a speck of factory grime was to touch her ceremonial dress. For, as the temple's vessel, she could only approach the Great Spindle Tree if uncontaminated. Beads of sweat gathered on the fair brow of a young maiden at Aroreh's hip. The hem of the young woman's dress slithered along the dirt street, unlike Aroreh's. She didn't envy the maiden's duty. From the wobbling smile on the young woman's face, the maiden didn't envy herself either.

Once more, she was complaining. A strange problem of late. One that was growing stronger the closer she reached her sixteenth birthday. Was her programming growing faulty? At times, it was if her mind was at the center of a battle. A prize to be won.

More pre-dawn wash women and repair men fell to their knees and pressed their noses to the dirt when her procession passed by.

Behind her, a temple maiden shouted, "Hail Queen Líeh! Hail Princess Aroreh!" loud enough to awaken the outer wheel of Rothlín.

Aroreh grit her teeth despite the warm smile she broadcast.

The rising dawn crested over the temple's rose-gold basilica in burnished layers of pinks and oranges. Fires along the forest's edge— to expand the spindle orchard and farming lands—always produced spectacular sunsets and sunrises. The temple's white walls and towers gleamed through the factory smoke and hazy sky. Ornate moulding crowned the front-facing roof lines in intricately knotted patterns of leaves and spun threads. Even the basilica was etched as though the delicate petals of a blossoming sweet briar rose. The same enchanted faerie thorns guarding the castle grounds and the royal insignia for the House of Rosen.

The toe of her boot caressed the first shadows of the temple's interior, and her shoulders relaxed a notch. The dusty pink, garnet, and coppery orange leaves and flowers of the Great Spindle Tree swallowed up her entire vision. A tangle of wires from surrounding machines dangled from the ceiling and ported into various limbs and selected areas around the trunk. Per tradition, her eyes were to remain fastened to the long, gnarled roots dipping into the moated faerie pool below the tree's sprawling branches—not gape about like a feral child from the streets, as she was oft scolded when younger. But, in her periphery, she noted runes scrawled across the monolithic stone walls, the marks glowing a soft purple as her nanotechnology interacted with the temple's. Upon seeing the goddess's illuminated approval, the maidens released the lacy hem of her asymmetrical gown. Aroreh heard soft sighs of relief from several of her attendants, followed by the rustle of garments as they slowed several paces to allow her mother, Queen Líeh, to walk beside her.

"Your Majesties." A temple priestess emerged from behind one of three machines feeding the Great Spindle Tree and faerie pool. The older woman dipped her head, hands spread out before her, palms up. "Aisling's blessings on you this holiest of days."

"Thank you, priestess," her mother intoned.

Aroreh stepped toward the elder woman, unable to contain her happiness. "Did Mother share how I received a visit this week from the Seer in Clifstán?"

"The old korrigan?" The priestess studied the queen a single heartbeat. "I thought the dwarf was to visit during your birthday celebration, princess."

"Yes, but she couldn't wait," Aroreh said, grinning now. "And she brought with her a wondrous mirror made entirely of gold. And yet, I saw my reflection as though it were looking glass."

"Did the . . . Seer tell you anything when you looked upon the mirror?"

"Oh yes!" Aroreh took the priestess's hands in hers in delighted laughter, joy that had longed to be set free since entering the temple. "She said that I was spun from sunlight and that my sacrifice to Rothlín would illuminate a new era."

The priestess's shoulders lowered, as if in relief. "The goddess sees your sacrifices and blesses you as our light and *beacon* of hope in the New Dawn Era. The korrigan speaks true."

The queen delicately cleared her throat. "Princess Aroreh brings a song to honor Spindle Day."

"Indeed. Let us purify you first, princess."

"Thank you." Aroreh extended her arms, palms up, like the priestess's greeting. Two temple maidens reappeared at her side and cradled her forearms with their hands while gently guiding her forward.

"Remember, Aroreh Rosen," the elder woman intoned, "until your spell-woven Fate is set upon the eve of your sixteenth birthday, the blessings gifted you at birth may be tried."

"I was created to bring others joy. I shall not waver in my dedication, priestess."

"The old korrigan showed you a favorable future, it is true. But faeries often speak in riddles." Her mother smiled at her, but in a way Aroreh didn't understand—thin lipped, eyes crinkling with fear instead of happiness. A look that matched the oddly cool tone of her voice. "Guard your heart and your mind, Daughter," she continued. "More so than ever. Aisling will turn her back on Rothlín, if you don't. And then we shall suffer the nightmare of her wrath instead of the beauty of her Dream."

Fear plucked at the tensing muscles in Aroreh's stomach. Had she displeased her mother by sharing the Seer's visit with the temple priestess?

Before she could fully panic, she pushed aside the confusion. Perhaps she had imagined the disapproval. Yes, she had simply overreacted. For why would the queen find fault with such a bright future? As a servant of the temple, it was Aroreh's sacred duty to guard her mind from impurities. Her mother was kindly reminding Aroreh of this sacrifice, nothing more.

The priestess dipped a copper bowl into the faerie pool and then poured the life-giving waters across Aroreh's fingers.

"May you only touch goodness all the days of your life."

Next she dipped the corner of a ceremonial cloth into the waters and then pressed the damp end to Aroreh's eyes, first one and then the other.

"May you only see that which is beautiful all the days of your life."

With the same cloth, the priestess touched Aroreh's lips.

"May you speak only what is pure and right all the days of your life."

Purification now complete, Aroreh knelt before the faerie pool. Giddiness swelled in her chest at the beautiful sight. Delicate ferns brushed the moss-dappled stones forming the lip of the moat. Red- and yellow-spotted mushrooms dotted the pool's bank, along with bluebells, snowdrops, and other bright and cheery flowers she could not name. The magical waters held secrets and healing properties. The tinkling lull of the light current was described by many as soothing, the sound of one's peace of mind. But, to her sensitive ears, she heard a different tune. The curiously soft, rhythmic lullaby of slumbering children who were carried into the night by vivid dreams.

The machines around her breathed the same whimsical melody. The faerie nanotechnology in her also resided in those younger, though for a different purpose. She had never known a wink of sleep nor experienced a dream. Among her blessings was perpetual wakefulness so she may never tire of her work for the realm of Rothlín, for the Kingdom of Ealdspell—her sacrifice. The dreams of children, however, kept the Great Spindle Tree alive and powered this particular faerie pool. The runes in their small bodies when lost to the subconscious state communicated with the runes in Aisling's machines.

Aroreh watched as a single garnet-colored leaf spiraled through the temple's shadows to rest atop the waters. A ripple of music graced her ears with earth's collision with water. A dancing sound—like a folk reel—and she smiled, this time for her own pleasures and not for obedient appearances.

A zap zinged inside her head and her muscles flinched.

She trailed her fingers along the pristine waters and then touched her forehead to acknowledge her goddess. A drip of water rolled between her eyes, down the bridge of her nose, and down her cheek, to plop onto her bodice, above her heart. A tear for those who didn't know The Dream. A tear made of faerie water since her other faerie blessing—a sunny disposition—brought smiles, not sadness.

The pleasure her smile brought others was pleasure for her as well. True pleasure, if she were honest, for her grace and beauty had inspired others to dream of a better future. A happier future. A life where only humanity's perfections remained awake and imperfections slept. Where women happily bore all the children necessary for Rothlín to rise from the ashes of the Cold Winds. Where those children were programmed from conception and again at birth to obey Aisling with desires to attain her every beauty.

A flush of pride heated Aroreh's cheeks. She was a faerie-blessed mortal of the New Dawn Era. Many more had been born after her. Those older, who earned the goddess's favor, could meet with the queen's spell weavers for upgraded beauty, gentle dispositions, as well as other virtues. No more anger, defiance, and other emotional hardships. Only cheer and goodwill.

Only complete surrender to a dream humankind could never manufacture until now.

The ache tugged in her heart once more. Her mind continued to spin happiness, but her soul wove a pattern of sadness. No, a stronger word than sadness, but one she couldn't fully conceptualize. Was this the temptation her mother had warned about? Even still, Aroreh pushed back the dark emotions. If her programming sensed negativity, she would receive another medicated dose from The Dream to suppress the unwanted traits. To question the ways of Aisling was to question one's dedication and to wish for what remained of Rothlín and Ealdspell to perish.

"Goddess be blessed," she whispered and then touched two fingers to her forehead once again. "I am ready." Aroreh held out her arms for her attendants to help her rise.

Queen Líeh placed the high priestess's veil over her crown. White lace fell across her mother's face. Then her mother quietly marched over to an altar. Nearby, the largest machine merrily rumbled lulling notes while digesting fresh dreams. Her mother lit a bundle of rosemary, meadow sage, lavender, and calendula. Writing runes in the air with the cleansing smoke, Queen Líeh faced north, followed by east, west, ending south, before brushing the bundled herbs over Aroreh. Ancient runic words fell quietly from her mother's lips and sharply echoed in Aroreh's ears, incantations that activated the control center of Aroreh's mind. The incense filled the hall within a matter of heartbeats and Aroreh's eyes fluttered closed.

Her pulse swelled with a symphony of fabricated emotions—joy, gratitude, peace, dedication. Each programmed feeling had a sound, each engineered sound became a note. The music threatened to fill every crevice of her being, but another song wished to be set free instead.

Independence. Curiosity. Fear. Fervor.

The crackling war in her mind grew louder until the building song in her soul spilled out.

CHAPTER 2

FÉLIP

Félip's breath formed small clouds in the ash-choked chill. This new day was a wee too quiet for one deemed celebratory. Street vendors still hadn't arrived and the clank of looms and whir of spinning machines didn't muffle all other bustling sounds. Those irritating grating sounds of industry and poverty meant to soothe the working class like a beloved crone's lullaby. To the non-Aisling addled, the persistent hum and rumble were more like an old man whose dreams died with every diseased, wheezing cough. Manufactured dreams were for horse-kicked fools, anyway.

But the stillness wasn't the most unsettling observation he had made this morn.

Faeries. Elves in full armor, to be exact. Their lean bodies slipping into the shadows of the spindle tree orchard. To passersby, they would see shadows of limbs or harvested logs for spinning wheel and spindle productions. But Félip knew the elves wanted him to see them.

Normally his pre-dawn stroll to Factory 23 didn't take him past the orchard. But the Thorns—Rothlín's faerie-sponsored spy and thieves guild—had requested his shadow walking skills to deliver a message unseen to an under-foreman in Factory 14. The same illusionary cloaking skills he had learned over the years from the very Dúnælven elves now hidden among the sacred trees.

Why was a whole cavalcade here?

And on Spindle Day?

Pretending to be mesmerized by the missive in his hand, he had simply trundled by—task turned bait. If faeries wanted to speak to him, he figured they would, like always. And if they didn't speak to him, the cheeky elves might be lured into the light by the secrets held within his fingertips. The bastards had been spying all over Rothlín for years, perhaps even all Ealdspell. Yet no one approached him or tried to tug the sealed paper from his fingers.

Suited him. He had work to do.

Félip pulled the edge of his cloak's hood farther over his face. Right now, his shadow walking cloak was turned out to the non-magical weave, allowing people to fully see his form. Normally he would prefer to hide rather than risk notice. But it was time to sweep Factory 23—his job.

The industrial alley ended in a few steps and he would emerge near the town square. A young wash woman twisted his direction when noting his clomping boot steps. He spared her a quick glance, any evidence of blight concealed. Her lips teased into a blushing smile—part of her feminine programming for Aisling, and partly a wee fancied look he foolishly allowed to settle in his heart a little. *Aye, a horse kick to the head it is, then.* She would spit curses his direction, if she glimpsed the truth. His body was a grave pit of hisses and rebukes.

Falling in love, or even a passing dalliance, wasn't on his life's horizon line. Not when his employer reminded him daily that half a copper was weekly payment enough for a floor-sweeping Blight.

Half a copper.

He couldn't purchase a rat-nibbled slice of cheese with a half a copper. Or a dozen rotting vegetables. At this rate of pay, he was destined to grow hunger enfeebled with elderly foster parents past their working prime. A burden he refused to place on their shoulders. After feeding and clothing him all these years, like hell he would let his mither and faither die of starvation because their blighted foster son made two measly coppers per month—and *only* if his employer was gracious enough to pay him in the first place.

The momentary tuft of pleasure from the girl's interest blew away with the factory smoke, like dandelion seeds on the wind. Not that anything would happen. Empty, black wishes, all of them.

"Your Highness."

Félip halted his steps. A stone dropped in his gut and splashed fear to every part of his body. The royal House of Rosen wasn't present. Who could this voice be addressing, then? Nobody knew he was a prince, except the Dúnælven, and even they referred to him only as Félip or Félip MacKinley to hide his dangerous secret. Royals didn't carry the shame of their ancestor's misdeeds, until he survived the dusting with a frostbite scar. But Félip didn't believe in the ways of Aisling or accept this false goddess's punishment for a crime he never committed. The Cold Winds took his family, took his realm. He was only a wee babe, an innocent. The injustice of it all threatened to send him into an even darker mood, so he redirected his mental focus.

The hoarse whisper came from the shadows on his right. To act natural, he lowered and fidgeted with his boot laces. From his crouched position, he slipped a sly glance toward a large stack of crates. A faerie met his cloaked gaze. The male gestured with his head to follow and then disappeared into the darker shadows of crates, cobblestone, and factory pipes.

Fresh dust fringed the edge of Félip's cloak and created lines across his breeches. Sighing, he brushed off what he could and then sauntered into the shadows—the pretty girl forgotten. Behind him, the temple gleamed a mocking white. Perhaps the only clean building in this forsaken realm. A beacon of false hope and lies.

"Here, Your Highness."

"Dinnae call me *that*, eejit." Félip moved into the darker shadows until he faced a tall, lean male with pale lavender eyes and long, charcoal hair, wearing black leathers with twin swords strapped across his back. A raven perched on his shoulder; the bird's black eyes fixed solidly onto Félip. His heart stilled a beat. The faerie warrior prince who made royals rise and fall called him an honorific title. Félip released a slow breath, then said, "Gedlen Fate Maker. It's been awhile."

The male bent at the waist and dipped his head. The raven flapped his wings. "Peace, Brandu," he said to his familiar.

Félip peeked over his shoulder and down a nearby spoke, then pulled the male up. "Ye daft? Naebody bows to a Blight."

"I'm here to enlist your service to Dúnælven."

Félip narrowed his eyes at the general. "The faeries in the orchard, aye? They're—"

"—attacking." Gedlen gently clutched Félip's forearm, an act of solidarity. The rock in Félip's gut sank deeper and fear rippled out to his pounding pulse. "Calling in a favor owed. We need your shadow walking skills."

"Ye have plenty of shadow walkers."

"No mortal ones."

An ill-humored chuckle slipped past Félip's lips. "Get to the point."

"There's no time, Your—"

"Listen, *charaid*." Félip yanked his arm away. Brandu flapped onto a nearby crate and cawed his displeasure. "Explain yerself or walk away."

A wicked grin flashed Gedlen's canines. "The House of Rosen has burned the forests edging Dúnælven—"

"—fer years," Félip finished for him, eyebrows pushed together. "Fer *years* the fires to expand spindle production have been burning. Why attack *now*? The people of Rothlín suffer plenty still, ye ken? We need food, clean water. Not war."

Gedlen stepped out of Félip's grip and tilted his head. "Pick a side Félip Batten."

"Dinnae use my House name, ye witless donkey pile." Félip's stiffened muscles deflated some as Gedlen humorously shifted on his feet. "And if I dinnae choose ye?"

"Protection services end and you become an enemy to Dúnælven, all blood ties forgotten."

Félip twisted away, gnawing the inside corner of his lip. *Blood ties?* What in the bloody hell did he mean by blood ties? The fae male was touched in the head and Félip sighed.

In the middle of the town square, the temple's rose petal basilica glinted in the rising sun. His eyes traveled down the unfurling lines. A longing was blooming inside of him too. A seed long planted now ready to fruit. He thought of the sealed message he had carried to Factory 14 and faced Gedlen. Everything made sense now. Why so few workers clotted the dust-coated streets this morn. Why the hidden Dúnælven weren't tempted by the secrets spinning in his fingers. They knew exactly what was scrawled inside.

And to not have Dúnælven's protection? Their favor? That was a life Félip had never known. A death price was on his head. For a realmless prince is surely in need of a new realm to claim as his own, or so the rumors milled about. And now the Fate Maker stood before him with an offer.

"Mither and Faither . . ."

"We'll escort them out of harm's way and ensure their every comfort. Food. Housing. Feather-stuffed beds and heavy quilts. The finest wines and sharpest cheeses in the cellars. The Dúnælven will treat them like mortal gods, I swear it."

"Fer how long?"

"The remaining days of their life."

Félip smirked. "And how long might that be?"

"Until they die of *natural* causes. We won't harm them."

That was all he needed to hear. "Aye, I'll join ye."

Another smile crept up Gedlen's angular face. "Go to the temple. The House of Rosen are performing ceremonies to the Great Spindle Tree. We need you to create a distraction."

"Desecrating the temple isn't shadow walking, *charaid*."

"You'll know when to walk the shadows, Félip Batten. I'll ensure you receive instruction."

Félip nearly rolled his eyes. "Och aye, faerie riddles, is it then?

And my last name is MacKinley. Ye ken the rules."

"The rules are changing today, Your Highness." Gedlen winked. And then the faerie general was gone, his raven too. Félip swore under his breath. What had he just agreed to? *Ye're the eejit, laddie.*

Blowing an unruly strand of hair from his eyes, he cleared his mind of all the mental clutter and observed the play of light and shadows around him. How each mote of dust glittered. The way the light spilled onto the streets, the buildings. The sun's angled position above the factories on Rothlín's east side. Light gathered inside each puff of smoke from nearby buildings and glowed outward until each beam evaporated into ribbons of chilly air. All of this he observed while melting into the cold, passing shadows, adjusting his enchanted gray- and black-mottled cloak to the shifting light as needed—a gift from the Dúnælven years ago. The Thorns didn't hire Blights as spies, only messengers. Though Félip could blend into his surroundings better than most and was the only mortal shadow walker in employ.

"Shadow walk, me arse," he muttered to himself. The Temple of Aisling—a massive pillar of reflective light—now stood a quick jog away. Nary a shadow touched the alabaster walls, nor her grounds. Walking shades of light was far harder. Grimacing, he mocked in a higher voice, "I'm here to enlist yer service to Dúnælven, Félip Batten MacKinley." A deep sigh left his body. Now *he* was referring to the forbidden name of his dusted ancestors. "Bloody faeries."

The town square remained still, as if all Rothlín were drawing in a collective breath of anticipation. The wool scratched his scar as he drew the cloak's hood over the blighted side of his face once more. Then he strode out into dawn's fresh light . . . and nobody shouted at him. Hurled insults. Or threatened his life for nearing their blessed temple. A strange thing, that. In a few steps, his hand made contact with the smooth exterior wall. His fingers caressed the pocked grooves in the alabaster. A tingling filled his fingertips. The wall, it was living. Vibrating with a heartbeat like factory walls when the machines were running. Félip tucked away this information as he slid into the first interior shadow.

Runes decorated stone walls and glowed a soft purple. He had seen similar runes before, made by a couple Dúnælven spell weavers who worked with the Thorns. But it was not the walls that captivated him most. Or the cloying herbal smoke graying the air. No, the Great Spindle Tree stole the dustless breath from his lungs. The dryad-made limbs seemed to ramble on forever. Perhaps three to four men could clasp arms to encircle the trunk. And the leaves could rival the sunset, their fiery brilliance nearly hiding the many ported cords. Félip couldn't imagine anything more beautiful.

That is, until a cluster of veiled women parted.

He didn't realize he possessed more dustless air in his lungs to lose. But out it went and, with his remaining breath, his good senses. A lass with long white-blonde hair stood in the middle of the circle of women. Layers of cream-colored lace in patterns of sweet briar roses cascaded from her waist to pool around her feet in dips and angles. A tight bodice, laced up in sage-green ribbons, hugged her slender waist and curves. Delicate pink roses were even woven into a crown of braids wrapped atop her fair head. She didn't need any more magic to bewitch him senseless. Yet his parched gaze couldn't help but greedily drink in how machine and candled light fairly shimmered off her smooth skin. She was, perhaps, the most beautiful girl he had ever laid eyes upon—a perfect dream. And for a moment, he forgot himself. He forgot everything. But not for long.

For a Dream is exactly what she represented, and he the Nightmare.

The distraction.

The desecration.

A fist seemed to squeeze his heart. The familiar ache in his chest returned, and he closed his eyes to hold back the angry tears. Locked away memories surfaced and dashed by his mind's eye—a wee girl in a different cream-colored dress with bonny flowers in her faerie-blessed hair. The songbird was the same Aisling-addled girl he was contracted to marry once upon a time. Not two different people, like he had previously believed. Like his fool heart had wanted. For the songbird was never a lie, unlike *her*. Muscles in his jaw clenched. If he walked out now, his foster parents would suffer. Possibly many innocents in Rothlín too. Not many options for a Blight. Not many options for a dead prince, either.

Damn you, Gedlen! Félip held back an angry laugh. *Better than two measly coppers.*

Félip's eyes snapped open, determined, bitterness roiling where nausea once sickened.

His toe stepped out of the shadows right when Princess Aroreh lifted her face to the Great Spindle Tree and began to sing.

CHAPTER 3

AROREH

The leaves shimmied and the Great Spindle Tree appeared to sway with every note that left her soul. When happy, the sacred Mother Tree's dryad would produce many life-giving seeds—the only way to grow new trees in the orchard. And new trees meant factories could manufacture more textiles for the Kingdom of Ealdspell. Wealth in Rothlín meant wealth for the other realms.

A temple maiden blotted a tear from the corner of her eye at the very sight, a smile on her lips. Everyone appeared moved, especially the tree. All but her mother. The queen's lips dipped in a slight frown. Her eyes narrowed only a pinch—like earlier. The displeasure was subtle, but still there. Aroreh nearly stumbled over the next note in guilt. She hadn't imagined it and confusion wove her thoughts into a frazzled mess. Was her mother's programming growing faulty as well? From Aroreh's periphery, she attempted to watch for the telltale zap of Aisling's strength. Surely a smile would re-form shortly. Her mother was the temple's high priestess, after all.

Or did she simply displease her mother?

Aroreh drew in breath until her lungs filled with more aching melodies. She opened her mouth to release another song when a scream shook her ears. Then more screams rent the incensed air followed by the loud caw of a raven. Aroreh spun toward where all the temple maidens gawked in horror. A raven swooped up to the rafters. Below the bird, the profile of a young man caught her gaze right before the glowing purple runes faded into the ancient stone walls. Candlelight flickered where light once shone a path for the faithful. Had the goddess fled? Why had the runes disappeared? Had Aroreh displeased Aisling as well as her mother?

And then Aroreh heard the awful silence. The absence of child-fed dreams. Now the tree and machines were like her—dreamless.

"Seize him!"

The queen's command echoed in Aroreh's hazy mind. The temple tilted beneath her boots and she took an unsteady step backward. A slow blink, a wrinkled brow, her own lips dipping into an uncharacteristic frown. For a few heartbeats of time, she felt weightless, as though the runes in her body faded into the wall as well. But those strange thoughts fluttered away as quickly as they formed. Palace guards materialized from hidden alcoves and marched by in a blur of black and red. The temple maidens circled around her and then lifted their prayer veils over their heads. They spoke not a word, but their eyes communicated fear with each shared glance. A loud grunt punctured the shuffling and shrill of moving leather and drawn swords.

"I come to wake Rothlín from the nightmare ye dare call a Dream," the man spoke.

"You have defiled the Temple of Aisling," her mother pronounced in reply. "For your crimes, your blighted blood shall be collected as an offering until you pass onto The Beyond."

"Mother!" the cry left Aroreh's lips before she could suppress the improper display. Who was she to question the queen, the high priestess? Why did she feel shocked? Her mother had performed many sacrifices. And yet, she found her feet moving forward and her hands pushing through the guards, though she couldn't remember choosing to move so. Her mind was swimming counter-current across undulating waves of foreign sensations. The unfettered energy zipping through her seemed to take control of her programming until even her body felt as foreign to her as the new sensations.

Forced onto his knees, a young man knelt before her mother,

swords pointed at his back. Wavy, russet-brown hair fell over dark, earthen eyes. His chest heaved, as though gasping for breath. She would think him lung sick if not for the simmering anger in the hooded gaze directed her way. Had she displeased him too? Guilt tinged the edges of her middle and she pressed a hand to her midsection. The way he looked upon her was strangely familiar, as though they had met before. Impossible, and yet, she couldn't shake the notion.

Gathering the layers of lace in her hands, Aroreh ignored the clamor of commands and exclamations and lowered herself before the man.

"Have we met?" she asked him. Her mother whispered warnings, but she ignored her too. This was the first time Aroreh had conversed with one so low-born and curiosity proved a stronger feeling among many presently clamoring for her attention in her quickly unspooling mind. "I feel as though I know you."

The young man drew in a quiet breath before looking away.

She tried again. "What do they call you, sir?"

"Félip," he whispered.

"Your family name, Félip?" The queen demanded. When he refused to answer, the queen's eyes narrowed, her skin growing sickly pale. Aroreh wasn't sure she had ever seen her mother appear so afraid. "Peel back his cloak and show me his neck." A guard wearing gloves complied and showed for all to see a rose-hued birthmark in the shape of interconnecting knots. "How . . . Where . . . " Why was her mother so upset? How did she know Félip? Before Aroreh could think on it further, her mother hissed, "You will *not* speak to Her Highness."

A guard struck the young man across the face. Félip's body recoiled before he righted himself. A drip of blood bloomed on his lower lip and fell to the temple's floor. Hands softly grasped Aroreh's upper arms but she twisted free of their hold.

"You shall not harm him!" She shouted, glaring at the men in uniform all around her. Did she just yell? What was wrong with her mind? She wasn't sure if she had ever raised her voice outside of singing. Then another voice emerged. A tone she had never asserted with anyone, let alone her mother's guards. "We are not forest wolves or mountain ogres who crave freshly spilled blood, are we?"

From beneath lowered lashes, the young man watched her every movement, riveted. As if fearful of another blow by the guards. As if fearful of *her*. Until her own gaze settled on a fascinating scar that ran down his hairline beneath his temple and curved onto his cheek toward his jaw—*blighted*. He was blighted. The man called Félip swallowed and lowered his head as a flush colored his neck and face. The open shame moved a piece of her heart. She knew to touch him was dangerous, but her mind screamed endless commands at her strangely floating body. It was if her hand moved of its own volition, her spoken words too.

"Beautiful," she whispered to him. "You survived when many had not." With a single finger, she traced the crescent-shaped scar along his cheek and jaw.

His head jerked up, eyes wide, a line of blood dripping from his lip down his chin.

Her mother sucked in a sharp, screeching breath, an agonizing sound to Aroreh's sensitive ears. Temple maidens cried out their horrors and burst into tears. A funeral wake spun around Aroreh as if she had died the moment her body made contact with his. Confused by the unhappy sounds, Aroreh considered her finger's tip. Nothing happened. Not the streaks of Blighted Rot that would eventually leech into her soul. Nor a heavy gust of icy wind that would dust a nearby loved one. She had only heard of Blights but had never seen one. For the very sight would sully her, or so she was told. All her programming prepared her to fear such an encounter. But she was drawn to Félip—to his mysterious presence in the temple, to the purpled scar on his cheek, the familiarity of his face, and the reverent fear he postured toward her in contrast to the pools of obsidian anger in his eyes. But mostly, though she had only heard a few uttered words, she was drawn to the lyrical melody of his voice.

Freedom.

His voice was a song of freedom.

The young man turned his head away and clenched his jaw, his long lashes blinking rapidly.

A clanking, thunderous strike boomed throughout the temple—a machine's engine turning over. Aroreh clapped her hands over her ears and gritted her teeth. Waves of pain lapped at every exposed nerve in her body. Then the lolling rumble of children's dreams soothed the hurt with their rhythmic lullabies. She felt the crackling zap in her mind before she saw the purple-glow of runes reappear on the ancient temple walls.

A warm smile stretched across her lips as her back straightened to an elegant bearing. Félip's dark brows pushed together as he studied her reconnection to the goddess. She blinked daintily.

"Princess Aroreh," her mother began, "I'll forgive your impertinence this once." The queen met the priestess's eyes before turning attention onto Aroreh once more, saying, "Separate yourself from Rothlín's filth. You'll tarnish your ceremonial gown."

"Yes, mother." Aroreh stood with the help of two temple maidens, who escorted her toward the faerie pool. A woman is, above all, subservient to her betters. In her great mercy, the goddess Aisling placed guardians in Aroreh's life to guide her every step and hold her choices accountable to The Dream.

"Priestess," her mother called out in a sing-song tone, "Please see to the princess's purification."

"Yes, Your Majesty." The priestess quietly strode to the machine near the altar.

Odd thoughts hazed before Aroreh's mind's eye, of a handsome young man with a beautiful scar and a melodious voice. Perhaps he was only a dream. A giggle escaped her chest and she grinned at the temple maidens who fussed over her dress and hair. "I do believe I dreamed," she said to them. "Is that not wondrous? I have always longed to know a dream."

"Indeed, Your Highness," a maiden replied with matching cheer. "What did you dream?"

"Of a handsome young man."

The temple maiden appeared lost for words. A strange reaction Aroreh couldn't reconcile. The maiden's eyes darted over Aroreh's shoulder, then she dipped her head slightly before meeting Aroreh's happy gaze again, saying, "A true dream, Your Highness. For a woman should only dream of her future husband, yes?"

The smile slipped from Aroreh's lips and a wrinkle formed between her delicate brows. She angled her head to peer over her shoulder. Mayhap she hadn't dreamed. The young man could be as real as her, and nearby. A name tingled on the tip of her tongue and she tried the sound on for size. "Félip," she whispered under her breath. But she wasn't entirely sure that was correct. Actually, she was unsure of many things save the Great Spindle Tree stretched before her and her endless duty to restore glory and power to the realm of Rothlín and the Kingdom of Ealdspell.

"Princess," the priestess greeted as she approached from behind the altar. "How do you fare now? Better, I hope?"

"Yes, thank you. Was I unwell?"

"Simply exchanging pleasantries, Your Highness," the priestess answered kindly. Aroreh smiled at the older woman, grateful for her warm considerations. "Did I share with you that a Seer from Clifstán visited me?"

"Indeed, you have."

She had? Aroreh tried to peer through her hazy thoughts, confused.

"You come today with a song?" the priestess asked.

"Yes," Aroreh said with a grin, all confusion forgotten, "my offering to the Great Spindle Tree this holy day."

"Wonderful, Your Highness. Allow me to purify you fir—"

A roar of shouts outside of the temple interrupted the priestess. Did a crowd gather to hear her sing? Aroreh stilled, awaiting instruction. Gratitude flowed in her veins for the people who would raise praises to the goddess from the streets. Temple maidens pressed in closer, their backs to Aroreh's body. Worry crinkled the corners of their eyes and knuckles whitened around their firmly clasped hands. A few whispered prayers rose with the altar's incense.

The priestess returned to the altar and conferred with the queen, who lit another bundle of herbs. Aroreh watched dutifully, hands folded before her, head held high, shoulders back, a warm smile always present. For a woman's beauty was more serviceable when she smiled.

Palace guards wearing gloves yanked a young man up from the floor, his feet roped and upper body unclothed, and then stretched his arms out wide. He strained and wildly fought the hold, shouting a single name over and over. *Gedlen.* She tilted her head. What a lovely voice he possessed—rather musical. The raven up in the rafters leapt into flight and swooped out into the morning's light.

"We're under attack!" A guard yelled over the frenzied shouts beyond the temple's walls.

The queen ran smoking herbs along the man's outstretched body with incantations. But Aroreh pieced out, "Dead you were and dead you shall remain."

"It's no shame to be born during the Cold Winds, ye hag!" the young man shouted back.

"Rules are rules, *Blight.*"

"Ye know who I am!"

"Royal *blighted* blood always spills richer." Delight twinkled in her mother's thinly veiled eyes. It was a happy look she often had before a sacrifice, though all other blood lettings were from beasts of the field. "The House of Batten displeased the goddess and so have the elf killers who no doubt hid you all these years. You only survived the dusting to carry your family's shame and redeem their souls. Would you now deny your kin their long-awaited happy ending?"

The priestess approached with a ceremonial copper bowl.

Aroreh blinked. He was a blighted royal? How was that even possible? And why would the faeries hide an abomination?

"I come to wake Rothlín from the nightmare ye dare call a Dream." He gritted each word between clenched teeth and the effect was profound. Aroreh closed her eyes momentarily with the passionate melody his declaration of freedom made. As though a true love's kiss on her heart. Her eyes fluttered open and she touched her blushing cheeks curiously.

Several guards ran to the temple's entrance while others cranked a wheel beside the altar. The young man was lifted into the air by his bare feet, the muscles in his body hardening and softening each time he screamed a name. *Gedlen.* He quieted only when a guard lifted a sword to the young man's throat. Félip would make a picturesque blood sacrifice for the queen's holy ritual this day. He was, perhaps, the most beautiful man Aroreh had ever beheld.

"Félip," she repeated aloud. Her brows drew together.

A false dream!

Something didn't feel right. A knowing ache tightened her chest. How did she know the man's name? And, if she recalled correctly, she normally couldn't watch blood lettings. The bellows of frightened, hurting animals and their sticky life source made her retch.

A zap sparked in her head and her entire body flinched. The young man's dark eyes found hers over the screaming maidens and the weaponed swarm of faeries now pouring into the temple.

And her kind smile for him grew wider.

CHAPTER 4

FÉLIP

Félip grunted when a faerie bumped into his head. Beneath where he dangled, palace guards and faeries struck steel and shouted orders to insubordinates. Where the feck was Gedlen? No matter. Félip needed to free himself from his restraints before a swordsman blindly lopped off his head. Or the queen still somehow managed to bleed him for her runic technology goddess—which he just learned when the purple runes had faded into the walls after he had unplugged the machines.

Curling at the waist, Félip moved up his body until his hands could grab the rope tied to his feet. Now what? The queen had him stripped to just his breeches. *Bloody hag.* Félip darted a calculating look toward the temple's rafters. At least if he fell, the ropes would break his ankles instead of his neck. The muscles in his arms shook and burned as he dragged his body up, his legs useless. His teeth clenched so tight, he feared they might crack. But he reached the timbered crossbeam and gasped for breath as he surveyed the scene below— still swirling chaos and fighting. So, he refocused on the excess rope sliding through an iron ring.

The ring was part of a large brace that wrapped partly around the beam. He didn't need to tug to see if the ring was loose enough for removal. The iron nails and pitch had solidly held his weight. Instead, he grabbed the rope and began rubbing the hemp fibers along the beam's sharper edge lines. Strands in one of the corded twines snapped. He pushed more muscle into the task, grinning with each snap. Laughing when the rope tied to his ankles separated from the rope tied to the crank wheel and levers below. Quickly, he untied the knots around his ankles and stood.

"Queen Líeh," Gedlen's voice rose above the melee. "Twice we have asked you not to burn our sacred forests. Twice now you have disrespected our wishes and set flame to The Wilds. And you hold your people hostage to increase production and personal wealth. You have committed crimes against the bylaws of Ealdspell set forth by the Druid—"

"I do not negotiate with faerie-killing warmongers, *elf*. Or those who desecrate the Temple of Aisling." Queen Líeh turned away, layers of finely woven cloth and robes spinning as she did so. "Come, princess. The goddess will slay those who wish us harm. We need not witness her wrath."

"Know this Queen Líeh," Gedlen shouted and the queen halted to peer over her shoulder. "Since you take from us, we will take from you. On the sunset of your daughter's sixteenth birthday, she will prick her finger on the needled splinter of a spindle tree—"

Before Gedlen could finish, the queen cackled in laughter and walked away. The kind of laugh that suggested absurdity. And perhaps it was. For when had the princess ever entered a factory? Félip didn't think the lass even knew how a spindle or spinning wheel worked. And if spindle trees were so dangerous to the queen's daughter, why surround the princess with groves of them? The hairs on the back of Félip's arms lifted.

"Change of plans," Gedlen said to his captains. "Retrieve the princess. We act now to save Rothlín. Send in shadow walkers and a rune whisperer."

Félip melted into the smoke-filled shadows and crept along the beams near where Queen Líeh, Princess Aroreh, and their entourage had disappeared behind the tree. A bevy of fae shadow walkers faded into the darkness.

The rope in Félip's hand grew taut the more distance he gained from the knotted end at the crank wheel. Tight enough that, perhaps, he could lower himself safely back to the ground along the Great Spindle Tree and out of harm's reach. He crouched and fed the rope to the air above the faerie pool. He could possibly swing toward the bank, near the altar instead of the tree. Slowly, he slithered down the rope, cursing Gedlen as the coarse hairs scraped against his bare skin.

Félip spun on the rope to glimpse the fight. He didn't want to jump into a dangerous situation. Well, more dangerous than it already was. He was unarmed and without armor—not that he had ever owned a sword or leathers. Still, a man wants to be dressed in more than he during a skirmish.

A woman screamed. A temple maiden thrashed in a male faerie's grip. The elf let go and she collapsed onto the floor with another shriek. Hiking up her skirts, she scrabbled to her feet and then dashed away after the queen, the male's laughter trailing after her. Félip was almost above the eejit. To pick on a hapless female was coward's play. He could drop onto the elf and then laugh at his fall. Or give into his boiling blood and lay the male flat with knuckled fists.

"Where's the rope?" he heard Gedlen call out.

"Disappeared above," another answered. "Appears His Highness is on the move."

"Find him," he said to Brandu. To the fae warrior, he said, "Then bring me the rope." Félip could hear the flap of wings and then he saw Brandu in the air, circling the melee.

Félip followed the sound of Gedlen's voice until he found the elf several yards away and out of reach. The general held Princess Aroreh's wrists in his grip. Panic seized Félip's pulse. What would they do with her? The lass didn't put up a fight. No, she was all smiles like a beam of sunshine in a sea of black and drab browns, as though Gedlen were escorting her to a white linen picnic in the spindle orchard. What a rotting pile tradition. Who wore white linen near burn fields? The queen, priestess, and temple maidens were nowhere in sight, either. Several palace guards laid face down in their own blood. Nor did a stream of guards clamor for the princess's rescue. A shadow walker must have quietly removed Aroreh as the royals passed by while a rune whisperer glamoured their minds to not notice. Still, the strangeness of it all hit him and the hairs on his arms rose once more.

"The prince could be anywhere by now."

Gedlen practically rolled his eyes. "Follow the rope lines."

"Up here, ye stinking heap of goblin balls!" Félip shouted down below. Brandu angled his direction and perched on the rafter right above him. If the raven shitted on him, he would snap its neck and give the carcass to the Castoff's Grandmother Killiney for her blackbird stew. To make sure Brandu received the warning, Félip shot him a murderous glare. The raven cawed his understanding—reluctantly.

Félip's core muscles flexed as he swung his body in the open air, a little at first. The momentum quickly built, however. Soon, his body was flying across fallen guards and canined grins.

"Watch yer heads, lads and lassies!"

Faerie soldiers began chanting "drop" and Félip howled over the raucous group as he rode the rope back toward the pool of water and released. Right before his irreverent arse plunged into the crystalline pool of holy water, he rolled into a ball. At the bottom, he straightened and pushed up with his feet and broke the surface, shaking water from his hair while wiping at droplets on his face.

He was alive.

Just minutes earlier, he was hung like a Spindle Day boar in the butcher's shop.

Félip strode from the pool toward Gedlen, dripping wet and pissed. The bastard had the decency to appear contrite. Still, Félip said in a mocking voice, "Provide a wee distraction, Félip. We need a mortal shadow walker, Yer Highness." He clenched his teeth. "I'll be a wanted man now, even more than before."

Gedlen flashed a toothy grin. "Thank you for your service to Dúnælven."

"I have half a mind to kick yer lying arse. The hag tried to bleed me like a bull put out to pasture!"

"Faeries cannot lie."

Félip rolled his eyes now. "More lies." Sighing, he combed fingers through his dripping strands. "Mither and Faither? They're safe?"

"And feasting on fresh caraway bread, goat cheese, and wine."

Félip's anger deflated a notch. "Now tell me what the hell's going on? And no riddles."

"After the princess sacrifices herself for the new dream. I expect more guards at any moment." Gedlen turned to Aroreh. "Right dear? You wish to help Rothlín?"

Aroreh's lips spread wider in a fevered smile. Her blue eyes seemed to sparkle as she took in the Great Spindle Tree. "Yes, kind sir."

Kind sir?

"Do ye remember touching a blighted royal, Yer Highness?" Félip asked her.

She softly laughed. "Royals can't be blighted. We're vessels of Aisling."

Félip shot Gedlen a slitted glare. "She's rune whispered. Feck, she cannae even recognize the cursed scar on me damned face."

"The whisper will wear off by eventide. Don't worry, she'll give you the reaction you expect soon enough."

Félip grabbed Gedlen by his leathers. "She dinnae ask to be pro-grammed no more than I asked to be blighted. Ye've sacked Rothlín and delivered yer warnings to the queen. Release her, general."

"Fetch the rope!" Gedlen hollered to a warrior over Félip's shoulder. The cool, lavender gaze studied Félip's grip. "I suggest you release me, Your Highness."

Aroreh laughed sweetly again. The innocent, girlish sound sliced through Félip's fury. For a single beat of his heart, he swore he could feel her finger trace along his scar once more. A shiver wended down his spine clear to his bare toes. "You are the one holding my hands, kind sir." Her voice was clotted cream and berries and he felt the pieces of what remained of his good sense flee.

Gedlen grinned at the princess. "Forgive me, I was speaking to the prince."

Fae warriors circling their small group stopped what they were doing and lifted ears to the wind. Boots. Many of them. Marching this way. Even Félip could make out the tell-tale sound. Brandu landed on Gedlen's shoulder and angled his head at the princess and fluffed his feathers. Oh he liked her, did he?

"Prince?" Her blue eyes traveled over to Félip and blinked. "Have we met? You look familiar."

Félip ignored her and leaned in closer to Gedlen, baring his own teeth. "The queen needs *her*—" he gestured toward Aroreh with his head "—to gain fervor among the people fer her manufactured goddess."

"Exactly why she must choose to lay down her life. Rothlín will not wake until she does."

Until she woke? Or laid down her life? *Bloody faerie riddles.*

"No, *charaid*," Félip countered. "If she dies, ye'll create a martyr people will worship. Let's take the puppet fer our own show, ye ken?"

The staccato clomp of boots in the distance grew louder.

"As you command, Your Highness." Gedlen dipped his head in a bow, a strange, calculating glint in his lavender eyes.

Was this a test? Félip watched a tiny smile curve the edges of Gedlen's mouth before the elf shouted, "Roll out!"

Dalbréath—a fae male Félip had known all his life—stepped forward with the rope and tied up Aroreh's wrists. She smiled like a lovestruck fool the entire time. Dalbréath simply winked at her and then threw the lass over his shoulder. The princess giggled—again— and Félip wanted to punch the arrogant bastard. He would have, except Dalbréath's mither had raised Félip until the age of five. For Dalbrenna, he would keep his fists to himself.

"Bloody faeries," he cursed under his breath for what felt like the hundredth time since waking this day.

Now where the hell was his enchanted cloak? The one spun from beams of light and woven with dark shadows? Hands on hips, he darted his gaze about. There. Beneath a fallen guard's head. Grimacing, Félip approached the unmoving, unblinking man. "Sorry, laddie. I need this more than ye." Gently, he scooted his faerie-made cloak from beneath the guard's head, as if the man were sleeping—not dead.

He turned the cloak inside out to the magical side and then shrugged into the gray- and black-mottled garment. Another shadow walker he knew dashed by as the temple emptied, switching her cloak around like Félip had just moments earlier. She grabbed Félip by the hood and pulled him in close. "Leave shadows shaped like evil shades as you leave. Meet-up in Leaf Curl," she said. "General's orders." Then she released Félip with a nod to follow.

The damned instructions Gedlen promised. Félip grit his teeth. Again.

Black smoke swirled around the temple and filled the streets. A factory across the way crackled and roared in a blaze of flames. Villagers shouted for loved ones and ran across the town square or down industrial spokes—their bodies in panic, their faces all smiles. Félip shivered despite the heat. The female warrior threw him a questioning look and he dipped his head in assent.

He was ready to walk the shadows and forget this goddess forsaken place.

"Be reassured, O King and Queen; your daughter shall not die of this disaster: it is true, I [the young fairy] have no power to undo entirely what my elder has done . . . but instead of dying, she shall only fall into a profound sleep . . ."

Scarce had he [the Prince] advanced towards the wood, when all the great trees, the bushes and brambles, gave way of themselves to let him pass thro' . . . and what a little surprised him was, that he saw none of his people could follow him, because the trees closed again, as soon as he had pass'd thro' them.

"The Sleeping Beauty in the Wood" by Charles Perrault, *Tales of Mother Goose*, 1697

CHAPTER 5

AROREH

The rust-hued factories, golden dust-colored sky, and sunset tones of the burn fields swirled together in Aroreh's jostling vision. Somehow seeing the world upside down allowed her to gain a new perspective. The warm leaf-fall colors were always present, season after season. Was Rothlín stuck in a perpetual autumn? Only death with no promise of spring? Aisling was a life-giver. The goddess rose from the ashes of the Cold Winds to protect mothers and children and unwed maidens. Why would she allow a reaper's plague after rising victorious from the grave?

Even more strange were the weakening zaps of runic adjustments as she journeyed from Rothlín to The Wilds. Though, in their place, were tingly sensations, like a bubbling brook skipping over rocks. The energy demanded every sharp attention to detail . . . building, building, *always* building. A funny, fickle thing too. One moment she would experience a newness with gripping intensity only to forget every shred of feeling she had just swum in, each dogged or merry transition marked with a fit of giggles. As if she felt everything and nothing simultaneously and all her body could do was celebrate in response.

The elf's armor dug into her side as he carried her and yet she didn't care about the pain, for the male had told her not to. Which resulted in more tingly sensations and more laughter. Whenever the elf suggested anything to her—notions that always seemed lovely, such as feeling no pain—the man they called Félip would materialize by her side with daggers in his eyes and lyrical poison in his voice, then fade into the shadows like dark mist.

"Your protector is a pain in my arse," the elf would say. "The fool lad and his hot temper."

"My protector?" She would laugh at the silly thought. "Why would I need protection from you, kind sir?"

"Just think of all the fun you will have soon, little queen."

Bubbly tingles had fizzed in her mind. "Are we running off to have fun?" she asked. "My mother will worry so." Then she would laugh.

A small part of her knew the elf meant something else entirely. Faerie struck? Did such a thing exist? She was uncertain though the word warbled in her head. Many notions warbled in her head, actually. Had she drunk more goblets of mulberry wine than proper? The world continued to tilt despite already being tilted herself.

The Wilds tangled thicker with brush and trees the deeper they pressed into the faerie woods. Oranges, yellows, and reds remained. But somehow cleaner. Crisper. Leaves blushed fiery shades all around her and fluttered to the ground like wayward embers. And oh the music they made as they fell! Unlike the leaves in Rothlín who seemed to tra-la-la and reel about in the wind, the leaves here sang soul-haunting notes as their skeletal frames fell toward their graves. Tears burned her eyes and fell to join the leaves who now rested in peace.

"Is he hurting ye?" The young man took shape before her eyes and she gasped at his sudden nearness. "Where does it hurt, lass?"

"No, sir." Her cheeks flushed under his inspection. Never had she wept, let alone before others, nor while hanging over the shoulder of a beautiful fae male in full armor. "I cry for the leaves as they sing their last song for the forest."

"Focus, Félip Batten," the elf said. "We're on a mission and you need to fall in line. I don't have time for your territorial—"

"Not speaking to ye, Dog Breath."

"Dalbréath, mortal. And your commander."

The man they called Félip ignored the correction and pushed his dark brows together. "Ye can hear nature sing?" he asked her.

"Shhhh, listen," she admonished, biting back a tearful laugh. Her eyes closed as her ears filled with a thousand melodious emotions—the melancholy leaves singing their goodbyes, the bones of their brittle bodies being crushed beneath each set of boots, the wind frolicking through the trees, the ticklish giggles of moss. More tears escaped to fly free with the playful wind. When she opened her eyes, Félip was gone. He had dissolved into mere mist and shadow once more. Was he even real? Or perhaps a figment of her sluggish mind?

"I am dreaming . . ." Another tear-stained laugh erupted from her body.

The changing world continued to spin around her, faster and faster. The energy inside of her was building, building, ever building. Beautiful, angular faces blurred by while shouting commands. Boots stomped in chorus, like the beatings of a drum line. The tingling sensation in her mind spread out to each limb. Bubbles popped in her feet as she tapped the air to the march. Perhaps she should dance. *Yes, the forest wants me to dance for her.*

"Put me down, kind sir."

"Not until we reach Leaf Curl," the elf answered. Dalbréath, was that his name?

"My feet must touch earth. The wind beckons me to twirl with the dying leaves."

The elf slowed and then she heard mercurial voices—hot, cold, rising and falling in pitch and passion. She could have focused on their words, but her heart was still too full of the sorrows and laughter all around her to fully listen. A couple words bled through, "madness" and "rune sickness." They were meaningless words. She needed their conversation to swell with music too. Anger simmered low in her belly. How dare they deny her music?

"I demand you release me!" she shouted. "I need to dance!"

Dalbréath swore under his breath and lowered her to the forest floor, his eyes wide. With fear? With humor? She couldn't tell.

The moment the toes of her boots caressed leaf litter and black earth, her body leaped away. She bowed before a female and laughed. Then curtsied before two males. The wind whispered encouragement to frolic, and so she did. The trees swayed under the melody of life. The leaves sang their haunting notes until they crashed to their death. Faeries laughed all around her, some even encouraged her to dance harder. She dipped, twirled, leaped—building, building, building— all the while her body grew more fevered. Music played in her veins and beat in her heart. Sweat beaded on her forehead. White-blonde strands fell loose from their braided crown and flew around her face in a sticky mess. She clutched at the pink roses in her hair and threw them around the forest as though petals in a parade. Breath came quick, ragged. She gulped heaving lungfuls of air as though drowning. Still she dipped, twirled, and leaped. Still the faeries laughed and encouraged her on. She couldn't stop dancing. She didn't want to stop dancing. Even though her stomach grew sick and her body trembled with weakness.

"Songbird," the young man snapped from behind. She spun in a twirl of melodious laughter toward him. "Ye need to rest yer feet before they blister."

"Let her dance!" a faerie tossed out.

"Shut yer ugly trap," the young man shot back. Daggers reappeared in his dark gaze. "She'll dance until she dies."

Aroreh spun around, her arms out wide, the young man's face moving in and out of view. "Then let me die content!"

"The palace guards are still chasing our trail. We need to run."

Unable to resist the urge, she grabbed his hands and pulled him into a dance. "Do you feel life sing? Isn't it heartbreaking and beautiful?"

"Yer having a withdrawal," he said softly, staring at their joined hands as if stricken. "Sick in the head without the hag's runes—"

"I am not sick!" she screamed at him. "Do not mock me!"

The young man clenched his jaw and lowered his eyes, then whispered, "Dance with me?"

"Feel life's heartbeat, Félip Batten." How did she remember his name? By the look on his face, he was just as astonished as she. But never mind. She placed his hands on her waist and he sucked in a sharp breath. "Now listen to the music."

Their bodies began to move and she hummed in delight the melody crescendoing all around her. A dance partner! And a handsome one too. They spun beneath the boughs of a tree and then another. He set their rhythm, a far slower one than she expected, but still he kept in tempo with the song she hummed. A song that was *building, building, building*. His fingers splayed across her lower back as his hold tightened on her waist. At his touch, her knees wobbled a step, and then another. This was her first dance with a man, and a stranger to her no less.

An odd cloak that reflected the forest covered his upper body. Though a sturdy garment, glimpses of bare skin still peeked through as they moved. She forced her eyes upward. Dirt smudged part of his cheek, just above a scar. The injury ran the length of his jaw, ending by full lips and a chin with a slight cleft. A smattering of faint freckles spilled across his nose. Russet brown hair hung in thick waves over his eyes, the very same dark eyes now meeting her curious gaze. He seemed curious of her too, openly staring for several movements of time, and yet he didn't smile. Rather, the corners of his mouth dipped in a frown. Why did everyone frown at her as of late? And why was he scarred?

"Do I not please you?" she asked, feeling tears form once more. Crying was an odd response to feelings when smiling was more convenient and less messy, she decided. But there were far too many emotions, perhaps even more than the grains of sand along Rothlin's coastal shores. Some feelings she didn't even know by name. She lifted her finger and touched the corner of his mouth where he frowned. "I was made to bring others joy."

His sigh brushed along her cheek as his steps slowed even more.

Gently he moved his face away from her touch. "What makes ye happy? Besides dancing and music?"

Building, building, building . . .

"I . . ." She tilted her head. A great many things made her happy, she was sure of it. A memory surfaced, despite the thoughts spinning faster than a wheel, despite the throbbing pain bleating in her head. *Songbird.* He called her songbird. She *did* please him. Gratitude swelled in her chest and she smiled. "Making other people happy is my joy. Especially when I please . . ." The words trailed off when her chest tightened with a familiar ache. A knowing. A pull toward something forbidden. Something entirely selfish. The goddess would surely disapprove. "You . . . you do not like to touch others, do you?"

"Only danced with me mither—"

"—I wanted to dance! Is it so wrong to please myself?"

Félip let go of her waist but didn't step away. "Aye, please yerself, Aroreh. Naething wrong with that."

"You are not mad at me?"

"Nae, lass." Félip leaned in close and whispered, "Forgive me, but ye look like ye swallowed a coal furnace."

"I feel all wrong inside," she whispered back. "The goddess has left me."

The hard lines of Félip's face softened. "Yer experiencing rune withdrawals. Faerie Madness, some call it. Yer inhibitions are dimmed and feelings are more raw. Thoughts too."

Sweat dripped down her forehead. "The music, I . . . I can't hear the forest sing—"

The world tilted once more and, this time, her legs gave way. And then she was falling, like a leaf. She clawed through the air for the young man, not ready to go to her grave. Strong arms caught her body before she hit the ground. Voices echoed and scraped in her ears. She grimaced as she curled up around her middle. Then air—blessed air—floated over her skin as her body moved through the forest, her face pressed to a warm chest. Everything hurt—her head, her legs and feet, her stomach, her heart.

She wasn't experiencing withdrawals. No, she knew exactly what was wrong.

"Blight Rot," she murmured while playing with the strings of a cloak.

The arms carrying her tightened as steps faltered. Her mother would surely never wish her return now.

She was ruined.

CHAPTER 6

FÉLIP

The Dúnælven fae stood on the edge of The Wilds, drawing their weapons and quickly making battle plans. Félip skidded to a halt near the line of light and shadows, where The Wilds gave way to Leaf Curl, the outlaying woods around the village of the same name. Panic rushed in his veins as a glacial finger traced down his spine. They were trapped, unless the Veil recognized the fae. And right now, it appeared the Veil refused to respond. Select fae would touch the silver mist and the mist would push back. Félip chewed on his bottom lip and squinted his eyes. In the mist, lines would take shape and disappear. *Runes.* He didn't remember spell weavers revealing their language in the mist before. Was this new?

"Why do the woods not open?" a warrior asked nearby. No one had an answer.

Aroreh lay limp in Félip's arms, though wide awake. Her glassy eyes stared straight ahead, her gaze vacant. But she babbled on about random things, like the Castoffs children did when ill with Wool Sorter's Sickness. Their lungs burned for air while their blistered bodies burned even hotter. And she was a furnace, seemingly growing more fevered since nearing the Veil.

His arms shook under her weight though she was a mere slip of a girl, as his mither would say. But he wasn't used to such a heavy workout. His days were spent sweeping threads and loom scraps from factory floors to prevent rats from nesting and furnace embers from sparking buildings into flame—not soldiering. Not muscle-grinding work when walking the shadows to deliver messages hither and dither for the Thorns either. Nor was his diet rich. His body looked more fae than human—tall, lean, agile. Only adrenaline kept his legs pumping now and his arms from dropping the load they couriered through the forest. And self-protection forced his mind to think of anything but the two words she had uttered in her delusion, or he might go mad too.

Blight Rot.

How he loathed those words. And his mark of shame—one the princess couldn't identify while faerie tranced. But the spell had worn off and her mind now suffered reality. And it was too much too soon. The sight of his face probably would be too. His hands itched to pull the hood over his head and cover his left cheek.

Behind Félip, a clash of steel clanked loud enough to wake the dead. He swore under his breath. The hag—the name he preferred for Rothlín's queen—probably ordered his return along with the princess's so she could finish her sacrifice ritual. Ice clawed down his spine once more. He would rather die here, in the forest, than in her temple of false gods.

All his days, he had heard only of the queen's beauty. At first glance, he supposed so. She was as fair and as unnaturally beautiful as her daughter. In all ways she appeared human enough, but a preternatural gleam darkened her otherworldly eyes. A predatory stare similar to the fae or mountain ogres.

Nasty beasts, ogres. Félip involuntarily shuddered.

War cries rumbled through Félip and snapped him out of his spiraling thoughts. Palace guards were cutting through brambles and brush. He had only a few heartbeats left to live. And this wasn't how he imagined his ending. Though, he had envisioned being chained to the locks many times, while starved, beaten, and left to die in the elements. A couple of years ago, another Blight met such a fate.

Did the royal House of Rosen descend from a line of creatures?

Queen Líeh created monsters to hide her own truth, he was sure of it. The woman wasn't natural. He was tired of paying for the sins of Ealdspell so the New Dawn Era could profit from the dusted realms. His gaze dangerously slipped to the young woman in his arms. Her cheeks were flushed, her bright blue eyes now dull. Folds of golden-white hair rippled over his arms. A faint melody rasped between her lips. A songbird, even now. Even as her technology overheated and programming failed. She paid for ancestral sins not her own too.

Félip considered her vulnerability as he readjusted the princess in his arms. But it was no use. To his shame, he wasn't sure how much longer he could last. He clenched his jaw with a grimace. Fire curled through his muscles. Any moment now, his arms would turn to ash and blow away. Just in time for his heart to become intimately acquainted with palace steel.

"Your Highness." Dalbréath held out his hands.

Félip didn't even hesitate. Gently, he rolled Aroreh into the male's waiting arms. With white hair, sky blue eyes, high cheek bones, and alabaster skin, Dalbréath looked as though he could be her sibling. A far older, womanizing bastard of a sibling. The male's calculating gaze swept over the fae warriors along the edge line before meeting Félip's appraisal. A blush warmed Félip's neck and he bit back another curse when the elf's lips tipped up. Men—or male fae—weren't his fancy, even if Dalbréath was pretty.

"Take one of my swords," the elf said. "You may need to fight, if we can't run."

"I cannae feel my arms." Félip mumbled. But, really, he had never wielded a sword before, nor held one.

"Use the shadows. Strike unseen or remain hidden." Dalbréath winked at him and, in such a way, Félip gathered he understood the real problem. "A sword is far lighter than she."

"Fine, ye frilly toadstool."

Félip casually glanced around the woods and noted how the various warriors held their weapons. He could do this. Kill a man?

From the shadows? This was less certain. But hold the weapon aloft as though ready to strike? Maybe. Drawing in a steadying breath, he pulled the finely smithed sword from the scabbard strapped across Dalbréath's back. Fingers of light touched the steel and Félip turned the weapon in his hand to watch the glint. He would need to work on angles to hide the reflective light, if he were to shadow.

"To run a man through requires more strength than slicing air," Dalbréath whispered to him, his gaze still darting about, calculating. "If you strike a guard in leathers, push with all your core and upper body muscle. But if a guard wears steel, stab the open areas between armor. Understand?"

"Aye."

"Position your feet and legs for optimal balance. Or strikes and blocks will knock you over."

Félip studied the warriors around him, measuring their stances and watching their footwork. "Do ye actually care fer me, Dog Breath?"

The elf never had a chance to answer. Palace guards pushed through their group. Reaching out a hand, Dalbréath touched a guard's face and spoke in runic, "The soldiers in palace uniforms are wolves. Kill them." Blue light sparked from the elf's fingertips, then he pulled away. The palace guard pivoted on his heel and lunged at a fellow guard. Félip watched in horror as the guard ran his sword through his comrade's gut. Rune whispered still, the palace guard lifted his blood-stained steel and searched for the next "wolf" to slay. Dalbréath touched another guard and then another, Aroreh curled safe in his arms. Félip almost laughed aloud. No guard would attack Dalbréath with their precious princess vulnerable to injury or worse. The queen would probably eat their entrails from golden platters, if they did.

The humor was short lived, however. Feet anchored in fear, Félip stood like a head-knocked eejit in the middle of the fray. Dalbréath's movements slowed as his energy waned. His spell weaving gift was a rare one, thank the false goddess. There were far more guards than fae warriors. Hopefully the wolf killers helped turn the tides in their favor.

"A Blight!" A guard kindly announced before his attack. Félip was able to prepare for the hit and lifted his sword to block. The steel hit his with bone-shaking force and his teeth clacked audibly.

"Feck me!" Félip cried out when he recovered. "Damn, laddie. What does yer mither feed ye fer breakfast?"

"Dinnae speak of me mither!" the guard shouted.

"It was a compliment, ye dumb oaf."

"No talking, Blight!" The guard lifted his sword for another hit.

"Shame." Félip blocked again, tensing every tired muscle in his body. "I talk better than I fight, ye ken?"

"Goddess save me . . ." And he swore the guard rolled his eyes as he muttered each word.

It was all the time Félip needed and he slipped into a nearby shadow and adjusted his cloak, finally pulling the hood over his wretched face. Sun rays shimmered between the autumn leaves. He could mimic the light to hide the glinting steel in his hand. A westerly breeze slanted the mid-day light behind him a few paces. He watched the dappled shadows shift and sway and then he moved accordingly. Angling his body, Félip toed the line of darker, colder spots. He preferred these areas. Less fiddling with his cloak to absorb the light and shape shadows.

The palace guard turned in circles a few times before jogging off toward his next opponent. Which just happened to be near where Félip was hiding. As the large man sprinted past, Félip stuck out a fallen tree limb and tripped the dimwit. Child's play, really. The guard fell with a satisfying *thwump*, his sword scattering across the forest floor. Another guard, who was walking backwards while fending off his foe, tripped over the man's body and fell to his arse. The fae warrior slid a quick glance Félip's direction and tipped his head in acknowledgment to the shadow walker he knew was there before running the guard through. Blood gurgled from the guard's mouth and

Félip wanted to vomit. The giant Félip felled first closed his eyes and pretended to be dead. And, in that moment, Félip hoped the lad was able to return to his mither alive.

Why did the Veil remain closed? They could all return home to their mithers if the damn mist would just part.

Alas, The Wilds remained a blur of steel and leather and blood and screams. Even Brandu joined the melee, pecking at eyes or ears. Along the Veil, Dúnælven threw fists at the silvery mist, shouting commands. Runes now glowed brighter inside the Veil than before. From the corner of his vision, a flash of white streaked the blood-soaked ground. The breath stilled in his tightening lungs.

Aroreh.

Her body lay sprawled in the moss and leaves, blonde tendrils wreathed around her head, her arms and legs in strange positions. Dalbréath lay nearby, his fingers clawing the forest floor to move toward her. Félip's feet kicked up dirt as he lunged out of the shadows and into the fray, fear worming deep in his gut. He dodged swords and axes, ducking, feinting left and right. But another fae scooped up the princess before he could. Relieved, Félip placed his hands beneath Dalbréath's arms and encouraged him to stand. The male was weak. Blood dripped from his nose.

The elf was nearly to his feet, woozy from magic loss. Félip grunted under the male's weight, almost falling over when the world began to spin at nauseating speeds until he thought he might truly be sick. The fae who had fetched Aroreh now held her up high for all to see the limp, broken factory doll. Then the faerie pulled from his pocket a sharp spindle tree splinter and shouted, "I'll prick her finger and she'll die!"

The palace guards circling the warrior lowered their swords and took a step backward.

"We demand another dream!" the warrior continued, quoting familiar Thorns rhetoric. "A New Dawn is coming for Rothlín!"

"Stop!" Félip screamed and launched forward. "She's innocent!"

Dalbréath caught his arm and started laughing quietly, a raspy, breathy sound that further stilled Félip's momentum.

"Are ye mad?" Félip's pulse beat like war drums against his ribs. His blood churned wildly, a torrential snow-melt river. Dalbréath yanked Félip close until he felt the elf's lips brushing against his ear.

"She'll just hibernate for a spell. Took most of my magic reserves. But I made sure of it." His voice became a wind that fluttered the leaves of Félip's mind. "But the guards and most of the Dúnælven's warriors don't know that. They believe she'll die, including the warrior holding her." Dalbréath's fingers touched Félip's temples and, in runic, said, *"Let them believe the lie."* A tingly sensation bubbled through Félip's head before fizzing down the length of his body. A hot breath left his chest in a cathartic rush. His fists relaxed and unclenched. Dalbréath collapsed at his side. Félip patted the elf's cheek, but the male remained unconscious, dangling beneath his hold.

Similarly, Aroreh's head lolled to the side. Dead eyes stared forward, but her lips moved to a melody all her own.

Even when the spindle prickwood slivered into the tip of her finger.

Ruby blossomed to a glistening berry of blood almost immediately. Then her body jerked, a single spasm at first. A heartbeat later, she quaked with convulsions, eyes wide and mouth parted in a silent scream.

A cheer erupted among the fae, growing in strength, right as her body stilled and eyes fluttered closed. The same moment the silver mist brightened. Trees groaned and bowed outward while shrubs moved the same direction to reveal a golden path made of corkscrew-curled leaves.

Still cheering, the faeries grabbed their dead and injured and dashed into Leaf Curl. A palace guard bumped Félip's arm and then stabbed another nearby with a guttural cry. The wolf slayers were thankfully still busy even though Dalbréath hung unconscious at his side. The bastard had saved Félip's life with his rune whispering. This twist in events probably saved other fae too. But the hunt wasn't over. A wolf noticed Félip's slack-jawed, immobile arse and Dalbréath's vulnerability and charged. A couple strides before his sword could run Félip through, a blessed Dúnælven arrow ripped through the guard's throat.

"Shite!" Félip slung another arm beneath Dalbréath's other shoulder, the sword still awkwardly gripped in Félip's hand, and then he began dragging the armor-clad male toward the parted Veil.

Sweat dripped down Félip's face and the muscles in his jaw ached. He was close, so close now. Thankfully the palace guards were too consumed with trying to subdue the wolf killers to notice his pathetic crawl toward the Veil.

"Your Highness." Gedlen slipped his longbow behind his back and grabbed the magic-depleted elf from Félip's arms. "You two are the last."

Félip's gaze jumped from tree to bush to the moss-dotted ground. "Aroreh?"

"Already in Leaf Cu—behind you!"

Félip spun, sword raised. A battle ax severed the faerie steel like freshly sharpened sheers sliding through yards of linen. The broken weapon clattered to the ground before his feet. Félip didn't have time to think of the ramifications. The battle ax slashed through the air once more and Félip ducked. From the distance, he heard his name. That was all the reminder he needed. Before the guard could take another swipe at him, he flailed headlong over the line of light and shadows, landing unceremoniously on his arse. The guard attempted to chase after him. But the Veil shoved him away from the line. Silver mist draped closed as the trees groaned back into position and the shrubs once more moved to block the golden path of corkscrew-curled leaves from sight.

The last thing Félip saw before collapsing in relief was the palace wolf being stabbed through the heart by a rune whispered wolf killer.

CHAPTER 7

AROREH

Black entombed Aroreh's entire vision. For what seemed like hours—perhaps even days—she had screamed for her mother, for her favorite temple maiden, and even for her music instructor. Their collective shunning oozed through these craggy stone walls like acid made from a starless night sky. The cackling drip echoed in her ears. A persistent mocking *drip, drip, drip.* And her hope began to corrode with every splash of rejection.

Was she in a dungeon cell?

She sucked in a hiccupped breath. Though she couldn't see her hand in front of her face, she knew she was rotting away—system corruption. This is what happened to New Dawn mortals who touched blighted souls. And she had, despite her mother's lifelong warnings. Aroreh curled up on the jagged stone floor and sobbed into the arms circling her knees.

"Goddess, please hear my prayers. I will not disappoint you again," she whispered to the darkness. A new wave of terror ripped through her trembling body and settled in her bones. "Don't abandon me!" she screamed. "Save me! Please . . ." Her fingernails clawed at the stone.

"So, you live. My guards reported you had pricked your finger and died by the Veil."

Aroreh's head whipped up at the familiar voice. "Mother. Oh Mother, you came for me . . ." Her voice broke into a sob.

61

"Your ceremonial dress is contaminated."

"I was taken from the temple—"

"Silence!"

Queen Líeh's form faded into view and Aroreh squinted her eyes against the glowing light. Long blonde hair rippled down her mother's back, each strand glinting the purest gold. Sapphire eyes sparked with disgust, her red-painted lips set in a thin line. But her nose was strangely different. More pert and less straight, regal. Her mother's voice snapped her from the odd observation.

"You are a disgrace."

Aroreh inspected her dress under the light that shone from her mother's presence. Torn lace dangled by threads. Grayish mud caked parts of her skirt and bodice and streaked across her arms. "I shall clean myself, if it pleases you. Simply guide me to—"

"Matters not. *You* do not please me, Aroreh."

Tears burned the back of her eyes. "Yes, Mother. How shall I bring you joy?"

"I fear you are beyond improvement."

"Please—"

"No sniveling!" Her mother's lips twisted into a sneer. "Where are your feminine graces? A New Dawn Princess of the realm doesn't *beg*."

"Allow me to make proper amends to Aisling after purification."

Laughter bounced off the stone walls and Aroreh resisted the urge to cover her ears from the painful sound. *Drip, drip, drip.* "Do you honestly believe Aisling will want anything from you?"

Aroreh remained silent, her hands folded at her waist, her eyes downcast.

"Smile! A woman's beauty is more serviceable when she smiles."

Her lips betrayed her heartache and stretched in eagerness to please.

"Why do you believe the Milfae took you?"

The Milfae?

"Perhaps because—" A slap stung her cheek and her head snapped to the side. Fresh tears pooled in the corner of her eyes. "It . . . It matters not what I think. Tell me, why you believe the Milfae took me?"

A satisfied smile softened the disappointment on her mother's face, and a ray of sunshine warmed a cold, frightened corner of Aroreh's heart. "Darling," her mother cooed, "you were manufactured by the goddess herself. And faeries are always attracted to beautiful, shiny objects."

Aroreh forced her smile to grow.

"And that is what you are—an object. Nothing more."

"I am honored to be a vessel of Aisling."

"*Were*, darling." Her mother leaned in close and Aroreh slowly lifted her gaze, her bottom lip trembling with the effort to not cry. "You honestly believe the goddess would want you back? That I do?"

The icy terror in her bones leeched back into her bloodstream. Fear-stiffened muscles shivered for any touch of warmth and her teeth clattered so loud, she could no longer hear the pounding of her pulse. "I-I shall do a-a-anything you ask of m-me," she managed to whisper. "I am e-e-eager to p-please."

"Your blood is frostbitten." Her mother tilted her head. "The Rot has progressed rather quickly, I see."

Aroreh choked back a plea of desperation and remained quiet despite her suffering.

A lady does not beg.

"Bring me Prince Félip Batten from the dusted Realm of Glenashlen." Her mother grinned and her eyes sparkled with delight. "When you do, as high priestess and as your queen, I shall forgive you and personally perform your purification."

Aroreh fell to her knees and bowed her head. "Thank y-you, Mother. You are m-merciful."

"And if you don't? I shall wipe you from my house." Her mother bent at the waist and angled her head to better see Aroreh. "And remember, darling, do not sleep. Even if your body fatigues without Aisling's strength. Should you slumber, your dream weaving will kill Aisling's blessings throughout Rothlín and then you shall be executed as a goddess slayer."

Dream weaving?

Queen Líeh's form brightened into a pure white light, and the shrieking light vibrations pierced Aroreh's ears. She threw an arm over her pained eyes instead of her ears, but her body was shaking too much to fully block the illumination's intensity. In a sparkling flash, the light disappeared save a single speck that danced above the jagged stone floor.

A *goddess slayer* . . . Aroreh swallowed painfully against the rawness in her throat.

The dainty blue glow seemed to call to her, pulsing ever so slightly, redirecting her troublesome thoughts. Aroreh found her feet and crept toward the tiny speck on shaking legs, uncertain if the light were friend or foe. But she craved light after screaming and crying into the darkness. When near, the little glow zipped around her head in a tinkling peal of laughing chimes before gamboling off into the black. Aroreh's feet dashed after the orb before her mind could even rationalize her primal response to escape from this prison.

The black world gradually lightened and consumed every heartbeat of her color-starved attention. The uneven rock floors tangled into sprawling tree roots and the stone wall softened into a chorus of fluttering leaves. Aroreh followed the speck as the dainty blue glow grew into the blue sky of daylight, growing larger and wider until she emerged from the mouth of a cave and into a moss-draped forest of golden trees with corkscrew leaves. A few steps away, a rainbow of wildflowers dotted the woods in reds, purples, blues, and orange.

A laugh danced free from her trembling body. Glacial rivers still ran in her veins, but she only cared about the wondrous colors wherever she looked, as well as the swaying flowers. Plucking one near a rune-etched stone. Picking another that had vined around a limb and dangled at eye-level. Birds sang melodies inspiring her heart to leap into the air and fly too. And perhaps it could now that she was free of the black cave and oozing Rot and her mother's chilly reception.

Aroreh paused, waiting for the full body flinch and Aisling's strength to correct her complaints. But nothing happened.

A trickle of laughter escaped her air-tightened lungs. The trees swayed in appreciation and the leaves shimmied, the same way the Great Spindle Tree moved when she sang. Had she pleased the trees in this enchanting faerie wood with mere laughter? Even the flowers dipped and bowed in merriment. Encouraged, Aroreh opened her mouth and allowed a few trilling notes to join the songbirds in the trees.

"Are ye lost?"

Aroreh spun toward the man's voice. All the mirth died on her tongue and she took several panicked steps backward.

His dark eyes traveled over her torn gown, partially unlaced bodice, mud-streaked arms and face, and the bouquet of wildflowers in her hand before settling on the nest of hair tangling about her face and down her back. "Are ye well, lassie?"

"No," she answered despite not wishing to speak. She had never lied before and didn't know how to even begin to do so. "I am Rotting away until I am naught but a breeze for the Cold Winds."

"Aye, there are a few people I would dust given the chance." A lopsided smile appeared just for her and she blinked. Did he joke? "Not a terrible magic to have, aye?"

He took another step toward her and she took another step back.

"Why do ye move away from me?"

"I am corrupted . . . by you."

He laughed and his handsome face transformed into a sight that left her breathless. The wind skipped through the brambles and tousled the wavy reddish-brown strands over his eyes. Long arms crossed over his chest and her gaze took in his narrow hips and long legs, then focused on his smile once more. Shadows caressed the high planes of his cheeks, as if tracing along the features of his face. In many ways, Félip Batten was more faerie than human. Was he fae?

His humor softened and their gazes locked. "Lass, if I were to corrupt ye, there'd be no suffering, ye ken? Only sighs and smiles."

A flush crept up her neck and she angled her head away in modesty. How did a woman properly reply to unwanted attentions? All her life, she was taught to smile and please. But every situation had seemed safe enough—until now. Though she couldn't explain why he made her uneasy. Was it her mother's request? Her conversation with Félip in The Wilds? Aroreh couldn't remember how she ended up in the dungeon cave. Strangely, she couldn't remember anything after she departed the temple with her mother. Beneath lowered lashes, Aroreh relished every handsomely boyish feature, from Félip's full lips, the slight cleft in his chin, the freckles across his nose, and—her breath caught. His scar was missing. Did he weave a new face from The Dream?

Confused, she considered her finger's tip, the very one that had touched him in the temple. Black lines now trailed down her finger, down her palm, over her wrist, and up her forearm. A startled cry left her dry, cracked lips and the wildflowers dropped from her other hand. The young man took another step toward her, followed by more. Lightning bolts of fear shot through her body. She tried to step back, but her foot touched the trunk of a tree. And he was simply too fast.

"Would ye like to dance?" he asked, offering his hand.

The word "no" trembled on the tip of her tongue and begged for release, but she didn't know how to politely refuse an offer.

"Dinnae ye want to make me happy?"

Nausea bubbled in her middle. "Yes, making others happy brings me joy," she heard herself saying. Clearing her throat, she added, "My mother demands your presence, in the Temple of Aisling."

"Do ye know what she does with the blood?"

"A sacrifice for the goddess."

"Spells." The young man grinned and, in such a way, the hairs on her arms stood on end. "Malfae spell weavers need fresh blood fer nanobots. Blighted blood is even richer."

"The ways of Aisling are—"

"Manufactured." He leaned in close now, their noses almost touching. His sweetened breath came quick and pulsed hot across her wintry skin. "Ye are truly the most beautiful woman in the realm, perhaps in all of Ealdspell, even when disheveled and in hibernation mode."

Hibernation mode? Did she sleep?

The strange thoughts dissolved quickly, however, and Aroreh smiled at his praise, unable to stop herself. A part of her longed to please him, to prove to Aisling that she was worthy of purification and renewal. The other part screamed at her to run. He wasn't Félip Batten, she was sure of it.

"Dance with me, lass?"

"I . . ." She swallowed. The words were thick and slow, as though honey pooled in her mouth and sealed her tongue in place. Ladies were never to refuse a gentleman and he hadn't actually acted uncouth. Aisling desired for women to be subservient, to smile and please. To ask him to leave might be seen as begging too. And Aroreh did long to dance. How she loved dancing! The forest was singing to her every winged heartbeat, and her pulse longed to take flight and join the birds in the branches. She opened her mouth to consent, but she still couldn't speak. Traces of icy terror still pooling in her bones leeched out once more.

"Simply take my hand," he encouraged, a handsome smile in place.

She lifted her hand—the skin shaded blue from the Rot's chill. If she refused . . . No, she *must* please Aisling. Her very life depended on it. Her eyes slid to his left cheek and studied the scar's absence as her frostbitten fingers touched his palm.

Pain seized her muscles almost instantly. Blood rushed to her head in pounding torrents. She couldn't move. She couldn't scream. And his hand was crushing hers.

"Beautiful," his breathy voice slithered in her ear. "Now fall back asleep and Dream."

A sharp sliver pierced the skin of her Rotted fingertip and then everything went black.

CHAPTER 8

FÉLIP

The last two weeks passed in a blur of activities. Félip's body ached something fierce, especially when lying about in bed with little distractions—like now. Ten days ago, he began combat training with Gedlen to satisfy his restless energy. Especially when the Fate Maker refused to share where they had secretly housed Aroreh from the other Dúnælven who thought her dead. Her system still hibernated despite all efforts to wake her mind too. Dalbréath's whispers proved more powerful than needed, it seemed. And as luck would have it, the general desired to personally see to Félip's suffering. The cheeky bastard. And the male worked him hard. Félip didn't know there were so many ways to kill a man, a few he might employ on his faerie overlord if Gedlen worked him as hard this day as well.

A sliver of sunlight crawled across Félip's grimacing face and he resigned to this morning's fate. Throwing off his covers, he grumbled under his breath as he rose to his feet and stretched. The cold air raced across his bare chest and back, a rush of goosebumps giving chase. He snatched his new elven tunic and threw it on, tying off the waist with a leather belt. In the corner of his room, he poured fresh water into a bowl and washed his face before shaving. Just the act of scraping a simple razor up his neck made his muscles weep. *Pull yerself together, laddie.*

Grooming complete, he trudged down the short hallway after tossing the dirty water out his window and pissing off a sleeping pixie. Mither sat in a cushioned chair at a table beside Faither. Félip slowed his steps to take in their soft smiles for one another. They were happy. In all his years with them, he couldn't remember a time when worry didn't line the corners of his mither's mouth or his faither's forehead. The abundance of food showed now too. Both of his foster parents had a healthy flush about their skin and eyes. These past two weeks he had fought doubt over his decision to aid Dúnælven in their attack, and the ones to come. But seeing his parents smile dusted many of his niggling fears.

"Good morning," he announced while walking into their private moment.

"Lad, what has bewitched yer hair?" His mither smothered a laugh.

Félip rolled his eyes. "Maybe my hair will scare that fae demon training me today."

His faither gestured toward a platter of hardboiled robins' eggs, bannocks, salted pork, apples, and candied flowers. "Break yer fast with us, Félip?"

"I'll see ye at midday. Already late, ye ken?"

"Aye, dinnae want to keep the fae demon await'n." His faither quirked a smile. Félip stared for several beats longer than necessary, wondering if he were still dreaming. His faither was *smiling*. At him. Were they rune whispered? And if so, did he care? They were happy. Though, Félip was unsure if he ever remembered his parents enjoying a day off in their life, not even when sick.

Blinking back the shock, he reached for a hardboiled egg, a bannock, and a couple apple slices and stuffed them into the pockets of his breeches. Then he kissed his mither on the cheek and shook his faither's hand before leaving their quaint cottage. Took everything in him to not scowl in pain as he clasped his faither's hand. No need to worry them after they had finally found peace. Did they understand the cost behind their retirement in Leaf Curl? Did he want them to?

Félip thought of these things and more as he ambled down the forest path, between other cottages, toward the training ring. This was the village he romped in until Rothlín. He was a faerie child until made a slave in the Castoffs. They even put his family in the same cottage as his first mither, an elven huntress who eventually moved to the other side of the mountains. For thirteen rotations now he had known endless dust, burn fields, dilapidated cottages, rusted textile factories, hatred, hunger, and survival. Shadows caressed his frame as he ducked beneath branches. Félip allowed the colors of Leaf Curl to seep into his very essence, allowed his lungs to enjoy breath after breath of clean air. Here, he wasn't feared for his frostbite scar. Faerie children laughed and danced around him then would scamper off to their next carefree adventure.

Guilt nibbled on the edges of his contented mood. His neighbors, those still in the factories, they remained in misery, many with unnatural smiles no doubt still beaming from their spell-woven faces despite their hardships. A factory loss would surely mean income loss too. The bits of food in his stomach soured. He was party to the attack on Rothlín. And now partly responsible for the problems they would face.

"Off to fight?" a voice asked from behind. He spun on his heel and met the green eyes of Cerwyn, a female warrior who appeared close to his age though he knew she was far older. Golden-brown hair twisted atop her head in a bun of sorts, held together with decorative cherry blossom twigs. "Is the prince's tongue tied in knots?"

"No," he replied softly. "My head is collecting wool. Training today?"

"Collecting dust is more like it," she said. "Do you actually use that brain of yours? Or are you just a pretty face?"

Laughter shook his sore body. "Aye," he answered with a wink to hide his embarrassment. Pretty face?

Cerwyn grinned and then leaned in and kissed his cheek before dashing down the trail, leaving him completely faerie struck. Over her shoulder, she called out, "See you in the ring, Your Highness!"

Félip's heart leapt to his throat where the rapidly beating organ remained lodged. She had kissed him. His fingers touched the skin still tingling from her lips.

His first kiss.

A blush heated his face as tears pricked the back of his eyes. A friendly gesture, he knew. Nothing more. The fae were freer with their affections, and Cerwyn had shown him lots of friendly attentions and touches for two weeks. But since fostering in Rothlín, no one outside of his foster mither had kissed his face—or touched his skin. Only his clothes or hair. Well, until Aroreh. And why wasn't his mither or faither ever afraid of him?

Blight Rot.

Images flashed by in his mind. Being spit on. Cursed at. Older boys stealing his meager lunch. The shame of sweeping a factory for a pittance. The shame of not being able to care for the very people who risked all to care for him. Being beaten with sticks and hit with rocks. The gleam of delight in the queen's eyes over spilling his royal blood. Over eliminating what remained from the House of Batten and the Realm of Glenashlen.

The sweet warmth in his chest heated to white hot anger. And more shadows joined the others dappling across his face.

Kicking up a flurry of leaves, he continued his march toward the training ring. His fists curled at his sides, and a scowl formed between his brows and at the corners of his lips. Why wasn't his mither afraid to touch him? Why had his parents taken him in? Surely, they knew he would never be able to properly care for them. And why had those questions never truly bothered him as they did this very moment? He knew the answer, though. There was naught time to think, only live from one moment to the next. And the Dúnælven were probably immune and spell wove immunity for his mither and faither as a form of payment.

The path disappeared inside his head and the village swallowed his moving form. People rushed by him. Voices shouted. The shadows slithered into one and then coiled tighter around his heart. Parts of him were snapping beneath each footstep like brittle twigs. His life continued to carousel past his mind's eye, but he only had sights for one person.

Félip grabbed a sword from the pile and strode into the ring. "Gedlen!"

The general's eyes snapped up to his. A slow smile spread across the male's pale face. Others in the ring stared wide-eyed over Félip's shoulder before running out of the arena. Shouts grew louder behind him, but Félip leveled his narrowed gaze at the elf dressed in black leathers with sword held aloft and canines bared. A war cry rushed from Félip's gut and then he lunged.

Steel collided and Félip grit back the pain. Gedlen's blade sliced through the air in a perfect arc. Félip swung his to meet Gedlen's counterstrike. Swords met once more and Félip shoved Gedlen back with a swift kick to the elf's stomach.

"Ye lied to me!" he shouted through panting breaths.

Gedlen tilted his head, tracking Félip's movements as they circled one another. "Faeries cannot lie."

"Bullshit!"

Félip grew vaguely aware of a thickening crowd streaming past the arena. But he never took his eyes off the fae bastard.

"My life," he continued, "what is it actually worth? Why would a starving couple from the Castoffs take in a blighted child?"

"Your Highness—"

"Answer me!" He raised his sword and charged, not sure if he was ready to know the truth.

The clamor and clank of metal on metal rattled his teeth. He struck, and then struck again. The muscles in his body quivered with every blow, but fury fueled him onward. Gedlen's sword slashed toward his chest. Holding the pommel with two hands and bracing for impact, Félip blocked the hit. A strike so hard, he stumbled backward a few steps. Before he could recover his balance, pain bloomed from his side and then his calf. The next thing he knew was a brilliant blue sky kissing his face—the warmth tickled where shadows had once roamed—followed by the earth, which merrily rose up to meet him as his bone-weary body fell toward the compacted dirt and crashed. Air punched free from his lungs. Hot pain sparked the back of his head and fired down his back. Even his toes hurt.

Félip slammed his sword to the ground in surrender and then closed his eyes. Sweat dripped down the sides of his face. His chest heaved for breath. And the sun continued to pleasantly warm his flushed skin. Feeling a shadow cross his face, Félip squinted open a single eye and groaned. Gedlen towered over his outstretched body, an uncharacteristic crease between his brows. Behind the elf, his damned raven circled in the sky.

"Your life, you ask?" Gedlen asked. "Halfling prince, you haunt my visions and have since before you were born."

Halfling? Félip ignored the shiver crawling down his spine at Gedlen's words. "I was happy here. Why the Castoffs?"

"A King who intimately knows the suffering of his people is a King who will shake the dust off his realm and ensure his people prosper."

Their eyes locked for one wild beat of Félip's heart. Disgusted, he turned his head and watched how leaves shadowed behind their illuminated fellows in the tree canopy. Anything to distract his mind from the fury he still felt. And the betrayal.

"Your foster parents took the risk for Rothlín," Gedlen said more softly. "And Dúnælven."

"Ye mean . . ." Félip's mouth fell open. "They knew? All this time they knew?" He pushed up on his elbows and spat, "I'm going to tear ye limb from limb, ye fobbing rump-fed maggot! Faeries cannae lie, my bloody arse!"

A bark of laughter rumbled from Gedlen. The breeze seemed to laugh at the sound too, rolling over Félip's overheated state in whimsy. Gedlen eventually sobered and offered his hand to Félip, who reluctantly accepted. Once on his feet, Gedlen leaned in and said,

"*You* were not to share with anyone. To trust a child's judgment was too great a risk. Not the same as us speaking on your behalf." The elf winked before walking toward Félip's discarded sword and picking it up. "As I've said, Your Highness, faeries cannot lie."

Félip brushed at the dirt on his breeches and tunic. "Then answer me this, Fate Maker. Did ye really plan to kill the princess before I stopped ye?"

"A sacrifice doesn't always mean death. You assumed that's what I meant." Gedlen sheathed his sword and dusted off his leathers. "But I'll not lie," he added with a sly look Félip's way. "I wanted you to rescue the princess. You now share a survivor's bond with her."

Frustration surged through Félip anew. "Why do ye *really* hold Princess Aroreh hostage? And if ye spin me a riddle or try to rune addle my brain, I'll punch ye in yer shriveled-up Dwarf balls."

An arrogant smile curled the elf's lips. "Your princess is an amplifier for magic. And possibly a dream weaver."

"General!"

Both Félip and Gedlen turned toward the sound. A warrior shoved past the gates and sprinted toward where they stood in the training arena. Brandu swooped down and settled on his master's shoulder with a loud caw.

"General," the warrior said once more when he stopped before Gedlen. "Something is wrong with the mortal. Seizures. A series of them."

Félip looked past the warrior to the main path. Crowds of fae flocked toward a building in the distance. Shouts rippled over the gathering, each one carrying updates or exclamations of how the princess lives. Panic cooled his temper but not his pulse. The pounding in his ears matched the hammer in his chest. Seizures?

"Gellynor requests your presence," the warrior added.

"Tell my sister I'll be there shortly." Gedlen placed a hand on Félip's upper arm. "From magic she is made, for magic she will remain. Her purpose slumbers still and only she knows when her true magic will awaken."

Félip frowned. "And what the feck does that mean?"

"Love." The older elf's eyes laughed. "The truest form of love."

At last he [the Prince] came into a chamber all gilded with gold, where he saw, upon a bed, the curtains of which were all open, the finest sight was ever beheld: a Princess, who appeared to be about fifteen or sixteen years of age, and whose bright, and in a manner resplendent beauty, had somewhat in it divine.

"The Sleeping Beauty in the Wood" by Charles Perrault, *Tales of Mother Goose*, 1697

CHAPTER 9

AROREH

Aroreh shot up and clutched the solid shape leaning over her "Help me!" she choked out between garbled breaths and tears. Tremors shivered down her body in an endless snowfall of discomfort. When would the ache end? She had disappointed her mother and the goddess, and Aroreh couldn't remember what she had done to receive their censure. But she would never forget the bitter cold or melancholy black of the dungeon cave until the glowing speck guided her out into the light of the faerie wood. And then back to endless black with only her terrified thoughts to keep her company.

"You're safe," a woman said to her. "Among friends. Stay with me this time, princess. Fight the program trying to hack into you."

"I only touched his hand and . . ." Aroreh splayed her fingers and inspected each one for Blight Rot, and nearly laughed when only spotting a bruise atop one. A tiny mark where she had appeared to be stung or pricked by something. Strange, though. She remembered her bluish skin, the black lines running up her hand and arm, and the frostbitten freeze in her veins. Just the mere memory of those horrors invited more tremors and her body quaked in response. "Thank you for your generous mercy," she prayed to the goddess. "I shall not disappoint you further."

"Disappoint me?" The woman chuffed. "Your mind is being attacked and you're worrying about *my* feelings?"

Movement caught Aroreh's eyes and she nearly forgot the woman's words at the sight. An undulating sea of blinking eyes crowded the small room. Even more pairs peered in from the doorway. They watched her. Blinked more. Heads tilted and lips whispered into ears. She could hear hushed sounds and excited breaths. Their voices held a strange lyrical quality, almost as if they uttered the language of nature.

"Well, you're staying present longer than the last two times."

Staying present? Dazed, Aroreh touched her cheeks, then her hair, lowering her eyes. She was in a shiny golden-walled room, stretched out on a bed made of leaves and flowers. Her skin appeared clean and her hair felt brushed. And she wore a periwinkle blue dress edged in midnight blue and silver elven ribbon. Bare feet poked out beneath the hem of her skirt, one ankle decorated in woodland daisies.

"Are you in any pain or discomfort?" the woman asked.

No, not a woman.

An elf.

The female's question was simple, but Aroreh's mind clouded with confusion. The many voices irritated her sensitive ears, too, though she relished the sound of their accent while speaking her tongue.

"Princess Aroreh?" The female placed her fingers onto Aroreh's forearm. "Do you feel safe now?"

"Yes," she whispered in reply.

A soft smile edged the elf's lips. "It's an honor to welcome you to Leaf Curl, Your Highness. I'm Gellynor, Chief Spell Weaver for the Dúnælven. And this," she pointed to a beautiful spotted owl perched atop a potted flowering tree, "is Tylluan." The owl hooted, almost as if angry. "My apologies, she prefers Tyllie. Owls are particular creatures." Tyllie hooted again. "What? Don't act like you're offended by the truth. You *are* particular." The spotted owl turned around on the branch and ruffled her feathers.

Through the haze, Aroreh registered the faerie's name. But she was most taken with the striking marigold eyes now inspecting her, the faerie's pale face framed by chin-length, wavy black hair. The owl—Tyllie—as if sensing Aroreh's curiosity, turned her head to look behind her and then blinked large yellow eyes.

A strange feeling fluttered in Aroreh's stomach and a knot formed in her throat. She attempted to swallow and grimaced at the dry ache.

"Your shields are tattered, probably from Rune Madness," Gellynor continued. "Bear with me today as I rebuild your walls. Hopefully you're not pulled under again or suffer another seizure."

"My throat is parched," Aroreh said in reply. She heard Gellynor's words but couldn't understand their meaning. What was Rune Madness? And how many times had she regained consciousness only to lose it once more? She couldn't recall waking even once until now. Perhaps the faerie was misinformed, for Aroreh couldn't sleep nor could she dream. All her memories, the pain, the twilight of fear . . . it had to be real. Yet she couldn't recall how she ended up in Leaf Curl either, nor when she had dressed in the beautiful gown currently draping over the bed of leaves and flowers.

Gellynor twisted behind her to a pitcher and wooden cup atop a side table. The many eyes continued to regard Aroreh's every move. Those in the front would speak to those behind, and then those few would turn and speak to their neighbors. The pattern followed out the door to the pressed-in crowd. Remembering her manners, Aroreh straightened her back and lifted a warm smile to the faeries.

The gold-eyed spell weaver drew dark, elegant eyebrows together before handing Aroreh the cup of water. Noting her smile, Gellynor slid a look toward the restless crowd and whispered, "Why do you smile so big?"

"A woman's beauty is more serviceable when she smiles."

The female burst into laughter. "Of all the mortal teachings . . ."

Heat crept up Aroreh's neck and she glanced at the crowd through lowered lashes.

"A mortal woman's beauty comes from her own magic," Gellynor said between breathy chuckles. "Take another sip of water, Your

Highness."

Aroreh obeyed, eager to make Gellynor happy. After swallowing an additional sip for good measure, she said, "Forgive me for displeasing you. How may I make amends?"

"Princess Aroreh, it's not your job to please me. Or to please them." Gellynor pointed at the crowd and then began waving her hands in shooing motions. "Out, all of—not you, Tyllie. The gossip mongering faeries." The owl hooted. "Yes, I know I said 'all,' I'm sorry." Heaving a great sigh, Gellynor said, "Fair Folk in the room, *out!* All of—"

She didn't hear the spell weaver finish. Stars bloomed in Aroreh's head—bright, sparkling, almost blinding—right before her vision darkened. Fire billowed up from her belly and fanned out to each limb until she swore her entire body had caught flame. Her muscles jerked. Then jerked again, this time more violently. The water spilled over her new dress and freshly brushed hair. Hands grabbed her incinerating body and held her down. Then fingers wedged a stick into her mouth just as her jaw clamped down—hard. Tears pricked at her swollen eyes, but she could still see the blurry image of Gellynor leaning over her as purple runes glowed in the air.

"I'm sorry, princess. Your mind is under attack. I've been trying to rune walk to find out who. I'll try again. You're not alone. Remember that. I'm with you." Gellynor turned away. "Tell Gedlen to get his pompous arse here. Now!"

The room spun, slow at first, as though she merely twirled about in a soft breeze. The hands holding her down gripped tighter. Voices shouted overhead. Runes painted her vision in vibrant shades of lilac and plum.

"Walk with me?" a familiar voice called from within her mind.

Aroreh felt herself falling and the golden room faded into a beautiful forest, filled with golden corkscrew-shaped leaves and a rainbow of wildflowers. She awoke in a patch of swaying grass and ferns. A cold wind blew out from the cave's mouth—like a heavy, sorrow-filled sigh—one that chilled her bare arms.

"Ye came back," Félip-who-wasn't-Félip said to her. "I missed ye, lassie."

Icy tendrils of fear curled around her chest. The air grew tight and her head light. She remained in the grass and ignored his proffered hand, though doing so soured her stomach. The goddess desired women who were soft spoken and subservient, not ungrateful for kind opportunities, such as walking through the woods.

Félip noted her hesitation and a slow, crooked smile crept up the side of his face, revealing rather boyish dimples. Everything about him was lovely and boyish and . . . dangerous. The false Félip turned his head and Aroreh held in a gasp. His scar, it had returned.

Was this perhaps the true Félip Batten?

"A lovely day, aye?" he said when she didn't reply. "Walk with me?"

"Who are you?"

"Ye don't remember?" He casually peered up at the trees. "We danced together, once upon a dream. Here—" his gaze returned to hers "—in these very woods, actually."

His eyes were strange—one the darkest earthen brown, the other emerald green. She didn't remember him having two-toned eyes before. And something about his voice didn't seem right. A hazy memory of his voice sang through the clouds in her mind. That lyrical voice conjured wondrous headiness to zip through her, even in her mind. *Freedom.* This Félip's voice sounded more like the drip of icicles on a wintry night.

"Aroreh," he whispered, offering his hand once more. "Be kind to a lad's breaking heart."

"I . . . I do not wish to make you unhappy."

"No, lass. Of course. Ye are gentleness herself."

Dread knotted tighter in her stomach. Still, she watched as her hand lifted from her lap, as if the movements belonged to an entirely different body than her own. As if her body obeyed his wishes though her mind disagreed. But why would she refuse him?

Her fingers reached out for his and—

"Don't touch him," Gellynor growled from behind. Aroreh's entire body startled at the unexpected sound. Trying not to gape, she peered over her shoulder. How was Gellynor even here, much less marching toward Félip with a sword held high? The Chief Spell Weaver settled on booted foot beside her and demanded, "What are you?"

Félip flashed fang at Gellynor and Aroreh's pulse sputtered.

"Shift!" Gellynor commanded. "Or I'll force you to shift with a rune sword in your chest, and then I'll steal all your magic's code."

The young man shot Aroreh a devilish look, right before his boyish features melted away—every freckle, his russet-brown wavy hair, his dimpled smile. And what remained was an enchantingly beautiful female in full armor. Golden-brown hair twisted atop her head, held in place with blossoming cherry twigs. Bright emerald-green eyes, glimmering with triumph, leveled onto Gellynor.

"Cerwyn?" Gellynor spoke the female's name softly. Disbelief seemingly gave way to sorrow as she asked, even more softly, "Who do you work for?"

"You were once no different than us, Gellynor."

"Who is 'us'?"

Cerwyn smiled, a sweet and endearing look as she pointed at Aroreh. "The same blood that runs in me also runs in her. She belongs to us, not the *mighty* Milfae."

Gellynor paled to a sickly pallor. "Aroreh, tell her to leave."

"I do not wish to hurt her feelings." Normally obedience would demand she listen to Gellynor. But her gentleness overruled the command. Aroreh wrapped an arm across her souring middle and whispered, "My purpose is to bring others joy, not displeasure."

"Trust me, princess—"

"She's the one harming you," Cerwyn interjected. "Her people stole you from the temple, from your own mother, killed your palace guards, and then kept you in hibernation for two weeks."

"I am unable to sleep," Aroreh countered. "How could I then be in hibernation?"

Cerwyn arched a single eyebrow. "Ask her, if you don't believe me."

Aroreh peered at Gellynor beneath lowered lashes, unable to stop her programmed obedience. "Did I hibernate?"

Gellynor stepped closer to Aroreh. "Ask her to leave, Your Highness."

"I cannot choose between you. Pleas—" She stopped herself. Ladies didn't beg. "My very life and the many lives of others depend on me pleasing Aisling. Don't you see?"

"You failed to guard your heart and mind." Cerwyn spoke softly, though the words were hard. "You are too easily tempted."

Aroreh hung her head. "I am sorry—"

"Join me on a walk." Cerwyn extended her hand to Aroreh once more. "I will explain everything to you. The Milfae are poisoning your weak mind."

"Don't touch her!" Gellynor knocked Cerwyn's hand away with the flat end of her sword. "Either ask her to leave, princess, or give me permission to force her out. I'll explain why later. Promise. But only *you* have power over *your* body right now. This is your program, not hers or mine."

"I know your father, Aroreh," Cerwyn added. "Would you like to meet him?"

Aroreh felt her traitorous lips dip into a frown. "I am a vessel of Aisling. She created me but chose my mother so I might inspire other women of the New Dawn Era to restore Rothlín to her former glory."

Cerwyn flashed her canines again and her eyes laughed with wicked delight. "Poor, sweet Aroreh, our fragile little Briar Rose."

"Aroreh!" Gellynor growled.

Panic gurgled in her chest. Whatever decision she made would either displease Gellynor or Cerwyn. And upsetting others wasn't in her programming. The very thought gnawed away at her middle—a spasming, souring sensation she loathed. Aroreh waited for her goddess to bring much needed strength and direction, this time not fearing the zap or the full-body flinch. But nothing happened, not even the tiniest bolster in faerie blessed gentleness, sunny countenance, or celebratory song. She looked between both females. Cerwyn was full of smiles and warm invitation—serviceable beauty and propriety. Gellynor's face was twisted into a scowl and her eyes sparked with anger—not reflecting a single glint of feminine grace.

Princess Aroreh, it's not your job to please me. Or to please them.

Gellynor's words circled about in her bruising heart. The pressure to decide grew and grew, until a melody of grief hummed in Aroreh's head. *Grief.* That was the very word she couldn't conceptualize in the temple as she prepared to sing for the Great Spindle Tree. And just like then, the notes seemed to sing their encouragement for her to choose an allegiance—her budding instincts or her wilting education. A choice that was ripping her apart from the inside out. But one she needed to make or suffer further.

"Leave," Aroreh said quietly, as if the single word were a dagger strike. "Please."

"She asked you to leave, Gellynor," Cerwyn said, her grin wide.

Gellynor's face relaxed into shock, her mouth parting and her eyes wide.

Then Aroreh remembered, though the memory was faded around the periphery of her mind.

Félip-who-wasn't-Félip. Her mother with the wrong nose.

Cerwyn had lied to her from the onset. Though, she hadn't called herself Félip, had she? Why did she appear as a man? And a blighted man, no less? At first, Aroreh thought Aisling was testing her fortitude and obedience, as the queen had instructed Aroreh to bring Prince Félip Batten of Glenashlen back to the temple. An odd request, as Glenashlen and all her people were dusted in the Cold Winds. But Aroreh was weak. One look at the young man—or who she thought was the young man—and happy notes longed to trill free from her fluttering pulse. *Freedom*. Like his voice suggested.

But it wasn't him. Never had been him in the enchanting woods all along.

Had her mother truly appeared before her in the black dungeon? Like Félip-who-wasn't-Félip, the transparent, glowing figure of Queen Líeh was a perfect rending save one physical flaw. Her nose.

A hot burning sensation pierced through the shuddering fear in her gut.

"Forgive m-me," Aroreh said again. "But I-I meant to address you, Cerwyn. Please leave our company."

Cerwyn hissed as her face darkened. "You dare displease your queen again?"

Tears gathered on Aroreh's lashes. She lowered her head and studied her hands—not blue, though she felt the Cold Winds gusting in her veins. Her whole body was trembling, for her actions had displeased a living, breathing being. How could she be so cruel? How could she dismiss another without regard to their feelings? She was selfish. Absolutely selfish. And obviously a sign that Blight Rot had indeed reached her soul.

An apology materialized on the tip of her tongue. She would beg Cerwyn's forgiveness.

But the faerie had disappeared before she could form a proper reply.

"You did the right thing, Your Highness." Gellynor sat beside her in the grass.

The gathered tears pooling along Aroreh's lashes now slipped down her cheeks.

"Come here." Gellynor opened her arms and Aroreh fell into her embrace and sobbed. "I see that more than your magic's barriers are tattered," she whispered into Aroreh's hair. "We'll help you repair your personal boundary lines too. But first we need to leave your mind."

"I'm in a faerie wood," Aroreh choked out. "Nothing makes sense to me anymore."

She could feel Gellynor frown into her hair. "That's what she made you see. A Malfae faerie trick. This space, a plane within your mind, is empty—black."

"Malfae?"

Why do you believe the Milfae took you?

The hair on her arms prickled. "I still don't understand."

"A full-blood Malfae shifter is in Leaf Curl and trying to re-possess your mind for The Dream. Cross-bloods can't shift, not even when in projected form, like we are now." Gellynor tightened her embrace. "Her existence is impossible. The Malfae were wiped out centuries ago in a civil war after they nearly destroyed humankind in their lust for power and control."

The same blood that runs in me, also runs in her.

Aroreh thought she might retch.

CHAPTER 10

FÉLIP

Gedlen shoved through the excited crowd. Faeries whispered garish tales to one another as Félip passed by. Stories spun by those reporting from inside the secret chamber where the princess had been held this past fortnight. Well, not so secret chamber anymore. The elves' incessant chatter was akin to the scuttling of beetles on stone. Blathering creatures, elves. Information to them glittered as brilliantly as the rare iridescent crystals found in the dwarven mines. Yet, one word nearly struck his feet immobile.

Malfae.

Who were the Malfae? And why were they attacking the Princess of Rothlín? Félip had heard tales of Mer in the coastal realms, of a halfling prince near the Spired Hills who terrorized his people, of dragons advising warriors in the north-western realms, and overworked dwarves readying to strike in Rothlín's neighboring realm, Clifstán. But the Malfae?

"Out!" Gedlen shouted at the cottage door. "You see she's alive. Now everyone out!"

Elves, brownies, pixies, and faeries he didn't know reluctantly left, many grumbling as they exited through the only door. Félip peeked inside and his jaw nearly hit the wild grass at his feet. The interior was made entirely of a gold-like metal. The Thorns Guild spell weavers once spoke of a golden metal from the Spired Hills that prevented runic spells from entering or leaving enclosures made from this rare material. Was this the metal they spoke of? Gedlen entered and Félip followed close behind, his fingertips trailing across the smooth, metallic surface.

"You," Gedlen said to a vase of flowers. "I see you hiding."

A pixie buzzed out from inside a large red poppy and stuck her tongue out at Gedlen before zipping out into the forest. Brandu cawed at the exiting faerie, then flew over to join a spotted owl on a flowering tree.

"Close the door," Gedlen said to Félip. "And lock it."

Félip arched an eyebrow but did as he was told. Candlelight flickered off the walls and turned the yellowish gold into beautiful shades of honeyed amber. The windowless room was circular inside, though the outside resembled a typical square-shaped home. All week, he had passed by this location and didn't remember seeing this particular cottage. Had they cloaked this space as an extra measure of protection?

A muted image of a bed reflected in the golden walls and he squinted to get a better look. Then he rolled his eyes at himself. *Still a horse-kicked eejit, laddie.* Perhaps he hit his head in the ring a wee bit harder than he realized. Peering over his shoulder first, he twisted toward Gedlen and searched for the bed, and stilled.

Dalbréath leaned over a body and whispered. Blue light sparked from his fingertips and then he moved away from the bed, arms clasped behind his back, as if awaiting his next instruction.

"What did ye do to her mind this time?" Félip asked.

"I simply gave her pleasant thoughts of me." An arrogant smile tempted the corners of Dalbréath's mouth.

Gellynor groaned. "He forced hibernation for a short spell. Her mind is still awake and can't fall into slumber. A built-in programmed failsafe of sorts in her magic system while she hibernates."

"Oh now, where's the fun, Gelly?" Dalbréath said. "Let the hot-tempered mortal stew a little."

The spotted owl hooted in what sounded like laughter.

"Gelly?" the female shot her owl a glare before glowering at Dalbréath. "I ought to weave a spell that keeps your arse firmly upon a bucket—"

"Too bad you can't rune whisper," Dalbréath interjected with a faint smirk. "Or I already would be."

"My spells are permanent. Not vaporous whispers!"

Dalbréath shrugged. "If you say so . . . Gelly."

The two elves continued to sling words back and forth. But the maiden stretched out before them held all Félip's attention.

Aroreh lay upon her back, eyes closed. Blonde hair, decorated in flowers and corded braids, spilled down her shoulders and across a pillow of moss. A lavender-blue dress hugged her curves before fanning over her legs and draping down the sides of the bed. A bed made of ferns, moss, and various wildflowers. He inched closer, breathing in her presence, his throat thickening with every rapid beat of his heart. He despised her family. Loathed everything she represented. Even now, his blood began to boil at the sight of her unnatural beauty. And yet, his legs grew wobbly and his breath quickened like a panting, love-addled fool.

What was it about her that riled him up so? She was an innocent—like him. Yet many a braw woman had yielded their hard-earned coin and denied their families food for pretty, spell woven faces and feminine graces—because of her. Because of The Dream. Aisling be praised, they would say as simple life gave way to New Dawn Era illusions. "Aisling be cursed," he muttered under his breath, not caring if others in this room heard him. Absently, his fingers grazed the nick on his throat. The place where a palace guard held a sword while Félip hung upside down like a boar for slaughter. Anger billowed out to each limb and he itched for a blade and another workout, despite how his muscles protested.

A finger pressed beneath his chin and pushed up until his mouth closed with an embarrassing clack. Laughter filled the chamber. Félip curled his fists into balls and glowered at Gellynor, who continued to laugh. "You looked like a fish sucking air from a pond's surface," she said between more chuckles.

"Cannae a laddie catch his breath after sparring?"

"Battling your 'growing' attraction is more like it," she said with a suggestive wink.

Félip's eyes narrowed to slits to hide the flush warming his face. "Tell me more of what I feel, Gellynor Death Talker, since ye ken so much."

"Enough, you two. *All* of you. Yes, even Brandu and Tyllie. I hear your opinionated chatter." The raven cawed at his master and then angled his head away. "Let us grown-ups talk." Gedlen crossed arms over his chest. "Now, sister, you requested me? The seizure ceased, I see."

Gellynor's sharp gaze cut Félip's way briefly. "A full-blood Malfae Rune Shifter is in Leaf Curl."

"That's impossible," Dalbréath rasped.

Gedlen sighed. "I always suspected a few full-bloods survived. Especially when the Druid went missing and the House of Rosen grew shadowed. But I never had proof, even with Aroreh's faerie blessings."

"Ye didnae bless Aroreh?" Félip asked.

"No," Gedlen answered. "Not any from Dúnælven either."

"The old korrigan dabbles in Fates. Just like Gedlen." Gellynor tapped at runes in the air before her. "We believed she gave Aroreh her faerie blessings and spell wove the other blessings for the citizens of Rothlín."

A chill swept over Félip's exposed skin. "And the Great Spindle Tree?"

"That is indeed our gift to Rothlín." Gedlen considered Aroreh, his dark brows pinched together. "The tree's dryad wanted to help rebuild Ealdspell after the Cold Winds. The old korrigan told her a queen spun of sunlight would save Rothlín and that she, the dryad, would save this fated queen."

"Well, Cerwyn shifted into an image of Félip to rune walk Aroreh's mind," Gellynor said, changing the subject. "She was trying to gain root access to hijack Aroreh's system."

"No doubt to see if she lived and remote access connect her to The Dream if she did," Gedlen muttered. "And stop our influence. Our *Milfae* influence."

"My thoughts too," Gellynor said. "And the queen chose Félip as the honeypot. Why? Does she know who he *really* is?"

All eyes slid to Félip. But he was too shocked to comment. Cerwyn? The elf he had sparred against off and on throughout this week? Who had seen to his care when wounded in the ring a couple of days ago? The one who had kissed his cheek just this morning? Dread pooled in his gut, followed by shame. He had marinated in her kind gestures, believed himself worthy enough of her platonic affections.

Dalbréath gestured to the golden walls. "But how did Cerwyn rune walk a contained space?"

"Rune Shifters can see through every glamour," Gellynor said.

"She shifted into the cottage while it was cloaked, then?" Dalbréath asked.

Gellynor nodded. "To the very walls of this room. It's the only explanation. I don't think she physically touched her, though. Cerwyn shouldn't be able to shift into Aroreh. I hope."

Félip blew out a heavy breath. "Contact is needed fer her to shift . . . into me?"

"Yes," Gellynor replied simply. "But for the spell weaving to work properly, she would need more than a touch. Blood. Saliva. Skin. Fingernail clippings. A strand of hair. The usual thi—"

Félip lifted a hand up for Gellynor to stop. "Ye dinnae make sense, lass. How do ye ken it's Cerwyn?"

"I saw her."

"In Aroreh's head?" he asked, disbelieving. Gellynor replied with a curt nod. "How?"

"Rune walking," she drolled.

He had heard her and Dalbréath use the phrase, but he didn't understand it. When he apparently still looked confused, she continued.

"She wove a spell that enabled her to communicate with another's runic technology. Think of it like a dream you can control but in the mind's eye of another. Most rune walkers create environments the other will trust to easily get permissions to further access that person's mind. Basically, it's a glamour. Every aspect feels real even though it's just runic magic communicating back and forth. Only advanced spell weavers can do this."

Félip wasn't sure if he was still confused or confused even more.

Seeing his expression, she said, "I'll explain more once Dalbréath's whispers wear off. I wanted to confer with you three before she awakes from hibernation." Gellynor faced her brother. "Aroreh's inner-personal needs are greater than we expected. The brainwashing runs deep. She has little to no boundary lines and a hazy sense of self. I fear she might not be strong enough for the future you saw."

"Every strong mortal woman I have encountered started out broken in some way. She'll reknit herself into a more impenetrable form once she has the tools to reprogram her mind and the knowledge to build her own truths."

Seemingly satisfied with Gedlen's answer, Gellynor side-eyed the white-haired elf with a baiting smile. "We have an evil faerie to catch!"

"Not all Malfae bloodines are evil," Dalbréath grumbled.

Her smile stretched into a wicked grin. "Oh yes they are. Terrible, evil things. Every last one of them."

"Traitor." A corner of Dalbréath's mouth twitched. "You're just jealous of my alluring good looks and seductive powers. I can't really recommend my Milfae heritage."

"Your Milfae heritage has kept you alive," she shot back.

Dalbréath lifted his shoulder in a humored shrug.

"Milfae?" Félip asked.

"The Milfae are now the Dúnælven," Gedlen answered. "The Malfae are our shadow race cousins and believed to be extinct, save those with halfling lines, like Dalbréath."

The cheeky white-haired elf winked at Félip.

"Och aye, I knew something was wrong with Dog Breath."

Gellynor burst into laughter. "Dog Breath . . ."

Dalbréath responded with a rude gesture toward Gellynor, which only made her cackle harder. "Careful, prince," he said to Félip. "Or you might find yourself licking your own arse."

Félip couldn't help his grin, even when Gedlen sighed with all the patience and annoyance typical of the old men training green lads in the factories. The familiar sound strangely comforted him a little. Félip considered Dalbréath again, then realized what Gellynor had shared and his self-satisfied smile slipped away.

"Yer faither," Félip said to Dalbréath. "Did the Cold Winds kill him and his kind?"

Dalbréath paled a little. A strange look for the arrogant elf. "The Milfae killed him and all of his traitorous kind over two hundred years ago."

"The Milfae—" Félip stopped himself and gaped at Gedlen. "Ye sanctioned the killing of his faither?"

"Not I, the Druid from Éireanna. The mortal who created the Kingdom of Ealdspell and appointed the Milfae as her protector."

"Éireanna?" Félip closed his eyes momentarily and grit his teeth. His anger was rising all over again. "This is why the queen called you a faerie killing, warmongering elf."

"Once, all faeries were the same," Gedlen began and Félip grit his teeth even harder. "And only two dimensions existed. Earth and Éireanna, the human plane and the faerie realm. But when the poison of war and hatred on Earth leached into Éireanna's soil, some faeries grew sick and shadowed." Gedlen watched Dalbréath partially twist away, then continued. "The Druid of Éireanna tried to heal the poisoned faeries with the life-giving sap of his sacred oak tree. But the faeries were far too corrupted and didn't want to heal. Especially those with shifting and whispering abilities—magic that could manipulate and control others. He called those with an insatiable, obsessive thirst for power and control Malfae and all others Milfae." Gedlen continued to watch Dalbréath, a frown tugging on his lips. "There is no goodness left in those who were poisoned. I and many of my warriors helped the Druid banish the Malfae from Éireanna to roam as unforgiven Underfolk in the Land of Mist. Then the Druid created a new dimension to preserve mortals and faeries should Earth destroy itself and all of Éireanna.

"The Kingdom of Ealdspell," Félip whispered to himself, not sure if he were still breathing.

"Yes," Gedlen said, nodding slowly. "An entire kingdom upon a leaf, one that is attached to the Druid's sacred oak tree. For who would search for an entire faerie realm on a single leaf? The Milfae he relocated to Ealdspell were renamed the Dúnælven. The same as our realm. And to better protect this dimension, the Druid blended Earthen technology with elemental magic for the Milfae. Runic technology has proven a stronger magic than the one we once knew in Éireanna. And I fear the Malfae have discovered this too, if The Dream is any indication."

A leaf? A whole kingdom on a leaf? Now Félip knew the Fate Maker was truly touched in the head. Faerie tales, nothing more. And his blood boiled once again with frustration. "Bloody faeries," Félip whispered between clenched teeth, rolling his eyes.

Dalbréath crossed his arms over his armored chest. "I wonder how many full-blood Malfae still exist?"

"And how they discovered Ealdspell?" Gellynor added.

"Félip, stay here with Gellynor," Gedlen said, letting the last two questions linger between them. "I need to alert the warriors."

"No," Gellynor quickly countered. "I don't think it wise for Aroreh to see Félip so soon upon waking. The Félip in her rune walked mind harmed her and she . . . allowed him to and almost allowed him to again."

"Faerie hunting it is, then," Félip practically spat. Heat spread to his limbs, as though his body contained the burning fields. "Can Cerwyn shift inside our mortal plane?"

"Yes," Gedlen and Dalbréath answered together.

Dalbréath finished, "And only full-blood Malfae can rune shift."

Félip ran a hand through his tangled hair and muttered, "Och, perhaps the hag will capture Cerwyn and bleed her out, if she dares wear my face in Rothlín."

Gellynor brought up more runes into the air and studied several lines. "I captured a few strands of Cerwyn's runic identity. But it's muddled and unlike anything I've ever seen before. Well, except Aroreh. They share similar base coding. I'll need more to established that fully, but—"

"Gellynor." Gedlen's pointed look held centuries of exasperation and Félip nearly laughed.

The female stuck her tongue out at her brother before saying, "Basically, the Veil believes she's Dúnælven."

"The Veil has for nearly a century." Gedlen crossed leather-clad arms over his chest.

"Yes, but now she holds Félip's Dúnælven code and can shift into him outside of Leaf Curl."

"I'm not Dúnælven," Félip interjected.

Gellynor ignored him and continued. "What if the Veil allows this Félip to bring in an army?"

Gedlen swore under his breath. "Still, she could have done that by stealing the runic identity of you and me."

"She probably has stolen our identities," Gellynor replied. "But we didn't have Aroreh then. And the Malfae probably don't have the numbers to defeat us, not then and not now. Cerwyn said Aroreh shared the same blood as her. Which means, Aroreh is part Malfae. The queen is Malfae and probably shifted to appear like Queen Líeh."

"You're suggesting she eliminated the real Queen Líeh and took her place?" Gedlen asked.

"The Cold Winds was a chaotic time. I'm saying it's possible.

The House of Rosen only shadowed since before the New Dawn Era" Gelleynor lowered her voice. "Right after the High Druid disappeared."

"Rònan," Gedlen said softly. Almost too softly. Why the sudden change in tone? He didn't speak of the High Druid with fondness before. "Do you think Aroreh—"

"A conversation for later, brother."

"If I had known sooner . . ." his voice trailed off. "Fate didn't feel I needed to know."

"Gedlen Faerondarl," Gellynor warned.

The general's gaze cut back to his sister's, then he tilted his head in acknowledgment. Félip frowned. Was the Fate Maker suggesting that Aroreh was the Druid's daughter?

Gellynor paused a beat, studied Félip, a strange look in her eyes, then continued. "The veil . . . think about it, brother. Would the Dúnælven believe you or I would lead an enemy army into Leaf Curl? Or any of our top warriors?"

"No."

"Exactly! But angry, wildcard Félip who grew up in Rothlín' Castoffs?"

All eyes turned his direction again.

A muscle twitched along Félip's jaw. "I'm not Dúnælven."

"Only fae can shadow walk." Gellynor ignored him again, this time his shocked expression at her implications, though she spoke directly to him. "The Veil granted Cerwyn full permission to leave, but she must return with another Dúnælven for the Veil to part—typical for many Dúnælven fae. Usually mortal or Malfae halflings. You? You have full permissions to come and go as you please—alone."

"Aye, a right fool thing to give me. A wanted man. In every realm of Ealdspell." Félip started pacing before shouting, "A death sentence is on my head! I already carry all the supposed fecking sins of my dusted ancestors. The entire Kingdom fears I'll steal a throne, if found alive. And the queen *knows* I'm alive, thanks to this headless bag of useless faerie meat." Félip jabbed his finger into Gedlen's shoulder. "Now I am to carry the deaths of Dúnælven fae too, if war comes? Change my fecking permissions!"

"The Veil grants permissions, not I nor any other Dúnælven fae." The blood drained from Félip's head. "Why?"

Gellynor looked away and Gedlen studied his feet.

Félip's throat knotted painfully. "I dinnae want to be a monster anymore." The words were hoarse, a shaky whisper.

Gellynor's eyes softened. "Then become the prince you were destined to be."

"Aye," Félip whispered. His gaze wandered over Aroreh, her preternatural beauty stoking the building rage tightening every sore muscle in his body. "The disfigured prince of ash and rubble."

"Unseelie faerie prince," Dalbréath said. "Why do you think the Dúnælven fae care so much about you? Even if you are half mortal."

"Dalbréath!" Gellynor bared her canines at the white-haired elf.

"Stop the theatrics, *Gelly*. He needs to know all the stakes here. This is *his* life, not yours." To Félip he asked, "Ever wondered why Gedlen isn't king? Or anyone else in Dúnælven? Or why the second-in-command of the Dúnælven army was tasked with partially raising you and training you to shadow walk? Any elf could have raised you."

Félip gaped at Dalbréath—part disgust and part horror. Unseelie faerie prince? Part Dúnælven fae? He couldn't process what Dalbréath confessed. Instead, he glared at Gedlen—the Fate Maker, the one who created this mess

"My and Gellynor's older brother, Félip Raven Shadow," Gedlen began, slowly, quietly, "is your father. His familiar was also Brandu's brother." The elf paused for a quivering beat of Félip's heart. "Your mother, Kæleen, was the mortal Queen of Glenashlen. Your father the Faerie King of Dúnælven, and your namesake. He was in Glenashlen when the Cold Winds arrived."

"My faither was mortal. I'm fully mortal!"

"Gellynor, I'm in armor. Show him."

The female lifted sad eyes toward Félip, gathered her hair in one hand, and then pulled down her tunic at the base of her neck. She had a rose-hued birthmark in the shape of interconnecting knots. Just like his. The blood rushed from Félip's head.

"All Dúnælven royals carry this mark. It's the Druid's seal."

Tears pricked the back of Félip's eyes. "What are ye telling me?"

"You're the heir to the Dúnælven throne," Gedlen said.

"My mother was dispatched to find you," Dalbréath added. "If she hadn't saved you, Gedlen would be king."

"So, *this* is the value of my life." Félip drew in a ragged breath. "My foster parents, they knew this too, aye?"

Gedlen stepped toward Félip. "We tried to find a royal house to foster you. But then the Druid went missing and . . . and I needed to hide you and in a place no one would think to look. I allowed the other realms to believe you dead."

Félip's heart grew sick. His father was a faerie king. People didn't speak of Glenashlen. Not in dark shadow or before the temple's beacon of light. He knew nothing of his parents or his heritage, only what he had dreamed his realm and family must have been like. But never this. Never fae. Then he remembered something else, a contract of marriage made while his mother carried him in the womb—and his heart grew sicker. The Dúnælven had wanted their royal line aligned with Rothlín from his very start. Probably the *only* reason he was kept alive.

"We were to marry"—Félip pointed at Aroreh—"before the Cold Winds destroyed everything. Is this why ye wanted us to have a 'survivor's bond,' as ye put it? And does she know she was once betrothed to Aisling's devil?"

"No, and it's best if she decides you for herself," Gedlen quickly replied, "if Rothlín is to awaken."

"Decides me?" A bitter laugh rumbled free as Félip walked toward the gold metallic door.

"Yes, decides you," Gedlen repeated. "For a blighted king who holds the light of three realms will help a queen spun of sunlight thaw the lingering remnants of the Cold Winds in their lands. But this vision only holds true when *she chooses* her future without another controlling her mind."

"Release me from yer gilded cage."

"Félip Batten MacKinley, Lost Prince of Glenashlen, Dúnælven, and Rothlín."

The use of his full name with the three realms each name represented stilled the roaring blood in his veins for a few heartbeats. Long enough that he could hear the Fate Maker's next words over the thunderous pulse in his ears.

"You were born to help Aroreh wake Rothlín from the nightmare they call a Dream."

Félip shoved open the door and marched toward the training ring. Let Cerwyn find him, if she was still in Leaf Curl. Or any other Malfae hiding among them. He was ready for another fight.

CHAPTER II

AROREH

A tiny pixie buzzed before Aroreh's face, singing a lively melody with a high vibrato. She couldn't understand the words, but the tinkling notes lifted her tired state some. Sunlight streamed through golden leaves and illuminated the pixie's purple dragonfly wings into magentas, lilacs, and a dark shade of grape along the veins. Her light green skin shimmered under the ribbons of light too. A smile trembled on Aroreh's lips at the sight, then faltered. Blinking back the embarrassment, she shifted in her chair before the window and rubbed at her arms. The pixie continued singing unaware of Aroreh's emotional fatigue. Confusion edged the line of her fading self-control, so Aroreh politely looked about her room and not at the pixie.

Many faeries had wished to bring her gifts since her waking from hibernation two days ago. A crown of wildflowers draped across her uncorded hair, with more flowers added typically with each visit, which came at all hours of the day and night. Acorns lined her windowsill and filled a bowl made from a small hollowed out, moss-covered log. The vanity table was now decorated in sparkling pieces of jewelry, all mismatching. No two earrings were the same. Nor were any dangles crafted to ensemble with a necklace or bracelet. Were these objects left for faeries to find? She had heard of her kind doing so long before the Cold Winds to invite the fae's favor. Though she thought such tales were just that—tales.

The song ended on a beautiful note and the pixie bowed.

"Thank you," Aroreh said. "You have a pretty singing voice."

The pixie spoke in her tinkling tongue and then dipped in to quickly plant a kiss on Aroreh's cheek. The soft, ticklish sensation elicited a giggle from Aroreh, and then the pixie flew out the open window and into the early-morning light. Aroreh allowed a twirling breeze to cool her warming skin before she closed the window and sighed.

She looked to her bed. Though she hibernated for two weeks, she still had never slept a wink in her life. Hibernating wasn't the same as sleeping, Gellynor had explained to her. For one kept the mind awake and the other slipped the mind into a subconscious state. Aroreh's fingers slid down the carved wooden post of her canopied bed as the queen's parting words of warning shivered through her.

"Why did you take me from the temple?" she had cried out shortly after waking last. Aroreh wanted to demand her return to Rothlin, but her mother had shunned her. Forgiveness could only be obtained through obedience. And was demanding similar to begging? For a lady should never beg.

Gellynor's lips dipped into a frown. "You are an amplifier for magic. Your magic works like a beacon. And the queen uses you to manipulate all of Rothlin for her gain."

Aroreh pressed herself into the wall with a whimper when Gellynor stepped closer. Then she remembered her manners and tried to relax her shoulders and unclench her jaw. But an overdrive of emotions surged her system. Lightheaded, she wanted to retch. Terrified, she wanted to run back into The Wilds.

"Maybe you should rest—"

"NO!" Aroreh shook her head vehemently. "I will not slumber. Is that why you took me? So I might sleep and slay my goddess through selfish dreams?"

"What? No. We wanted you to choose your future and, thus, the future for Rothlin and all Ealdspell. Can't do that under mind control." Gellynor crossed her arms over her chest and shifted on her feet. "If you dream, you'll kill Aisling?"

The piteous look in Gellynor's marigold eyes was her undoing. Aroreh had yelled at the kind faerie. Tears brimmed dangerously on her lashes. A lady never raised her voice nor asserted her opinions over another's happiness. Ducking her head, Aroreh bunched her shoulders to make herself smaller and quietly said, "I'm so sorry, my lady. I am utterly ashamed at my behavior. How may I make amends?"

"You're allowed to speak your mind here." Gellynor took another step closer. "Our thoughts are not programmed by runic technology. Or a royal."

Fear skipped through Aroreh's pulse. What if Aisling heard their blasphemous conversation and further punished Aroreh's defiance?

"Your goddess is a manufactured lie."

"I beg your pardon?"

Gellynor placed a hand on Aroreh's shoulder and whispered, "Aisling is a machine. And it programmed The Dream to control the people of Rothlin for the queen."

Aroreh ran her fingers along the plush blankets of her bed.

She should feel angry over this lie, she was told. Or perhaps sad. Aroreh didn't know how to choose anger. She didn't know how to choose any emotion, really. Well, except fear and confusion. A fog swirled over her mind often. Even so, her faerie blessings from birth no longer operated the same. They were there and yet they were not—their presence weaving in and out of reality. Was this the temptation her mother had warned about? Was that even her mother? Were the faeries lying to Aroreh? Cerwyn seemed to think so. But Cerwyn had deceived her as well.

And now Aroreh felt everything and nothing.

The thoughts in her head spun faster than the spinning machine she once saw demonstrated to her as a child. The word "betrayal" tingled in her heart's periphery. Yet, she didn't know whom to feel betrayed by—her mother, the temple, or the faeries? For faeries had blessed her at birth as a holy sacrament for Aisling and had also used magic to create The Dream. And faeries were the ones who gifted the Great Spindle Tree to Rothlín after the Cold Winds turned most of the orchard to ash and made the remaining trees unable to bear fertile seeds. Yet her mother designed a New Dawn Era daughter. Not for pleasure or goodwill, but for a beautifully woven lie to gain power beyond Rothlín. One Aroreh had unwittingly spread in her duty to the temple and to Aisling.

What did betrayal feel like? Was it the pockets of confusion and exhaustion she felt now? Or a sickening, like the horror stories of wash women and wool-sorting children who fainted at the factories, never to wake again?

Everything and nothing.

Rune Madness had surged uncontrollable, bold emotions through her body at once, as though she were an unspooling bobbin of thread.

And the wandering nothingness now burned in every emotion's void.

Her body dragged and a strange pressure bloomed behind her eyes—a discomfort she hadn't experienced until now. But she wouldn't complain. A lady was grateful, even for pain. Though why one should be grateful to ache so, she couldn't say.

At her vanity table, she dipped a rag into a basin of water and pressed the cool fabric to her brow. Respite from the flush shuddered through her at the touch. Her body fevered on occasion as her runes adjusted to life beyond the temple's reach, such a contrast to her frost-bitten blood while hibernating. Aroreh studied her fingertip, the one that had touched Félip. Was the boyishly handsome young man even real or was he manufactured by the runes in her system too? She was unsure of everything and nothing anymore . . .

A light rap at her door echoed in her chamber. Aroreh drew in a fortifying breath, then answered, "You may come in." The door squeaked open and Gellynor's head popped into view. Tyllie flew into her room and perched onto the windowsill and then hooted her greeting. Aroreh lowered the cloth and squared her shoulders to appear more presentable.

"Overheating again?" Gellynor asked.

Aroreh simply nodded while gesturing to a chair beside the one she lowered into.

Gellynor plunked into the seat and leaned back, an appraising eyebrow arched high. "I see you shut your window."

A group of faerie children played a game in the glen, a stone's throw from her window. She imagined it must be a cheerful, babbling sound, like water merrily spraying off rocks. But she wasn't certain. Since awaking from hibernation, she hadn't been able to hear music in seemingly everyday things as before.

"Will I offend the Dúnælven, if I rest for a spell? I do not wish to be selfish—"

"Your Highness, peace." Gellynor sat forward and draped long arms across her knees. "When the magic of earth, sky, and water gives, it also takes. An exchange happens. Sometimes a fair exchange, sometimes not. Sometimes re-balance is needed. Do you understand?"

She fidgeted with her skirt. "I fear my head is rather muddied."

"When the sun visits, he takes water to the sky but gives light to the earth. Sometimes he takes too much water and the sky swells while the earth parches. Sometimes the water gives too much and the earth floods and the sun's warm light is needed to wick the excess water away." Gellynor paused a beat and leaned over her knees, as though sharing a secret. "Earth, sky, and water adjust to strike balance without permission from the other."

The imagery bloomed in Aroreh's cobwebbed mind and her shoulders relaxed a notch.

Gellynor continued. "You have given Dúnælven personal magic, simply by entertaining our visits. Now it is your turn to take." Gellynor's eyes were as gold as the corkscrew leaves in the forest, as mischievous too. "We fae understand the exchange of magic, the rhythm of give and take. We don't deem you selfish or unkind, nor do you need our permission to strike balance within yourself."

"What shall I take?" She pointed at all the glistening baubles, shiny acorns, and the wilting flowers atop her head. "I have already received so much."

"Time." Gellynor smiled. "For time you have given, now time you shall take."

"Time . . ." Aroreh whispered to herself. Her attentions returned to the children outside her window. Adults didn't supervise their play, nor dog their every step with instructions for improvement. Their time was their own. "Time is a strange personal commodity."

"And one of the most precious. It's in this personal space where one learns who they are."

Aroreh felt her lips fluttering into a familiar automatic smile. "I was created to bring others joy."

"You are an amplifier, yes." Gellynor tilted her head. "Answer me this, princess. How does one go about bringing others joy?"

"I . . ." Aroreh's brows wrinkled. A slap ghosted across her cheek and she nearly shriveled up into herself with the memory's sting. "Matters not what . . . I think. How do you believe I bring others joy?"

Gellynor's soft smile faded into a frown. The merriment in her eyes dulled too. "Time," she said simply. "You'll know the answer to your own question . . . in *time*."

"Time," Aroreh repeated.

"Would a walk outside help cool your system's flush?"

"Oh yes, a walk would be lovely." Aroreh darted from her chair, eager to leave this chamber and join the freedom outside her window. A curious, tiny smile ghosted the corners of Gellynor's lips.

Outside, the breeze caressed Aroreh's skin in soothing touches. She longed to open her arms and embrace the wind. Instead, she straightened her back and matched Gellynor's long strides with dainty ones of her own. Tyllie hooted and then departed for a golden apple tree and found a branch high above to watch Leaf Curl, blinking her large yellow eyes. The faerie children noted Tyllie and stopped their game, then dashed over to dance around Aroreh. Their laughter was infectious and Aroreh found herself joining in their happiness. The autumn wind was a fickle wind, though. The children twirled and breezed back to their game as quickly as they gusted over to where she walked.

Their laughter remained with her, however.

Despite her cheeriness, exhaustion rippled through Aroreh and she hid a yawn behind her hand. Last night she had yawned for the first time, a terrifying experience. What if her body couldn't remain awake? What if she accidentally harmed others, her goddess, by falling asleep? Noting her rising panic, Gellynor glanced her way.

"You could sleep in the gilded room. The Aurelienne ore blocks magic from entering or exiting. You would do no harm to Leaf Curl or any other."

Aroreh considered the possibility. "What if I do not wake?"

"Well, we could try, and if anything goes awry, I'll wake you. I have a suit made of the same ore. My magic will still operate with proper connections to you. I know sleeping scares you. But without The Dream running your system, your body will need proper rest, or you might die of exhaustion."

Die of exhaustion? Fear seized her heart—again. The queen didn't warn of this setback. Did her mother—or Cerwyn—truly wish for her die rather than sleep? To physically sacrifice herself for The Dream?

"I'm an amplifier for magic when awake." Aroreh fidgeted with the ribboned ties of her bodice. "But what might happen should I sleep?"

"I'm not sure." Gellynor slowed and faced her. "What do you think?"

"Matters not what I think."

"Okay, you keep saying that . . ." The faerie narrowed her eyes. "I disagree. But for the sake of conversation, if you amplify magic while awake, it holds reason that you may dampen magic when asleep."

Aroreh shuddered at the very thought. What if she unwittingly harmed another who depended on magic? And what if the faeries lied and Aisling was truly spirit, not technology as they insisted?

"There's always a chance that nothing happens," Gellynor continued with a shrug. "Either way, like I said, the gilded room would be safe."

"I was told my dreams would be dangerous."

Gellynor nodded. "A weaver of dreams is dangerous to someone who craves control."

Aroreh closed her eyes, conflicted. Emotions continued to unspool in her mind. Endless temptations created endless fears with endless questions demanding answers that would never satisfy her paranoia. She was simply not equipped to make decisions or own them.

Everything and nothing.

Yet . . . she *did* wish to choose her own future. Yearned to, actually.

Aroreh's eyelids fluttered open to a dawning azure sky filled with pink and lavender clouds. Did the sun seek permission to sleep so the moon may rise? She thought of Gellynor's explanation of earth, water, and sky. Of the give and take to find balance and harmony in a relationship founded on mutual respect and trust. She placed a shaky hand to her midsection and breathed out slowly.

"If it is no trouble to you, I shall attempt sleep in the gilded room."

"No trouble, Your Highness."

"Thank you."

"For letting you sleep?" The faerie laughed. "Your needs aren't an inconvenience, princess. Especially basic needs."

Aroreh wanted to thank her again for the kind encouragement and reassurance but didn't want to displease Gellynor once more. So, she settled on soaking up her surroundings instead. Gellynor's strides never broke once, her head straight, her hand resting on the pommel of her sword. Ears pointed out from ruffled chin-length black strands. Golden eyes casually took in the rustling forest, the passing fae, and Aroreh's barely veiled curiosity.

Thatched stone cottages lined the path, separated by narrow footpaths and enchanting gardens. The wondrous, brilliant colors and textures dazzled Aroreh. Mothers called for their wild, dancing children. Warriors pushed each other around with teasing laughter. Young lovers hid beneath the shadows of large trees, oblivious to anything but each other.

Aroreh smiled. But this smile felt different. This smile was entirely for herself as she secretly enjoyed the happiness all around her. A happiness she wasn't responsible for manufacturing. As her smile grew, the colors around her brightened to a more vivid hue. The laughter too. An entirely new warmth filled her body as she passed through the village. Not the flush of an overheating system, but of personal pleasure.

That is, until a breeze fluttered by and a young man materialized while crouching in the shadows of a large fallen log. Wavy hair made from autumn leaves fell over dark eyes shaded by the richest earth, the freckles across his nose stark against his paling skin. Her smile fell as the memory of iced blood flowed in her veins.

"Félip," she whispered.

Their eyes collided in a swirl of churning emotions she could name—fear, anger . . . attraction. Her system overheated again, and once more not from lingering Rune Madness.

CHAPTER 12

FÉLIP

J ust the mortal I seek," Gellynor practically chirped.

Félip's steeled gaze remained riveted onto Aroreh—the way she dipped her head but gazed at him through lowered lashes; how her shoulders were rounding, as if trying to make herself smaller; the way fingers of light caressed her skin into a blush; and how the wind played with her dress and hair. The rising and falling of her chest quickened and he clenched his jaw. Of course, she feared him. Everyone in Rothlín feared him.

He brushed the cloak to rest behind his shoulders and then stood from his crouched position, unsure of what had happened. He was simply skipping through shadows to hide from Gedlen when the light grew intense and shifted. As if the light itself was drawn to another's warmth and radiance. Had it been? A vague memory surfaced of fading sunlight seeking out the songbird when she sang in the stone circle.

"Your Highness," Gellynor said, punctuating each word. Félip crossed fatigued arms over his chest and angled away from Aroreh and Gellynor, being sure the princess had a good view of his disfigurement. A reminder to keep her distance. But, when neither he nor Aroreh responded, Gellynor barked, "Félip Batten MacKinley!"

"Aye?" Félip slid an annoyed glare the elf's way. Before she could say what he wanted him for, he asked, "Did ye find my double yet?"

"You know we haven't." Gellynor's eyes narrowed back. "She fled Leaf Curl."

"How do ye know I'm not the Rune Shifter?"

"You are pieced together too perfectly," Aroreh softly interjected, another blush reddening her neck.

Félip's chest constricted. "Perfectly?" he choked out.

She touched her cheeks and rushed out, "Forgive me, I shouldn't have spoken so freely." She lowered her eyes farther and added, "Matters not what I think."

"Nae, lass. Never apologize fer speaking yer mind." Félip stepped toward her and Aroreh stepped back, her eyes darting around the path. He dropped his arms back to his side and gentled his tone. "What do ye mean by 'pieced together'? Maybe we can learn how to spot a Rune Shifter in the future."

Aroreh studied the ground as she twisted a layer of her skirt in her fingers. "When you first appeared to me in a golden forest near a cave, your face wasn't . . . scarred." Her fingers left the lace of her skirt to rub her upper arms. "Then . . . then, when you appeared once more, a different time, one eye was green, the other dark brown."

"Interesting." Gellynor considered Félip, head angled in thought. "Anything else?"

"Yes," Aroreh replied just as softly as before. "That Félip Batten seemed taller, leaner. More angular, perhaps. And his voice . . ." She swallowed and then drew in a shaky breath. "His voice wasn't beautifully musical, like yours." Her eyes snapped to his. "When you speak, I hear freedom. I cannot hear music around me anymore. But I still hear the melody in your voice. Even now. That is when I truly knew it wasn't you in the woods. For you carry a song of freedom."

Félip was speechless. A song of freedom? She found his voice beautiful? Now it was his turn to blush. He pulled away from her curiously fearful gaze to gather himself.

"I'm sorry to displease you." She continued to rub at her arms, as if cold. In fact, her entire body was shaking.

Did she mistake his need to process as rejection? Now he understood Gellynor's comment yesterday, about her inner-personal needs.

She was nothing like he expected, far more timid, far more fragile. The young woman who had defended his life and traced his scar was gone. Her defiance was probably the result of a glitch from switching off the machines. Hopefully Gedlen was right about strong women. The Princess of Rothlín had a lot of work ahead of her to awaken a new dream—to set her realm free. That is, if she even wanted to join Dúnælven's war plans to save Rothlín from the hag's mind-controlling magic. Maybe she would rather return to her previous life.

Noting his inspection, Aroreh tried to smile, but struggled to do so. Then her eyes widened. "I hope I didn't sound like I was begging for a compliment, for a lady never begs. I simply don't wish to upset you, and if—"

"Yer Highness." Félip removed his cloak, turned it inside out to it's normal weave, and then draped the garment around her shoulders when she didn't move away from him. "I'm not upset. Only processing yer words a spell. I asked ye to speak yer mind, aye?" She gently nodded and pulled his cloak around her tighter. Gellynor watched him, a calculating glint in her impish eyes. Dread knotted in his gut, knowing what the faerie was thinking. "Och! Gedlen is expecting me," he said in mock surprise, not giving the meddling faerie a chance at matchmaking. *Oh sure she was looking fer me, my arse.* Gellynor wasn't fooled by his outburst, however, and arched a dark eyebrow.

"Félip!" Gedlen hollered down the trail, behind his twin sister. "If you continue to jump shadows to escape training, I will take away your cloa—" The Fate Maker stopped short when noting who now wore his Cloak of Light and Shadows. Félip wanted to groan. He was an eejit. One kind word from a bonny lass and he offered up his most valuable possession without a single intelligent thought. "Well then," Gedlen continued with a pointy grin, "problem solved."

Brandu circled Félip before landing on his head. Félip batted at the annoying raven, who seemed to take pleasure in tormenting him too—like his master. "Ow!" Brandu's claws tugged on Félip's hair before flying over Gedlen's shoulder. "Damn bird. I'll use yer feathers fer a pillow, if ye do that again!" The raven cawed back his own threat.

Gedlen stroked Brandu's ruffled feathers. "Giving lessons, prince?"

"She was cold." A few choice words begged for release when Félip's reddening ears burned even hotter at his ridiculous excuse. To cover up his embarrassment, he quickly tossed out, "Cannae keep up with shadowlings these days, general? We need to work on yer tracking skills." Félip flashed a taunting smile of his own. "Just keeping yer old bones agile."

"Are you challenging me, prince?"

"Is the obvious a challenge, *charaid?*"

Gedlen slapped the back of his head. "Come, you have many more rounds to finish before your lessons are done for the day."

"Brother," Gellynor said. "After lessons, see me. And bring Dog Breath with you."

Félip couldn't help himself and laughed, until he glimpsed a wicked curl to Gedlen's lips. Dammit. He was about to pay for his shadow walking stint. Gedlen gestured with his head for Félip to follow. Rolling his eyes, Félip maneuvered to stride past Aroreh. As he passed, she whispered, "Thank you," and brought the edge of his cloak's hood to her cheek.

"Aye, lass," he whispered back in reply.

He was a right fool, and Gedlen was about to demonstrate just how much.

Hours of training later, Félip soaked in the cold stream outside the village proper. Every muscle burned and trembled. And his ribs felt bruised, areas of his legs and arms too. But he should thank Gedlen for the workout. After shifting into the light before Aroreh, he buzzed with a furious riot of emotions. His initial reaction was to release his pent-up anger over her mither's injustice. To shame Aroreh for how children went hungry and cold because their mithers preferred a pretty face over their own babes. How men now pressured their wives, daughters, and sisters to follow the ways of Aisling with hopes of surrounding themselves with fabricated beauty, mindless obedience, and unnerving gentleness. How other blighted children had suffered and even died under her mither's fervent religious beliefs. But his damn heart refused. Especially when she quavered in his presence and averted her eyes. So, he released his turbulence in the ring, striking steel and learning footwork. Preparing for actual war.

Did she fear him or his disapproval? Or both?

He sighed and then dunked beneath the water's surface. For all his frustrations, Aroreh was still a far safer thought than processing how he was the heir to Dúnælven's throne. The glacial water tingled across his bare skin. Any stubborn remnants of temper cooled.

Tiny bubbles floated from his lips as he pushed up toward the blue sky and broke the water's surface. Droplets raced down his face. He shook the water from his hair and then wiped his face with a wrinkly hand. Satisfied, he strode from the water and onto the bank, where he sat on a rock to dress. Birds sang lullabies overhead as he laced his breeches and then his boots. An evening breeze wisped by cold tendrils of the night sky to come. Goosebumps shivered across his back in reply. The chill felt good. More than good, actually. Though he didn't dare complain about the warmth when his tunic covered his arms and brushed down his chest and torso. He began to reach for his belt and stopped. A twig snapped behind him. And over his shoulder, an unnatural shadow moved.

Félip lunged for his new sword and spun toward the shadow on drilled-in instinct. The belt dangled from his other hand. But he raised the supple leather to use as a whip, if needed.

A girl gasped, frozen—half in light, half in shadow. Details came into sudden focus. White-blonde hair. A mottled, faerie-made cloak. Eyes as blue as a summer sky.

"Aroreh?"

"I apologize, Your Highness." She quickly turned her back to him. Félip cringed with his honorific title on her tongue. "I didn't realize you were bathing."

He glanced down, eyebrows drawing together. He was dressed. Did he forget an article of clothing? A water droplet rolled down his face and he deflated in relief. His hair was wet. Of course. Félip lowered his sword to the ground. "But ye knew I was here?"

"Gedlen shared where I could find you so I may return your cloak."

"Cheeky bastard," Félip muttered to himself. "Turn around, lassie." The quickness at which she obeyed startled him. He had never answered if he were still bathing. And now she regarded him like she was eager for his approval. Was she? Or just acting on muscle memory to please those around her? To test his growing concerns, he pointed and said, "Ye can sit over there."

Aroreh faced the direction he indicated. "In the red patch of flowers or in the golden pile of leaves?"

"Where would you like to sit?"

"Matters not what I think. Where do you believe I should sit?"

Her voice was soft, almost afraid. His concern grew larger and settled heavily in his chest. Félip took slow steps toward her, not wanting to spook her fragile sense of self. She pressed her back into the trunk of an oak tree and watched him, eyes large. Her gaze begged him to be kind; her body cowered in anticipation of cruelty. The concern tightening his chest ached at her reaction. The kind of ache where he knew she was now wrapped up into his anger. But not at her.

For her.

He stopped a couple of strides from where she stood and whispered, "Do I frighten ye?"

Her rounded eyes roamed over his face and settled on his scar. "My memories of you are frightening. Is . . . is Blight Rot real?"

"I'm not a cursed monster." He heaved a sigh and nudged the forest floor with his boot. "My foster mither and faither dinnae have Blight Rot. They've touched me many a time, even my frostbite scar. Others have too, accidentally, and they were never infected."

Aroreh looked away and appeared to be blinking away tears. "Everything seemed so terrifyingly real. I felt the frost in my veins. I saw the black lines leading to my heart. Even when Cerwyn harmed me as you, I experienced pain."

"I would never harm ye." She looked at the sword in his hand. Feeling dumb, he tossed his blade and leather belt onto the forest floor, then said, "I mean it, lass. I would never harm ye."

"I believe you, Félip Batten."

"Yet ye came here anyway, even though ye thought I might harm ye? Is my good opinion of ye truly worth yer safety? Yer life?" She daintily gnawed the inside of her lip, refusing to meet his eyes. "What did she do to ye?"

"I am not sure," she whispered back. "When the false Félip, I mean Cerwyn, would touch my hand—"

"Nae, lass," he gently corrected. She blinked several times again. A small wrinkle formed between her brows. When she finally met his waiting gaze, he said, "Yer mither. What did she do to ye?"

"I am to bring you back to the temple." The words released with a groan, as if she fought the confession spilling out of her mouth. Was she battling her programmed obedience? Félip wasn't sure if he should stop her. It was obvious she didn't want to share. But her next words came out too fast. "If I fail to do so, I won't receive purification. Or be welcomed home. My . . . my life depends on it."

Disgust burrowed through Félip.

Kicking up a storm of leaves into the air, he said, "So the queen let ye go into the hands of the faeries to drag me back, and then sent a Rune Shifter to torment ye into obedience." Her eyes searched his as the kicked-up leaves clattered all around where they stood—the only sound in their strained silence. After the last leaf fell, he quietly asked, "Yer life truly depends on me returning to the temple?"

"Yes."

"She would kill ye? Her own kin?"

"I . . . I am not sure, actually. She threatened to wipe me from her home." Aroreh flinched and then looked away once more.

"Did she physically hurt ye? Yer mither?" He grit his teeth. "The way ye tremble . . ."

Aroreh didn't reply. Shoulders raised, face grimaced in grief, her fingers furiously knotted a ribbon from her dress.

Fury re-stoked the embers in his veins until they burst into flame. He didn't want to know if Aroreh would accept his blood as a holy sacrifice in her mither's precious temple to earn back the queen's favor. He didn't want to know if she still believed him a monster because the Cold Winds traced a frostbite scar across his cheek. Instead, he leaned in closer until she was forced to look at him.

"I will teach ye the ways of light and shadow, if ye want. I will help ye take back the power stolen from ye at birth."

A tear crawled down her unblemished cheek, but she remained silent as she continued to hold his heated gaze—strangely unafraid of him now.

"I know factory wash women with more power than ye. They at least choose to be faerie blessed or no, even if their bairns are connected to The Dream." He clenched his teeth together and spat, "Let yer mither wipe ye from her home. She dinnae deserve ye, anyway. But ye deserve to control yer own mind and to live without fear. The people of Rothlín too. I've glimpsed the strong woman ye are, Aroreh Rosen."

"Strong? I hardly know how to feel in my own skin lately. I hardly know what to feel . . ."

"Ye put yer life before mine in the temple, to defend me. A stranger to ye. Ye also shouted at me in The Wilds and demanded I respect yer choices. That woman still exists. She's simply hiding in the shadows right now. We'll find her."

Aroreh closed her eyes and a feather of a smile appeared. A genuine smile. And it was utterly breathtaking.

"Freedom," she whispered to the wind and the setting sun. "Your voice is the loveliest song I have ever heard."

Félip's legs grew weak as his treacherous heart hammered behind his bruised ribs. The most beautiful woman in all Ealdspell spoke of him with sighs, a true smile on her lips. He was afraid to move, afraid to breathe even. Aroreh's eyes fluttered open and locked with his bashful gaze. Whatever was holding his legs upright inched closer to liquefying before her feet. But somehow, he still managed to say, "Someday, yer voice will be a song of freedom too, lass. More so than mine."

"Teach me the ways of light and shadow, Félip Batten." Then her smile widened. "I have . . . time."

CHAPTER 13

AROREH

Aroreh smothered a giggle with her hand. Félip crept by within inches of where she hid in the shadows of a large stump decorated in mushrooms and blackberry vines laden with plump fruit. A spot she specifically chose near the rushing water of a stream to hide her breathing and small movements, as he had instructed. Félip's dark eyes slightly narrowed while he searched the underbrush. His lips pursed and then he angled his right ear to the wind. With face upturned toward the light, she could see every rascally freckle across his nose.

So focused was he on his hunt that he missed how the toe of his boot snagged on a partially buried limb. His arms pinwheeled the air as he stumbled forward and she erupted in laughter. At the sound, he swiveled her direction on his rocking heel and righted his balance. Félip still couldn't see her, but his attentions remained on where she crouched. Aroreh was half-tempted to slip into a different shadow. But she also wanted to be found by him, again, and again, and again.

Félip regained balance and practically swaggered toward the stump. A smile tilted his lips up and his eyes danced. She remained very still, biting back another rush of laughter. Slowly, he approached, and her heart threatened to flee her breath-fluttered chest. A couple of hours had passed since she found him in these very woods to return his cloak. And each time he found her, Félip Batten erased more of her hibernation terrors and claimed a few beats more of her wildly thrumming pulse. He encouraged her to speak any thoughts she wished to share and to own her personal pursuits of happiness without shame. There were moments she almost forgot what it was like to cower before her own self, to feel obligated to please those around her. And all this after a mere couple of hours playing in the woods. What would happen if she knew him for a lifetime?

A smile stretched across her face as giddiness rolled through her. Seemingly in the same moment, the wildflowers around the secluded glen brightened in hue. Rays of fading sunlight widened and moved across the grass and ferns in a gentle caress. Félip halted his steps and considered the forest, studying both shifting light and waning shadows. He did this each time happiness found her while hidden, each time her heart trilled melodious notes of freedom. His eyes tracked the beams as they moved until his gaze locked with hers. Golden warmth tingled the skin of her face and her smile widened.

"Ye have a shadow walking fatal flaw." He gestured toward the scintillating beam above her head.

She considered the sunlight. "You searched for how long this time?"

"Light is attracted to ye when yer happy."

"I have a sunny disposition."

He rested his hip against the stump and crossed arms over his chest. "If ye remained grumpy and bitter like me, ye would shadow even longer."

She grinned, unable to contain her building mirth. "If you would watch where you walk—"

"Och, it's my fault, is it now?"

She rose, her smile dimming. The light around her waned and the wildflowers muted back to their normal vibrant hues. "Forgive me, I didn't mean to unfairly accuse you of my own failings."

"Aroreh . . ." He said her name softly, the way one whispers a name in secret. Félip reached out and tugged on the cloak's hood until her face partially dusked. "I was jesting."

"But you could have taken my words as a genuine accusation."

"Aye. I could have." His eyes roamed over her face. "I know yer ways, lassie. But let's pretend I was someone who wished to harm ye."

"I wouldn't be happy then."

He laughed. The kind where his head fell back and a hand pressed to his stomach. She bit down on her bottom lip, pleased, while taking in the shifting shadows and twinkling pockets of remnant light. His mirth tapered off and settled into a handsome smile. "Now, back to the lesson. What would ye—"

But Aroreh anticipated he would return to training and jumped into a nearby shadow, tiptoeing away from the stump toward a large oak tree. Félip's smile stretched into a grin.

"Cheeky," he said to the empty forest before him.

She pressed her palm to her mouth to hold back the laughter wishing to spring free once more. Forcing Félip to seek her out again was a form of bliss unlike any other. But catching him off guard while doing so? Even better. Joy tingled in every limb and she skipped through the shadows, a merry tune on her lips. Until the ferns she walked through swayed—loudly. She stilled, like a spooked deer in an archer's sight. Despite wanting to play, he was teaching her a valuable lesson. Giving her an element of power—an ability to control her presence in any given environment.

"Ye're not helpless," he had told her. "And this is one way ye can protect yerself, aye?"

"What if I'm found?"

"Trust yer instincts. Ye'll know what to do."

"I don't know how to trust my instincts."

Félip had searched her eyes then, as if he were lost in them. "Ye can't fully trust anyone but yerself, ye ken? People will use ye, spit on ye, wish ye dead for their own agenda. Even the faeries are manipulating us fer their own plans, not ours. But it's up to us to agree or not agree, princess." He swept a soft gaze around the forest. "Light and shadow surround us, always. Let the environment sing to ye, like when the forest sang to ye in The Wilds. Ye'll know what to do. Just wait and see, lassie."

Aroreh focused on the world around her and not the swelling emotions in her thundering chest. No wind rustled the undergrowth. Félip noticed this too and focused on the shadow where she hid. A lopsided smile alighted his face as he ambled toward the oak tree. He found her and so quickly, and all because her heart floated above the clouds. But her angle in the shadows still concealed her form. The light was shifting, though. A beam rested on a patch of mossy earth. Walking shades of light was more difficult than shadows. But if she were escaping another who wished her harm—such as a faerie or perhaps even her mother—would the risk be worth the chance of discovery?

The toe of her boot slid into the light, still beneath Félip's faerie-made cloak. Moving between light and shadow was a dance, she decided. And she did enjoy dancing. Now all she needed was a song.

A warm shaft of light reached through an opening in the boughs above her head. Tufts of cottonwood seeds floated by, as though melodic notes gliding through the air. She couldn't hear the forest sing to her anymore, but she still found music around her, nonetheless. The soft melody whispered in the evening's air pulled her body forward and she gracefully leapt onto another illuminated patch of moss, her arms and legs gliding like cottonwood tufts in the breeze. She was a wild, dancing faerie child, the cloak swirling around her, and the music grew louder, more persistent. She continued to spin and move, her body floating through the air, until she found a suitable hiding spot in the shadows of a large rock.

Félip reached her previous shadow and smiled like a fool—at nothing. Her laughter threatened to break free once more.

"All right, lassie. Reveal yerself."

She bit into the cloak to remain quiet, her body shaking with laughter.

"Aroreh, I know ye're hiding here." His smile dissolved into a thin line when she didn't reply, and he raked long fingers through his riotous hair. Then, as if afraid to touch her, he carefully extended a hand into the shadow, nearly yelping when he fell forward and touched the tree. "Cheeky," he said again, pleased. "New lesson," he continued. "On a count of three, I want ye to dart out into my line of sight then disappear again. Ye may need to run and think quick on yer feet." He turned in place, talking to the forest from all directions. Excitement prickled down her body. Her muscles tensed, ready to dash out into the open. "One . . . Two . . . THREE!"

Adrenaline surged and she shot out of the rock's shadows. Félip spun toward her, a calculating smile spreading on his face when he caught a glimpse of her body leaping through the air toward the darker shadows. She was a wild hart, bounding through the woods in graceful, dancing steps to escape the hunter. As she ran, she could almost envision a herd of deer flanking her sides. Behind her, the thump of Félip's boots gained purchase as he chased her.

She jumped off a small rock, unable to contain her laughter—not wanting to—and glided through the air into another shadow, landing light on her feet. Then she was off again, as unfettered as the wind, as carefree as a bird, as graceful as a doe. But her hunter caught up and reached for her cloak. She twirled out of his reach and melted into a beam of light and froze. He squinted his eyes, and then his gaze darted around the woods. They both stood still, their heaving breaths giving them away if not for the rustling leaves. Perhaps she could inch backward until it was safe to run once more.

But she didn't want to run, not from him. No, she wanted him to find her. Again.

Shadows moved across his face—like soft kisses, as if they knew him intimately. Strands of russet hair fluttered over his dark eyes. Flushed lips remained parted for ragged breath after ragged breath, and she was tempted to reach out and feel his skin beneath her fingertips. This time not out of fear or curiosity, but for the pure pleasure of doing so. An entirely selfish, unladylike desire, and one she wouldn't apologize for. The world around her illuminated in wondrous shades of glittering rose and golds as happiness glowed inside her—a light brighter than the one surrounding her cloaked body.

Félip's eyes tracked the fingers of sunset-hued beams that combed through trees, ferns, and wildflowers until the rays tickled her exposed skin in delicious warmth.

His eyes locked with hers. A breeze pressed his tunic against his chest and reeled through his hair.

"Yer happy again," he whispered.

She whispered back, "You make me happy."

"Ye made yerself happy. Look at what ye did, lass? Och, ye walked light and shadow, better than most new shadowlings in the ring. I dinnae think I would have found ye, if the sun wasnae drawn to ye."

"I drew the sun on purpose." A blush warmed her cheeks and she whispered, "I wanted you to find me."

He softly blinked and his breath quivered. "Aroreh..." Her name was spoken as a caress once more—as a secret delight upon his lips.

"I have never played before, not like this evening." She pulled his cloak up to her nose and then buried her face in the enchanted wool. "Thank you for gifting me a slice of happiness."

He cleared his throat, then looked around the woods, rubbing the back of his neck. "We should return, before Gedlen sends his pesky raven after us. Stupid bird."

A smile stretched across her face as she fell into a shadow. When she was several steps down the trail, she hollered, "Come find me!" And then, like a wild, dancing faerie child, she tumbled away in the autumn wind, her laughter trailing behind her.

CHAPTER 14

FÉLIP

The Princess of Rothlín continued to surprise him. She was, perhaps, the happiest person Félip had ever met. Her laughter was magic, her smile too. Even the setting sun wanted to bask in her radiance. The arrogant, cold-hearted girl he once believed her to be didn't exist. No, she was as gentle as a faerie's feathered wing and as unexpectedly strong as a spindle tree—except she didn't realize the latter. Félip stood immobilized in her laughing wake, beguiled by her clever, mischievous nature. And the way her body slipped through light and shadow when he chased her? *Breathe, lad.*

Wait.

. . . chased her.

Och, he a was slack-jawed, panting eejit!

Félip jogged to his sword and belt, fastened them around his waist, then dashed down the wooded trail after Aroreh. Her laughter skipped along the path, carried by the wind. His legs pumped harder, determined to catch up—to catch her.

I wanted you to find me.

His feet faltered a step and he almost stumbled forward. He righted his balance, then scooped a handful of leaves. The chase continued, a wicked grin curling his lips. Her merriment grew louder. Almost close enough . . . almost. The muscles in his legs burned. His grin grew wider. The draft made by her movements breezed over him and he followed the rush of air as she zig-zagged between light and shadow.

Only when he knew he was upon her did he throw the leaves. The rain of brittled gold hit her frame and outlined her position. She halted mid-stride and re-appeared before him, a leaf in her hand.

"Shite!" Félip's boots skidded across the moss. He threw his hands out to grab her, hoping this would lessen the impact. Blonde hair whipped across his face as they tumbled through the air. Félip twisted, Aroreh in his arms. His arse hit the spongy moss first, his head next. Breath punched from his lungs and he grunted—then grimaced.

They remained silent for a long spell, embraced in each other's arms. Trees swayed overhead and wild grass bent around their bodies. Their pulses echoing in the quiet. Aroreh eventually lifted her head from his chest, her face ashen. Blue eyes traveled over him, her shaky breath fluttering across his cheek, his lips.

"Are ye hurt?" he whispered.

"I'm so sorry, Félip. How thoughtless of me to stop so."

"I startled ye with the leaves."

A slow smile softened her mouth. "I was startled by your brilliance."

"Aye, I can track and hunt." He lifted a slow smile of his own. "Shadow walking isn't just games of hide-and-seek."

"Teach me to track and hunt?"

Félip laughed. "Then how will I sneak up on ye?"

Even in the first twinklings of starlight, he knew she blushed and the air in his dust-filled lungs stilled. A gibbous moon brushed her waves of hair and smooth skin in silvers. Her body remained cradled atop his. And he became increasingly aware of his hands on her back, the way her chest rose and fell with every butterfly-winged breath.

"I didn't mean to beg," she whispered. "A lady never begs."

His fevering blood cooled. She thought he laughed at her valid request?

Gently, Félip nudged her body off his, keeping his hands on her waist until she settled beside him. Then he propped up on his elbows and peered intently at the night sky. If he looked at her right now, he might pull her back onto his lap. To comfort her. To comfort him. Feeling her body pressed to his awakened a longing so deep, it terrified him. People in Rothlín didn't touch him—not willingly. And he wanted to be touched, to feel the physical warmth and comfort of another.

"Ye didnae beg, lassie," he said. "I was jesting again."

"But you could have interpreted my request as begging?"

"Cannae say I would complain much." He smiled at the stars. "To have ye beg me, fer anything."

She caressed a fern frond for a few heartbeats. "I thought men preferred agreeable women."

"A man should prefer a woman who knows her own mind." He rolled to his side and rested his head onto his hand. "Now, ye were begging me?"

Aroreh's eyes rounded for a blink and then she burst into laughter. "Are you always full of jests?"

"He's full of horse shit," a voice said from the shadows. Gellynor moved into the moonlight, hands on hips and eyebrow arched. If not for the humored slant of her lips, Félip would think her pissed at him. "Do you know what time it is?"

"I'm not a wee bairn, ye swamp-souled meddling faerie," Félip shot back. "Leave us be."

Tyllie landed beside Aroreh and hooted at Félip. "She says you're full of ogre shit," Gellynor translated for Aroreh's benefit. "I stand corrected."

Félip playfully glared at the owl and pointed at the ground beside him. "Come here and hoot at me like a man, ye spotted chicken."

"Hoot!"

"Och, ye need a woman to protect ye, do ye now?" Félip lunged at the owl. Tyllie flapped her large wings at Félip without cease though he kept batting her away.

"Hoot!"

"All right, all right . . . I yield." Félip lifted his hands up in surrender and grinned. "The princess is strong enough to protect us all."

"Hoot!"

Félip sighed dramatically. "Aye, ye're a beautiful, fierce owl and can protect yerself too." He peered at Aroreh and winked. "But still a spotted chicken."

Gellynor roared with laughter and Tyllie fluffed her feathers before turning her back to them. "Oh, don't give me that look, Tyllie," Gellynor managed through more laughter. "You wanted the prince to insult you." Tyllie continued to ignore Gellynor, so the female turned her waggish attentions onto Félip. "Gedlen is looking for you."

Félip fell back to the earth with a *thwump* and groaned. "What does the old male want now?"

"Best you ask him."

He closed his eyes and sighed. "And what if I want to sleep beneath the stars? This lass wore me out," he said, blindly pointing Aroreh's direction. "The fae demon can find *me*."

A sharp jab poked his side and Félip jumped to a seat, a scowl pinching his face. "Fae demon?" Gedlen asked, flashing fang in a delighted grin right before poking him again with a large stick.

"Do that again, *charaid*, and I'll show ye exactly where to put that stick." Félip flashed Aroreh a playful glare, making sure his lips twisted just slightly into a smile. "Ye could have warned me. I thought we bonded out there, jumping shadows."

The princess studied his face, tilting her head as if in thought. Then her face brightened, realizing he was jesting once more. Warmth spread through his chest in response. She trusted him, could relax around him.

"Do you like Gedlen to chase you?" Aroreh asked. "How I like you to chase me?"

"Och, that's cold, lass." Félip screwed his face up in disgust and she laughed.

Gedlen smiled, almost fatherly at Aroreh, then tapped Félip's leg with his boot. "Come, prince. We must talk."

"Fine, ye bannock-brained mouse dropping."

Félip pushed off the ground and then dusted the leaves and grass from his breeches. Gedlen offered his hand to help Aroreh stand and Félip nearly rolled his eyes at himself. That should have been him and Gedlen knew it, flashing him fang in another delighted smile. Perhaps a trick of light, but the elf appeared disappointed when Félip didn't react to the latest prod. Good. Served the bastard right.

"Your Highness." Aroreh offered the Cloak of Light and Shadows to him, and Félip pulled his attentions from Gedlen to her. "Thank you for the kind lessons this evening, Félip Batten."

"MacKinley. I want to honor me foster parents, ye ken?"

"Of course," she replied in a near whisper. "Félip Batten MacKinley."

"*Beg me* fer a wee lesson again soon, Aroreh Rosen. Aye?" A girlish smile lit her face, followed by soft laughter. She was going to murder him, one smile at a time. Even now, he felt her steel in his chest, twisting his heart. "Ready?" He turned toward Gedlen a little too cheerfully. A lad must be in a desperate place to call upon the fae demon, and he was desperate—desperate to breathe again.

The Fate Maker draped an arm across Félip's shoulders and directed him away from Aroreh and Gellynor. Félip glanced over his shoulder at Aroreh and dipped his head in a slight nod. She lowered her lashes and smiled. *Breathe, lad.* A hand clapped his back and he barked a surprised cough, daggers in his eyes as he whipped his head toward Gedlen.

"You seemed like you were struggling to draw breath."

"I was breathing just fine, *eejit*."

Gedlen grunted in humor. "I don't think I'm the idiot here."

Now Félip did roll his eyes. "What did ye want to talk about, *charaid?*"

"Nothing."

Félip stopped and spun toward the elf. "*Naething?*"

The male threw his head back and laughed. "You're too easy.

Come on, boy." He grabbed Félip by the back of his tunic and forced him to keep walking. After a couple of steps, Félip yanked free from Gedlen's hold. "Peace, Your Highness. Gellynor simply needs a private moment to ask if the princess wished to sleep tonight or tomorrow night."

"Aroreh is to sleep?"

"She knows true happiness now." Gedlen slid him a sly look. "Time to show her true sorrow."

"Faerie riddles . . ." Félip's pulse spurred into a gallop. "If ye control her mind, then ye're no different than the bloody hag on Rothlín's throne."

Gedlen slowed his steps and faced Félip. "You go too far, prince. I'm nothing like the queen and you would do well to remember it."

"Aye," he whispered under his breath, regretting his hot-tempered words immediately.

The remainder of their walk was cloaked in silence, Félip lost to images of Aroreh running in the wood and Gedlen lost to—well, who knew what a centuries old faerie thought. Félip didn't want to know, either. They parted words only when Félip reached his cottage and disappeared into the warm glow of candlelight.

"Félip," his mither called from the kitchen. "There ye are, laddie."

He leaned in and kissed his mither on the cheek. "Sorry to worry ye. Lessons ran late."

"Yer flushed." She placed the back of her hand to his forehead. "Not fever'n. Let me see yer eyes." Félip's shoulders sagged, annoyed with the unnecessary fussing and worried clucking. But he let his mither cradle his face and draw him lower toward her, trying not to flinch. Hazel eyes, crinkled at the corners, inspected his wary gaze. Then her face relaxed. "Yer happy. I see the smile in yer eyes. Ye wear the flush of contentment."

"Aye, it's a relief to see ye well care fer, Mither."

"Nae, laddie," she admonished, still holding onto his face. He raised his eyebrows. "Another makes yer soul smile so. A mither knows these things. May she deserve yer heart and be stubborn enough to put up wit yer fool ways." She patted his cheek and walked away. Heat crept up his neck and he opened his mouth with a smart reply, but clamped it shut when he saw the state of the kitchen.

"What's this?" He pointed to the crates filled with dishes and linens lining the floor. "Are we changing cottages?"

His mither fussed with a tea towel. "Me and yer faither are mov-ing up the mountain tomorrow."

"Why? And where's faither?"

"He's fetch'n firewood. And fer our safety, the faeries said. War is come'n to Leaf Curl."

"War . . ."

"Och aye, that's what I said. Are yer ears filled with wool?"

Félip swallowed back the rising panic. This is why Gedlen was looking for him, and his heart sank. "I'll help ye pack."

People came in from every quarter in great numbers; they threw water upon the Princess's face, unlaced her, struck her on the palms of her hands, and rubbed her temples with Hungary-water; but nothing would bring her to herself.

"The Sleeping Beauty in the Wood" by Charles Perrault,
Tales of Mother Goose, 1697

CHAPTER 15

AROREH

Aroreh edged onto a freshly made bed of moss, ferns, and wild flowers. The gilded room glinted in the candlelight, a lovely shade of golden amber. A yawn crept up and she daintily placed a hand over her mouth. There were moments she struggled to keep her eyes open, which should have jolted her into fresh terrified alertness. But she didn't. Her body's needs outweighed her own fears.

Dalbréath played card games with her through most of the night and Gellynor stuck by her side today until she could no longer stomach the idea of staying awake. Last night, she was still too frightened over the idea of falling asleep. But if she were truly honest, she had wanted to think on her time walking light and shadows in the wood, afraid those memories and lessons might disappear should she dream of other things.

Gedlen and Gellynor conferred nearby, talking in low whispers as Gellynor manipulated runes in the air. Brandu and Tyllie perched by their masters, watching them argue. Aroreh's mind continued to reel after her many conversations with Félip in the outlaying woods.

He thought her strong? The very idea rattled her notions of how a proper lady should behave. What man desired a woman who demanded he respect her choices, even if they displeased him? Women with subservient natures made for better wives and mothers, she was told. And a woman's gentle demeanor—a prized feminine trait—pleased the goddess she served.

And yet, he declared that a man should desire a woman who knew her own mind, then scandalously demand she beg him for another lesson. That afternoon into evening, she forgot what it was like to fear displeasing those around her. She forgot her own sense of propriety and just . . . played. Even the sun rejoiced in her happiness. The land brightened in hue and in light, and her heart beat with fluttering gratitude for the boy who gifted her permission to savor this self-aware power unabashedly.

"So, he returned?" she heard Gellynor ask her brother. The concern in the female's voice cut through Aroreh's wandering thoughts.

"Yes, a couple of hours ago. He's angry."

"He's always angry."

Gedlen sighed. "They're the only real family he's known, Gellynor. But a promise is a promise. He knows this, even if his heart doesn't right now."

Did they speak of Félip? Is this why she hadn't seen him all day? For a spell, Aroreh believed she had upset him. She searched for the impish young man around the training ring and near the wood where they played the evening past. She even knocked on his cottage door, terrified of how his mither or faither might think on her for darkening their doorstep to see their son.

"Cold feet?" the female elf asked.

Startled, Aroreh pointed at her own chest. "My apologies, but do you speak to me?"

"Yes." Gellynor settled on a stool beside Aroreh's makeshift bed. "You look peaked."

"I suppose I am." Aroreh wrinkled her brows. "Do you think me strong, Gellynor?"

"Matters not what I think," she said, parroting Aroreh's trained response to questions. "Do *you* think you're strong?"

Leather armor squeaked in the following silence. Gedlen shifted on his feet, his mouth pressed into a thin line, and then he crossed well-armored forearms over his breastplate. Those violet eyes now studying her unsettled Aroreh's nerves further. As did the twin swords strapped across his back.

"I'm not a warrior, like you," she eventually said to Gellynor. "Nor do I command others."

"A woman can be strong without being a trained warrior."

The pull in Aroreh's middle persisted. "I fear I am too agreeable to be strong."

"I'm not agreeable?" Gellynor grinned, followed by a wink. Tyllie hooted behind her. "I *am* agreeable. Hush."

Aroreh lowered her lashes and studied her hands. She understood the faerie teased. But Félip's words danced around in her head endlessly. Did he lie to her? His voice sang of freedom, but when away from him a loud part of her still remained wary of the young man. Of everyone. When with him? She longed to know only his company all the days of her life.

"Strength wears many faces, princess," Gedlen said softly, yanking Aroreh out of her ever spinning thoughts. "Some mortal women choose steel and battlefield mud. Some choose compassion and kindness as their weapons. Some fight by leaning on well-sharpened intelligence. While others inspire those around them simply with their willingness to become vulnerable. There are as many examples of strength and courage as there are stars in the sky."

Gellynor added, "Gentleness is *not* a sign of weakness."

Aroreh considered Gedlen's words as she caressed a delicate blossom resting against her leg. Was she like this petal? Beautiful, pliable, yet fragile? Curious, she tugged at the petal's tip until a piece ripped free. Her brows pushed together. The petal possessed remarkable strength despite its fragility.

What anchored her strength?

Darling, you were manufactured by the goddess herself. And faeries are always attracted to beautiful, shiny objects. And that is what you are—an object. Nothing more.

Her mother's words echoed fresh in her wounded mind. And wounded it was, she realized. An injury had taken place. Everyone around her seemed so certain of who they were and who they were not. They didn't quake in fear over sharing pieces of themselves, nor agonize if their behavior was acceptable. They freely laughed, clenched fists in displays of anger, and tossed aside any rule that encumbered them from being . . . *them*.

"The language of earth, water, and sky," she quietly reminded herself. The language of cycles and balance, of give and take. Recognition gleamed in Gedlen's eyes and a faint smile softened the hardened lines of his angular face.

The pink flower twirled between Aroreh's fingers, back and forth, back and forth. Each petal had unfurled in their own way—loose, tight, passing into another petal's space. She compared the flower in her hand to the others dotting the bed. Each one was unique, even hues of the same kind differed subtly. And yet, each flower bloomed bright despite how they were plucked and displayed. Unlike Rothlin. Unlike home where service to the goddess required a uniformity of set perfections.

Earth, water, and sky . . .

Aroreh's heart sank. "How am I ever to repair myself?"

Brandu cawed and Gedlen considered his familiar a heartbeat.

"If you could dream," Gedlen began, not really answering her question, "what would you dream about?"

She didn't reply right away, mostly taken aback by his abrupt change in subject. Or so she thought. The Fate Maker often spoke in riddles. Nor could she speak Raven or Owl. Perhaps Brandu encouraged the question. Her first instinct was to ask what the faerie twins thought she should dream about. But she had always wanted to dream. To truly experience that magical place so many already knew and cherished.

The flower in her palm recaptured her attention.

"Sweet briar rose," Gellynor said. "The blossoms have magical properties to help one sleep. Did you know this?"

"No," she quietly answered.

"Eating the petals, drinking a tea made from the blooms, or even sleeping in a bed of briar roses will help a mortal fall into a deep sleep."

And it was her House insignia—a fitting symbol for a realm who currently slumbered to a false dream.

Did she wish to dream of her home in Rothlín? Of the emotional ignorance and mental captivity? A hot feeling bubbled up from deep within. How did she know the faeries didn't lie to her too? What if this were a trick to steal her mind once more, and she ruined every chance to reunite with her mother? After all, Aroreh had never slept a wink in her life.

And faeries are always attracted to beautiful, shiny objects. And that is what you are—an object. Nothing more.

No.

She may have been deemed an object since birth, but that wasn't the future she wanted.

Aroreh lifted her head and met Gedlen's intensity with her own. "I wish to dream of a world where I am my own person without apology. Strong and fearless."

A slow, calculating grin stretched across the faerie's face. "A magic unlike any other."

Gellynor jumped off the stool with a resounding "Yes!" and then clapped her hands in a giddy riot of laughter. The boisterous reaction startled Aroreh at first, but she quickly joined in the celebratory joy. For she had declared her dream without fear or apology. Nor did she feel selfish for longing to have a basic need others had known their whole life.

Well, not right away.

Doubt crept back into place, as well as the paranoia that she had displeased her goddess—a deity she was told was manufactured. Surely her mother would disown her now. Maybe even bleed her out as an offering for the temple. Not only had Aroreh failed to bring Félip back, she had defied the queen, asserted herself in The Wilds, and even now she spoke with a power she struggled to rightly possess. The ache returned and bloomed bright in her chest until the fear crowded out the air in her lungs.

Overwhelmed, she watched her fingers twirl the flower in her hand. The tip of her finger no longer remained bruised. And, thankfully, black lines still hadn't streaked to her heart. Aroreh stilled the spinning stem and blossom.

"Why was my finger injured so?" she asked.

Gedlen cleared his throat. "In The Wilds, before the Veil, a fae warrior pricked your finger with a sliver from a spindle tree."

"Pricked my finger?"

"Yes." Gedlen took in a deep breath. "The rumor was that you would die, for your amplifying magic was woven from spindle tree blossoms. The poison in the wood would counteract the spell from the flowers. But Dalbréath rune whispered your system first to ensure you would only fall into hibernation. The Veil opened immediately following your system's sleep. The mist refused to open until then, which we realized was because your overheating system was jamming the Veil's program. Your hibernation saved many, princess."

Her mouth parted in shock. "Dúnælven wished me dead?"

"No, not really. This is war, princess. The Fate of Rothlín rests in your hands." Gedlen stepped closer to Aroreh and she sucked in a quiet, trembling breath. "The queen gains strength from your amplifying magic. You are the reason she can influence so many. Without you, her reach is limited."

Horror welled up from Aroreh's middle until she feared she might be sick. "And if I'm no longer alive?"

"We're not entirely certain. Though some believe all light will flee Rothlín when your heart no longer beats."

She clapped a hand over her mouth. Tears gathered on her eyelashes and rolled down her warming cheeks. Brandu left his perch and flapped into her lap and rubbed his head against her chest. Then Tyllie settled beside her on the bed and hooted a sad note.

"My mother," Aroreh began in a trembling voice, "She warned that I would slay the goddess Aisling with my dreams."

"We suspected you were a dream weaver," Gedlen said. The blood drained from Aroreh's head. "Forgive me," he continued. "Simply put, your dreamscape is the world around you. Always. And what you do in your dreams affects reality. That requires a significantly large draw of magic, which is why you may dampen the magic around you while sleeping. But this is also why you're an amplifier while awake."

Gellynor shot her brother a dark look, baring her canines at him. "Tell her the good part."

The male sighed. "I see visions but they're only in part. Fate is a ribbon that threads our lives. Our choices build the weave that Fate ties together. I . . . have seen your death as an answer to dissolving a Kingdom-wide war." Gellynor growled at her brother. "But," he quickly added, "I have also seen your life, in a separate vision. Several visions, actually. And it is far more beautiful than you can even imagine, full of magic and full of love."

"I am so sorry. I am so very sorry."

"Sorry for what?" Gellynor asked sweetly, though she still glared at her brother. "You're not responsible for the rules of your magic, no more than I or Gedlen are responsible for ours."

Aroreh collapsed onto the bed and the birds took flight. The beat of wings echoed in her pounding ears. Then a heaving sob gave way from her too-tight chest. Anger blushed her blood hot while grief cooled the edges of her heart. The sourness in her middle strengthened. But it was the bleating pain in her chest that throbbed most. This pang, this injurious sensation was perhaps the most bitter sorrow she had ever known. A sadness laced with fury.

Betrayal.

This must be betrayal.

The faeries intentionally risked her death for their war. Her mother had wanted her so she could control the Kingdom of Eald-spell. Aisling was artificial intelligence, she was told, and The Dream its program—not a life-saving goddess. Not the goddess she fervently served since first recollection.

And that is what you are—an object. Nothing more.

"Leave," Aroreh said, her voice muffled. After a few wild beats of her heart she shouted, "Leave!"

The shuffle of footsteps quickly followed her outburst. She should feel shame for behaving so. A lady didn't raise her voice or speak unkindly to another. The overwhelming sickening of spirit and body tamped down all rules of etiquette, however.

All rules belonging to a lie.

Aroreh curled her legs up to her chest and buried her face farther into the flowers. Another sob wracked her body. She didn't have control over her body. Never had, never would. Not even now. Her body demanded sleep without The Dream controlling her runic system. Félip was wrong. Strength wasn't in her programming. Only eager obedience—a faerie blessing her mother chose—and one she fought endlessly since before arriving in Leaf Curl. Factory wash women had more freedom than her, Félip declared. But were they truly free? If still subjects of The Dream, if still followers of Aisling?

"I was created to bring others joy," she murmured to the dark space inside her arms. Now she understood their darker meaning. She murmured the words again and again—angry and disbelieving. The words repeated until they formed a drifting melody that floated up from her soul. The shaky notes escaped her mouth and she quietly sang to herself. This was the first time she had sang since Rune Madness in The Wilds, and the feeling was both exhilarating and comforting.

The bitter, hollow words eventually melted into arias from her past. Ones her instructor had taught her over the years. Aroreh rolled onto her back, an arm draped across her eyes. Drawing in a deep breath, she prepared to sing yet another song of childhood. Instead, the haunting notes of autumn leaves falling to their death in the forest gusted free. This song soothed the betrayal chilling her resolve to go on, to care about fulfilling the dreams of others. The true Blight Rot, she realized with a hiccupped note as her throat knotted painfully.

"Songbird," a soft voice whispered nearby.

Her entire body stilled, the song on her lips halted. Slowly she peeked out from beneath the arm draped over her face. Dark eyes met her tear-stained gaze. His mussed hair haloed his head in warm reds and browns. Dropping her arm, she pushed up onto her elbows bashfully. An earthy scent filled her nose, one richer and spicier than her bed of moss and wildflowers. Like the scent of freshly felled trees and a warm rain on the horizon.

He didn't say another word. He didn't need to; the grief was written across every handsome feature of his face.

Félip Batten MacKinley lowered onto the stool Gellynor had vacated. The corners of his lips dipped into a frown, his forehead wrinkling with shared sadness. Did he know the truth of her now? Did he realize how weak she really was? The strong woman he believed to have glimpsed, the one who danced between light and shadow with him, was still controlled by others—simply malfunctioning.

Then she remembered what he had called her.

Songbird.

Strangely, this pleased her. It was the same name he had called her in The Wilds when she had wanted to dance until she died. And just like then, his melodic voice stilled her chaos—if but for a moment. A small weight on her chest lifted and her lips trembled into a sad smile. She didn't even know such a smile existed.

"I yearn to choose my happily ever after," she said to him. "Not my mother, Gedlen, or even you. I want to know the power of my own mind."

Félip nodded thoughtfully. "I yearn to remake my once upon a time. I want to know my birth mither and . . . faither. And see the hills and crags of Glenashlen. I would not be reviled there." He worried the corner of his bottom lip. "Can ye imagine a life where the Cold

Winds didnae come?"

She whispered, "I exist because of the Cold Winds."

"I should have died with my family."

"What are we to do, Félip Batten MacKinley?"

He searched her eyes a heartbeat. And then another. "Fight."

Fear knotted in her middle once more and she shivered. "May . . . may I hold your hand?"

"Aye," he whispered, but hesitated before lacing his fingers with hers. "Sing yerself to sleep if ye need. Dinnae mind me."

"I'm afraid."

"Of what, lass?"

"What if I never wake?"

"I'll wake ye." His gaze traveled to her parted mouth and lingered there for a heady spell. Then his Adam's apple bobbed and his long lashes shuttered in a slow blink. "Afraid . . . of anything else?" he practically croaked.

"Yes." Heat wended up from her middle as his warm gaze caressed the lines of her jaw, curve of her cheek, to lock onto her sleepy gaze. "I fear that I shall finally gain a dream only to lose it."

He tucked a tangled strand behind her ear and whispered, "I won't let ye lose yer dream."

Her eyes fluttered closed under his comforting touch—a touch she no longer feared.

Just the mere whisper of his voice sang to her heart. A melody all her own yearned to answer his call, and so she hummed softly to herself. The notes cradled her bruised emotions until her hand grew limp in his and their song faded into the calming darkness of her mind. The last thing she remembered was his beautiful voice whispering in her ear, "I want ye to find me too, Aroreh Rosen."

CHAPTER 16

FÉLIP

Félip's thumb caressed the silky-soft back of Aroreh's hand. A few weeks ago, before he knew his songbird and the princess were one and the same, he would have felt only disgust at the slightest thought of her skin on his. Sure, just their hands touched right now. But people didn't reach out to Aisling's devil for physical comfort—well, any comfort—most especially the figurehead of the New Dawn Era. A princess he had never seen but loathed with all his being. *Once*, that is. Now? She stole the very breath from his too-tight chest.

Steady, laddie.

His pulse wobbled like a newborn foal taking steps for the first time. Perhaps his heart was learning how to beat all over again. His breath quivered, afraid he might awaken her and ruin the spell over him. The memories of her haunting melodies still played in his mind. When a lad of eight rotations, he once believed the songbird sang for him. A kindness to wipe away the wrongs of his world. Ten rotations later, he knew without a shadowing doubt that the final song warming her lips was entirely for him. The beauty of the moment lingered still. He wanted this heady feeling to last forever.

But luck didn't exist in Ealdspell.

The door cracked open and the faerie twins slipped in, wearing golden armor in a hue similar to the walls. Brandu and Tyllie swooped in and gracefully landed on their favorite flowering tree. Félip released

Aroreh's hand and jumped to a stand—his heart now hammering in his throat. The shadow walking cloak lay clumped in his arms. No time to blend into the dusky ambers of this room. But he also didn't want anyone, especially Gellynor, to get the wrong notion. The princess was afraid, he simply sat by her bedside until she calmed to sleep, her lullabies lilting the moon to slumber along with her. That was all. And she had only just fallen to sleep.

Gellynor halted her steps and quirked an eyebrow. "Your Highness, this is unexpected."

"Ye and Gedlen were arguing outside the cottage."

"Yes, but why are you here? It's not safe."

Not safe? Félip swallowed against the pulsing lump in his throat. Suddenly the room felt suffocatingly warm. "I remembered something I forgot to tell her. In the woods." He hastily pointed in the direction of where he had bathed the day prior. "When she returned my Cloak of Light and Shadows, that is. I told her, though, before she fell asleep." The dark eyebrow arched higher on Gellynor's face. "I know I sound like an eejit—"

"You sound like a man desperate for another glimpse of a beautiful girl." A tiny smirk replaced the frown.

Anger sparked at her words. "Once more, Death Talker, tell me how I feel."

"I just did."

"That was sarcasm, *charaid.*"

"Was it?" She started laughing. "Hard to tell with you."

Félip rolled his eyes and muttered, "I heard yer fight and was concerned, *Gelly.* No more. Aroreh invited me to stay." Gellynor's lips twitched and Félip groaned. "Och, I'm not a besotted fool. She's far more than a pretty face, ye frolicking goat scat."

Gellynor burst into more laughter. "You have the best insults in all of Ealdspell, I'm convinced." Tyllie hooted and Gellynor's face twisted into offense. "Would you like him to insult you again too, why he's at it? I'm sure he has something special more to say about your feathered brain." Another hoot echoed in the room. "Spotted chicken," she muttered back.

"Might I stay?" Félip swallowed back the ache in his chest. "I . . . dinnae want to be alone tonight."

"I suppose you can stay since you seem unaffected. Strange, but maybe we were wrong about her magic."

"She has magic? Not just faerie blessed?"

"Yes. I'll explain in a bit. Now scoot so I can monitor Aroreh's runic system."

He stepped aside for the huffing faerie and her oddly quiet brother, surprised that Aroreh remained asleep. The rollicking elf wasn't known for being quiet, or considerate of other people's personal space—unlike Gedlen. No, the fae demon just spouted pretty words and then pounded Félip into the ground. *Bastard.* His raven too. *Bastard bird.*

Gellynor plunked onto the stool and then pulled a thin, golden rectangle—two hands high and one- and one-half hands wide—from a pack at her side. Her brother stood beside the bed and placed three fingers onto Aroreh's temple.

"I'm ready," he said to his sister.

With a tap, the rectangle's surface glowed to life and Gedlen's eyes turned an eerie shade of white. Félip sucked in a sharp breath, wanting to look away. Unable to look away.

Tyllie alighted into the air and hooted. Her large wings beat near Félip's ear and he flinched. The spotted owl circled his body several times and hooted again.

"Tyllie, he doesn't need much poking to insult someone. Stop being so dramatic—" Gellynor stopped, her gold eyes growing large as she stared at the device in her hands. "I haven't seen anything like this in centuries."

Félip ignored the flustered spotted owl and inched closer to peek over Gellynor's shoulder.

"Why did ye dress to match the walls—"

His words turned into a sharp hiss. Hot pain flared from his scar. Félip dropped his cloak and pressed his palm to the cutting sensation tearing across his face. Tyllie hooted, a loud warbling sound. Then the room began to spin. But only for a moment. He could feel his eyes rolling to the back of his head just as his legs gave out. His head hit Aroreh's bed first before his body crashed to the floor in convulsions. Every muscle spasmed until his back arched and a scream scorched his throat.

Hands grasped under his arms and yanked. An animal of some kind gently landed on his chest with a feathered thud. Frost crackled down his body at that same moment. He could feel every jagged, sharpened ice crystal stabbing his arms, his chest, his torso, then his legs. His breathing grew ragged, erratic. The air in his lungs was crystallizing as well, he was sure of it. Especially when a violent shiver scraped down his spine and his teeth began to chatter.

"Almost there," he heard a strained voice—Gellynor's. Feathers caressed his face with a soft, whispering hoot. "No, don't say that, Tylluan."

Sunlight assaulted his pounding head. The sudden warmth scalded his frozen skin and he cried out.

"What happened?" A faerie asked.

"He's like ice!"

Others shouted, "The prince!"

"Alert Gedlen!" Gellynor screamed. "Now! He's tranced. The prince's life is in danger."

Voices faded in and out—too loud, then too quiet. Bone-shaking convulsions seized him again. He wheezed for breath. Each intake sent daggers to his chest. He was dying. All the pain, all the torment, and he didn't live long enough to avenge the wrongs. He wanted to tell Gellynor to pass along to his mither and faither that he loved them, but the words wouldn't form. His lips were freezing shut. Black edged the periphery of his vision, the light growing smaller and smaller.

A final ice-laced breath rattled free from his frosted lungs. The animal on his chest leapt into the air.

And then he felt nothing.

CHAPTER 17

AROREH

The castle gardens in Rothlín sprawled out before Aroreh. A sleepy sun hung low in the dust-tinged sky, spilling gold and amber colors across the landscape. Her plum-colored skirt flapped against her legs while the same autumn wind flurried strands of her hair to dance. The clover lawn undulated in the light breeze and climbing sweet briar roses nodded their petaled heads to the same lazy beat.

Aroreh descended the steps leading down from the Great Hall to the gardens. A celebratory feast roared on behind her—a coronation feast. Though she didn't know who was made queen or king of Rothlín. The sounds of laughter and music carried out to her through the opened windows. But she didn't belong there. The Wilds beckoned her to dance to the drum and pipes of the fae. And the leaves trilled her name in a haunting melody that sang to her rune-programmed blood. She just wanted to run away and learn to be free. The kind of freedom that offers the truest form of purification.

May you speak only what is pure and right all the days of your life.

A contented sigh passed her lips when her bare feet sank into a soft patch of clover. She ambled down the green path toward the far end of the grounds, encouraging bombinating bees and praising the chirping birds. The language of earth, water, and sky flowed off the tip of her tongue and curled through the air in a brilliance of bright colors.

A raven circled above and cawed repeatedly. She peered up to

the tea-stained sky and asked, "Come join me?" The black-winged
bird swooped down and landed on her shoulder.

May you only touch goodness all the days of your life.

Aroreh merrily stroked the back feathers with a single finger before continuing her walk. There was something she needed to find.
Something buried beneath the ancient standing stones the walls and
enchanted sweet briar roses guarded.

Moss draped down the side of the largest menhir—an upright
prehistoric monolith. Swirls and inner-locking knots decorated the
stone. Aroreh traced the designs in wonderment. As a little girl, she
had sat before these very stones and sang to the gardens, and to her
goddess. These carved rocks had probably existed since the formation
of Ealdspell. Her fingertip dragged down the rough surface, noting
each craggy rise and dip. An energy vibrated beneath her finger. Curious, she placed both hands flat against the large menhir.

The raven hopped off her shoulder and flapped to the top of the
stone and cawed. Beneath her bare feet, the ground began to shake.
Aroreh stumbled back a step and gasped. Her head swiveled back and
forth to take in the trembling castle grounds. Black wings stretched
out wide, and then the raven leapt off the menhir and alighted into the
darkening sky.

May you only see that which is beautiful all the days of your life.

Purple magic glowed from the base of each stone and glittered
into the air and out over the clover in twinkling wisps. Aroreh spun
on her heel, her mouth agape and eyes rounded. Runes glowed on the
surface in shimmering dark purple light—her runes. The code of who
she was; the very carved lines written on her bones, written across her
soul. Not the false dream glamouring her truest magic.

Behind the stones, thick clouds swirled around the burnished
sun. A raindrop plopped onto her upturned face. Thunder cracked
across the horizon, followed by a flash of lightning. More drops fell
from the luminous, cloud-ruffled sky. Aroreh laughed as she slowly
turned in place. Her glittering inner-magic twirled around her body

and danced across her fingertips.

Then she remembered: she needed to find something buried in this sacred place.

A small voice whispered under the clover. Runes sparked off her finger and she touched the ground, sucking in a delighted breath when a little girl sprouted from a beautiful patch of honeyed clover. White-blonde hair rippled down her back; blue eyes considered the swirling sky and splattering raindrops; her cream lace dress fluttered wildly around her.

"Princess Aroreh . . ." The little girl spoke her name before slowly turning toward where Aroreh stood. A small hand grasped hers and tugged. "Come, you must see."

Magic still swirled around Aroreh's body like glittering falling stars as they stepped toward the giant gate. The brambling sweet briar roses curled thorned limbs around the iron bars and pulled. A loud caw sounded from behind before Aroreh felt a weight on her shoulder and soft feathers on her neck. She knew this raven, she realized. Wasn't this Gedlen's familiar? The little girl peered up at the bird and tilted her head. She knew Brandu too?

That expression prickled the hairs on her arms. The way her delicate brows puckered just so, the curious glint in her eyes. Aroreh gasped. The little girl was her. She now held the hand of her former self, a more innocent version.

"Where are we going?" she asked her younger self.

"To wake your mind."

Beyond the gate, the vivid gardens gave way to dust-choked streets and factory smoke. They walked down a familiar spoke, the one Aroreh had stepped through during the Spindle Day procession. Wash women, some with babies strapped to their backs and toddlers playing at their feet, stirred bolts of linen in large vats of mineral dyes. Beatific smiles stretched their dirty, worn faces. Their arms trembled from hours bent in labor. A small child clung to his mother's skirts, crying. His emaciated frame shook with each wail. But still his mother smiled—wide—and without stopping her task.

"Do they not have food?" she asked her younger self, growing more disturbed.

The little girl blinked and then pointed.

Crates of rotting, maggot-ridden vegetables stacked behind the wash women. "Are these for the dyes?"

Her younger nodded. "Dyes and food."

A sickening horror welled up from Aroreh's gut. The child cried from hunger and his mother's spell-woven smile mocked his pain, and all to please the goddess. Before Aroreh could ask another question, the little girl tugged on her hand. Perhaps she could return with fresh food from the celebratory feast. The thought quieted her roaring pulse. At the castle, they ate until their stomachs stretched with discomfort while the children of Rothlín cried with hunger pains.

"In here," the little girl said. The soft, innocent voice cut through Aroreh's grief.

Before them lay Factory 8, where wool and flax were spun into threads. The low hum of machines droned in her ears. Brandu flew off her shoulder to the ground and hopped around, pecking at the dust for bugs and scraps. Aroreh placed her hands on the rusted door frame and then stepped through. A chorus of squeaks rose up from every cold shadow, and she involuntarily shuddered when a rat scurried out from a dark corner and darted across the dirt floor. Sensing Aroreh's hesitation, the little girl clutched her hand once more and tugged. They walked down a short hallway that opened into a factory floor.

Women sat behind mechanical spinning wheels, treadling to the *tap, tap, tap* of a uniformed whirring rhythm. Their deft fingers moved with programmed grace as they fed wool or flax to the machines. Glowing runes hovered above each spinning machine. Were they a count of how many bags of fiber they had processed? Men paced down the lines and barked orders. Women with spell-woven faces smiled at the men and dipped their heads in eager obedience. One such woman had spun several bags, far more than others. But she grinned at the opportunity to produce even more, though her fingers bled, nearly swooning in delight when one of the under-foremen patted her head appreciatively and said, "Good girl." Women without spell-woven faces wore the haggard expressions of exhaustion and despair.

"Ye are a worthless cow!" A man spat at a trembling woman. "If ye just smiled more, ye might actually be of use to Factory 8. The machines don't want to hear yer ungrateful sniveling either."

"The spinning machine is broke, sir," she quietly replied. "Just the same as hers." The woman pointed to a younger woman with a spell-woven smile.

"Her beauty is serviceable. Yers is not." He pointed to the hallway. "Out! Yer sacked. And don't even think about collecting wages fer this week."

"Bu-but me bairns," she stammered out. "They need to eat. Their bellies weep with hunger. I'll work an extra shift. Please sir—"

"Perhaps if their mither cared about pleasing the goddess, they might have food on the table."

Tears streamed down Aroreh's cheeks. "I never knew. My heart," she choked out, "I do believe it is sick."

The little girl peered up at her with pity, then gestured toward a corner of the factory.

A large group of children sorted and cleaned freshly sheered wool. A girl barked a deep, wheezing cough. Sweat beaded on her flushed face. The beginnings of a boil blistered on her neck. Another girl nearby coughed as well.

"Wool-Sorters Sickness?" Aroreh asked her younger self.

"Yes. They will die soon from the lung sickness."

Aroreh sucked in a ragged breath as another sob loosed from her aching chest. Images of the wild, dancing faerie children reeled in her carouseling mind. And their carefree laughter drowned out the droning machines for a single, haunting heartbeat. "Why do these children even work in a factory?"

But she knew the answer to her own question. Hunger. They

were all hungry.

"The goddess taught women to bear many children," she said. "But why if there's naught enough food and sickness plagues their homes?"

"Sleeping children dream, hungry or full. Sick children too."

The Great Spindle Tree formed in her mind and, for a moment, she could hear the lulling notes of slumbering children softly echoing off the runic walls of the temple. A sob formed in her chest. "The Dream, it's a program . . ."

"Yes," the little girl answered simply. "To steal dreams and replace them with the queen's."

"A manufactured lie," Aroreh choked out. "Why suffer your people into the grave? What benefit is there to gain?"

The little girl peered up and frowned. "The queen desires increased production and expansion."

"The burn fields . . ."

"People who know their own mind aren't controlled by pretty lies."

Aroreh started to turn back toward the hallway and paused. In the far corner, a blighted young man swept up fallen threads from the floor. The room sweltered, but he wore garments that covered every inch of skin below his neck, including hide gloves. Sweat dripped down his gaunt face and across a zagging purple scar that puckered part of his cheek. Sandy brown hair was cut close, close enough that she could see patches of disease on his scalp. As his waif-like form passed by, people hurled insults at him. Some even spat on his clothes.

Was this the life Félip had once known? Was his mother a factory spinner or a wash woman? Did his faither repair the machines or break the spirits of those who ran them?

She couldn't see anymore, couldn't bear anymore grief for causing this much pain to innocent people—to children. She could choose a different ending to this story. Aroreh spun toward the exit. But she didn't get very far. Brandu flew in and fluttered before her face, wings flapping, his caw insistent. Then he circled around her body and swooped out into the hallway.

The little girl grabbed her hand and took off into a run. "Hurry!"

"What is happening?"

"The prince," her younger self said. "He needs you."

"But the citizens of Rothlín? The children?"

The girl didn't stop running. They dashed down a spoke, and then another. Past smiling wash women and crying babies. When they reached the castle gates, the brambling sweet briar roses granted them entrance. Brandu flew just ahead of them and glided through the air toward the circle of ancient stones. Landing on the largest menhir, he cawed and the ground began to rumble. Purple magic glowed from the bases of each stone. The runes appeared once more and twirled around her like sparkling will-ó-the-wisps.

"We shall meet another time," the little girl said.

"What if I never dream again?"

"Remember, princess . . . there are as many examples of strength and courage as there are stars in the sky. Do not fear your own mind."

Aroreh desperately looked around the gardens. Clouds now swirled violently around a blood-red sun. Tears continued to roll down her cheeks. She opened her mouth to ask yet another question, but the little girl released her hand and stepped back. The raven cawed once more and the ground stopped shaking. Her younger self lifted a small hand into the air and Brandu swooped to perch onto the pad of her thumb.

The little girl began to fade, the raven with her. Before disappearing, she said, "Wake up."

Aroreh shot up from the bed.

CHAPTER 18

FÉLIP

A world of mist unfolded before Félip. He trundled through an unfamiliar wood toward a shimmering waterfall of clouds. Every step felt weightless, as though he glided on winged feet. His first instinct was to melt into the shadows to assess his surroundings unseen. But shadows didn't dapple the forest floor here, nor did his shadow walk alongside him.

Where was he?

A strangled cry floated through the trees. Félip pivoted on his heel to peer behind him, eyes wide. In the distance, a warbling image of Leaf Curl faded in and out of the mist. Did the sound come from Dúnælven? Another screeching cry vibrated through the air, followed by another. His head whipped back toward the ethereal waterfall. The cries echoed off the writhing mist, a sound akin to a flock of angry, wailing blackbirds.

Félip steadied his breathing and squinted his eyes. The wall of falling clouds textured into fast-moving shadows. Faces blurred into focus only to disappear, their bodies soaring through the glistening mist as though birds in the sky.

The Veil of Souls.

"No," he whispered to the oddly translucent trees. A chill prickled down his body. Wait. How did he still physically feel sensations if dead? Curious, he studied his hands and curled his fingers. Then he punched his thigh—hard—just to see if he were still living. Bruising pain shot through his leg. He bent at the waist, air sucking through his teeth in a sharp hiss before he spat, "Fecking eejit!"

"I could have told you that on the mortal plane."

Félip twisted toward the familiar voice. Gellynor strode toward him, arrogant smile in place. Her midnight blue tunic and short black hair ruffled in a breeze he didn't feel. Not even leaves shuddered in limbs above where she stood.

Then it hit him.

The Death Talker. She was here because he was dead. Félip looked back toward Leaf Curl. A thousand emotions hit him all at once. Regret. Anger. Mostly anger. And he groaned with the effort to not scream in fury. He couldn't be dead. Not after all he suffered.

"The Cold Winds should have taken me," he practically growled at her. "Why did I cheat death only to live a cruel, short life?"

"Anger is normal," Gellynor said. "Most souls aren't ready to depart for The Beyond. Especially young souls, like yours."

"I'm not dead." Each word left his mouth raw, as though grit by sand between his teeth. "I'm not dead!"

"You're right. And also wrong."

Félip bitterly laughed. "And now ye come to mock my final moments with faerie riddles, have ye?"

A horrible horde of inhuman cries shook trees in the distance. Félip's fury dissolved and his eyes darted the woods for evil shades, banshees, a prowling monster. He reached for his sword and came up empty. A lad couldn't take weapons into The Beyond? At this realization, whatever was left of his mortal heart pounded on the coffin of his Otherworldly form.

"What the feck is *that* cry?"

"The sluagh." Wisps of hair flew around Gellynor's face as she searched the forest canopy. "A host of eternally decaying, banished Malfae Underfolk. They sense your misery and impending death and want to steal you away."

"I thought I was already dea—" Félip blinked. "Steal me away?

From what, lass?"

"A happy afterlife."

"Right. Only an Underfolk would want my blighted soul—"

"There's a time to be rightfully angry and a time to rightfully listen," Gellynor snapped, her gaze still roaming the trees overhead. "What do you choose?" Félip rolled his eyes, then gestured for her to continue. "I can't remain here with you, so beware. If stolen by the sluagh, you become a creature more vile than Death itself."

"Orc shite . . ." Félip ran a shaking hand through his tangled mess and his fingers snagged. Not even the Otherworld saw fit to have mercy on his unruly hair. "Do I go through the Veil of Souls then?"

"Only if you truly wish to die."

Félip's gaze shot daggers at the faerie. "Ye ken the answer to that question. Now, what am I then, if not dead?"

"In-between. You're in the Thin Place right now, the Land of Mist. Behind you is the mortal plane, before you is The Beyond. Your soul is given a choice, it seems."

"How . . . how did this happen?"

Gellynor placed a hand on his shoulder and he couldn't feel the pressure of her touch. Was she not here?

"The spell keeping you alive was shattered when Aroreh fell asleep. You remain preserved in ice and not even Aroreh's waking is thawing the runes encasing you. We're working on a solution."

"Ice . . ." He slowly touched his cheek, his jaw dropping open as shocked fury returned. "Ye mean, my scar is spell woven?"

"For magic given, magic is taken. Matter isn't newly created, Your Highness. The energy is simply refashioned and transferred. Visible scars were the price of our inoculation against the Cold Winds." Gellynor removed her hand when an angry tear crawled down his cheek. "It was the only way to save the children. The only way we knew how. The Cold Winds took so many from Ealdspell. The Kingdom would perish without the magic of children. By the time we perfected the spell, it was too late. So many children had already perished. But the few we saved?"

"I dinnae want to hear more." Félip's voice trembled and he grimaced to hold back the flash flood of pain roaring through is body. Stumbling back a step, he said, "Another lie. All faeries do is lie and manipulate!"

The horrific caws of angry, weeping blackbirds shook the trees again, this time louder, closer. He could almost hear the gusting wing-flapping rush of the soul hunters—hundreds of them, by the sound of it. And yet, the terror of their nearness paled in comparison to Gellynor's confession.

Gellynor's spectral form yanked back, as if being pulled. "My time is up."

"Aye, go then. I should have died eighteen rotations ago, anyway."

"Félip Batten MacKinley, you need to hear this—"

"Go!" he screamed.

Gellynor's entire corporeal body deflated as sorrow lined the angular planes of her face. "Stop walking the shadows long enough to meet your shadow-self, nephew. Then learn to walk within the shades of light."

From the west, a swarm of black devoured the mist and swallowed trees as the sluagh approached. The Thin Place darkened and rumbled. Ghostly leaves rattled like bones and the wind howled the cawing fury of demon souls. Félip threw his arms over his head and crouched low, unsure of what else to do.

Félip . . .

The wind's raspy voice whispered his name.

Regret choked his soul, clutching his pulse and immobilizing his body. Threads of images spun in his mind, of his mither's soft touch, his faither's perseverance . . . and Aroreh's song, just for him. Tears wanted to fall and his fists wanted to fight. But more than anything, he didn't want to be a monster—not in the mortal plane, not in the Land of Mist, or The Beyond.

Félip . . .

"Run!" Gellynor's fading voice bled through his terrified haze.

Félip sucked in a steadying breath as Gellynor became swirling mist, and then he dashed to his feet and ran.

. . . it was even whispered about the court, that she [the Queen] had Ogreish inclinations, and that, whenever she saw little children passing by, she had all the difficulty in the world to refrain from falling upon them.

"The Sleeping Beauty in the Wood" by Charles Perrault, *Tales of Mother Goose*, 1697

CHAPTER 19

AROREH

Faeries gathered close, whispering, pushing, staring. Appointed guards kept the insatiably curious fae from dangerously pressing in close. Despite demands to leave, the faeries remained and watched.

Gedlen paced between the cottages shadowing where Gellynor lay beside Félip—tranced—with Tyllie on her chest, also tranced. Aroreh had awakened in a panic, terrified of what she had seen and confused on why the prince needed her. But she wasn't prepared for what she now faced.

Unable to touch him, unable to contain the tears weeping down her cheeks, Aroreh shielded Félip's body with her own, afraid he might shatter with any accidental bump by the circling crowd. The Death Talker roamed the Land of Mist in search of Félip's soul. And if dusted, then he would truly die and Aroreh knew a piece of her would die with him.

Guilt ached and writhed in her gut. This was all her fault. She sucked in great, heaving breaths, wanting each one to be her last—instead of his. And instead of the last breaths of innocent children forced to work in filthy factories. Blissfully unaware yesterday, she had carelessly chased sunbeams while entire families suffered in Rothlín. She laughed and played and watched the stars with a handsome boy while babies cried for their smiling mothers to spare them a scrap of unspoiled food.

Her mother was right. When she dreamed, she destroyed the magic around her.

"I am despicable," she choked out. Furious tears dripped off Aroreh's face and splashed onto his cheek, crystallizing upon impact.

"You are not to blame for this tragedy," Gedlen said.

Aroreh's entire body shuddered with anger. "My mind does reason this, but my heart disagrees."

"A breaking heart weeps for answers and a battered soul aches for relief. Do not confuse the two."

Was it true? Did her soul, in her heart's breaking, profess wrongdoing to relieve her building agony? Gedlen was prepared to kill her and now the prince lay near death. Why would she trust anything he said? And yet, she could feel the old programming bashing against the circle of stones in the garden of her mind. The stones that protected her true magic. But the wild emotions lashing at her pulse pled a sacrifice of some kind. Her hands balled into fists. She wanted to beat on Gedlen and scream until she tired of it.

Instead, Aroreh ignored the Fate Maker and focused only on Félip. Her garments rippled over the young man in a slight breeze and froze at the hems. She was careful not to brush any part of her exposed body across his, or her skin might blight as well. Perhaps even her blood. But she yearned to touch him, like she had in the temple, like she had wanted to in the wood. The memory of her body pressed to his in the meadow shivered through her—the feel of his arms around her waist, the warmth of his hands on her back, her cheek flushed against his rapidly beating heart. Starlight had bathed him in midnight blues, moonlight in alluring whites and silvers.

With a trembling finger, she pretended to trace the frosty curve of his cheek, the freckled area across his nose, and then just over the slight cleft in his chin. His riot of wavy hair had frozen like dancing blue flames of ice. He was so handsomely boyish, as though a part of him were a wild, rascally faerie child, the rest an embodiment of stubborn resilience, laughter, and twirling, embered sparks of fire.

"You survived, when many had not," she whispered for his ears alone. "Survive again, lost prince."

Dark images from her dream—the wailing children, the programmed smiles, the women whose fingers bled in the factories—cloaked her waking mind in sorrow. Félip was to teach her more ways of light and shadow, to track and hunt, and help her regain the power stolen from her at birth. She couldn't imagine a world without his voice. Even now, his song of freedom beat like war drums in her veins.

"You shall have your new once upon a time." Her heart drew in a shuddering breath, and then she echoed his words to her. "I won't let you lose it."

A horn sounded from outside the village. The fae stilled in the silence that followed and pointy ears tilted to the wind. Gedlen's eyes cut first to her just before a booming voice sliced through the village sounds.

"We're under attack!"

Gedlen shot to his feet. The faeries crowding her and Félip scattered like beetles under a rock exposed to sudden light. The shrilling ring of steel and thundering stomp of marching boots spilled out of the golden forests around Leaf Curl. Gellynor's body shook, her eyes rolling to the back of her head. Gedlen knelt beside his sister and whispered into her ear, taking her hand in his. The mischievous faerie blinked her marigold eyes then rested her gaze on Gedlen.

"I found him," she rasped out. "The sluagh . . ."

Gedlen seemed to pale at his sister's words. "We must move him to a safe location."

"He might dust, if moved!" Aroreh cried out.

The elf met her panic-stricken gaze. "You have my oath. The prince will not join his ancestors this day."

Warriors dashed by where they crouched. Shouts rang out all around her, and mothers grabbed children and rushed into nearby cottages.

Aroreh slowly sat back on her heels, reluctantly nodding her understanding.

Gedlen grabbed a male warrior and spoke instructions she couldn't hear. Together, they removed their upper armor, followed by their tunics. Aroreh would have looked away, but she was too terrified that any movement would shatter the boy who made her heart sing. Gently, they wrapped their tunics and under-armor over their hands. Then, as though a well-choreographed dance, the two males cradled Félip and slowly carried him into the gilded room. The precision of their movements struck Aroreh and, in such a way, she knew this wasn't the first mortal they had saved from the Cold Wind's frostbite. She followed them into the gilded room and watched, helplessly, as they lowered Félip's frozen body onto the bed of moss and wildflowers. The other warrior left shortly after, dipping his head at Aroreh on his way out.

"Gellynor," her brother called out. When his sister approached the bed, he said, "Seal Félip and Aroreh inside, then hide the cottage—"

"General!" A female warrior shouted from the doorway, cutting off Gedlen. "Palace guards are now in the village! And taking our children!"

"Why the children?" Aroreh stumbled back a step, the blood rushing from her head.

Gellynor placed a hand on Aroreh's arm to steady her. Neither twin answered her question, but she already knew the answer. Leaf Curl stole the queen's daughter and so the queen would steal from the Dúnælven. And the queen would use the dreams of innocents to power The Dream—her dream—and increase spindle tree and textile production. The anger stoking inside Aroreh's belly spilled out to her pulse and set her heart on fire.

Unwrapping the tunic and under-armor from his hands, Gedlen began to re-dress. Seeing this, the warrior fetched Gedlen's gilded leathers before leaving, her sword raised. The Fate Maker gathered his long hair and twisted it into a warrior's knot atop his head, then sheathed two swords across his back. Brandu settled on his shoulder with a caw and fluffed his wings, as though flexing muscles for a fight. Dark purple runes decorated the air as Gellynor manipulated the symbols, but her eyes continually wandered back to her twin. Worry creased the space between her brows and pinched her lips.

"I'll be fine," Gedlen said, when catching his sister's troubled gaze. "Must we discuss your worry each time I march for battle?"

"If you make me walk planes again today, I'll push you into The Beyond myself." Tyllie hooted behind Gellynor. "She'll help me."

"I love you too," he said with a humored grin. To Aroreh, he bowed and said, "Do not fear your own strength, little queen spun of sunlight. The earth, water, and sky watches over you."

Aroreh felt her panic rise anew as the faerie dashed out of the room, followed by a jaw-snapping yawn. She hadn't slept long, and exhaustion tugged hard at her eyelids. It didn't help that a headache now bloomed behind her swollen eyes too, pounding whenever she moved. But she must remain awake, or she could harm the Dúnælven who currently fought her mother's guards. They didn't wear gilded armor like the faerie twins.

Armor . . .

A wild thought hit her, the idea so bold she clapped a hand over her mouth to hold in the excited gasp. Aroreh pivoted toward the bed of leaves and wildflowers. Sweet briar roses wilted near the edges; many had frosted into ice where fragile petals and stems touched Félip. Then she noticed something odd. Aroreh squinted her eyes and slowly approached the blighted Prince of Glenashlen. He wasn't wearing his cloak. Her eyes darted around the room, her pulse thrumming loud in her ears. On the ground, beside the bed, lay his enchanted Cloak of Light and Shadows. She gathered the garment into her arms, turned it to the enchanted side, and then plucked a handful of wilting sweet briar roses from the bed.

"What are you up to?" Gellynor asked over the shimmering purple runes.

Aroreh shrugged into Félip's cloak and lifted the hood. "I must free Rothlín."

"The queen will enslave you once more." Gellynor's eyes widened. "We're under attack!"

Aroreh melted into the candlelight and dashed toward the only exit before Gellynor could grab her by the cloak.

The chaos outside threatened to spear her resolve. But she would be brave. For the children of Rothlín and Dúnælven, she would fight, even if she faced the point of a sword to free them.

Peering over her shoulder, she took in Félip's frozen body and whispered, "Come find me." Then she fell into a shadow and ran.

CHAPTER 20

FÉLIP

F*élip*...
The dark wind's raspy voice whispered his name again. Sweat dripped from his face as he ran. If he wasn't so terrified, he would laugh at the absurdity of a soul sweating in the Land of Mist. The Thin Place might be the strangest experience of his life, or death. Och, he didn't know what to consider this state of existence. How is one in-between?

Mist slithered across the color-dimmed landscape. The glow of mushrooms clustered around various trees and reflected off the ghostly fog in eerie ribbons of blue and green. A black cloud of ravens haunted each of his steps. Their weeping caws shuddered down his spine and rattled his bones. Félip leapt over a fallen log and hit the ground in a jarring thud. But kept running. He felt like a little boy all over again, running from the older lads who had tormented his childhood. Anger surged with the memory and he clenched his jaw. The damned scar on his cheek was spell woven. He suffered for a faerie blessing he never asked for. If not for Gedlen Fate Maker and his bloody riddles, Félip would have died as a wee babe and reunited with his dusted family.

Now he did laugh. A bitter, furious laugh. Here he was running for his life while lamenting on how he hadn't died already.

What did Gellynor mean by his shadow self, anyway? He already knew how to walk in shades of light. Well, at least, he could. He was better at shadow, always had been. Would he even have time to unravel her faerie riddle? Bloody elves. Spinning pretty words and weaving confusion. If Gellynor wanted him to survive so fecking much, why didn't she just tell him how to fight the sluagh? Unless a soul couldn't do so.

The ground beneath his feet began to rumble. Shadow wings darkened his path—the *only* shadows in his cursed place.

Félip . . .

He couldn't outrun them. He couldn't outrun the hatred and poverty in Rothlín either.

Coughs wracked his dust-choked lungs. The muscles in his legs burned. The muted-colored trees melted away and the moss became iron-tinted dirt. Rusting textile factories rose up on either side of him, the smoke of coal furnaces now slithering between his legs instead of spectral fog. His malnourished body ducked beneath drying garments strung between the factories. Wash women screamed when spotting his disfigurement. A rotting vegetable hit the side of his head and he stumbled a step. Angry tears pricked the back of his eyes.

"Scat Blight!"

"Rules are rules."

Félip wiped his face and shouted, "I'm not a monster!"

A door slammed open from the side of a factory. Félip's gaze snapped onto the red-faced man snarling in the doorway. "Where 'ave ye been, Blight? The floors dinnae sweep themselves. Get in 'ere and start work'n or I'll garnish yer faither's pay."

Laughter spilled from the wash women and their beautiful spell-woven smiles contorted their grime-smudged faces into wicked delight. Fury trembled through Félip at the sound, a quaking roar of flames that painted his skin with shame.

"What are ye gaping at, Blight?" The man spat. "All yer kind are the same. Ungrateful and lazy. Against me good senses I offered ye a job, even though the blessed Aisling shuns ye. And this is how you repay me mercy, Blight?" The veins in the man's face visibly throbbed as he clenched his teeth and threw a full-body work uniform at Félip's feet. "Get to work!"

Félip painfully swallowed against the knot in his parched throat. The factory rooms were suffocatingly hot from the furnaces. Nobody cared that a Blight like him dangerously overheated in these mandatory uniforms. Or that his skin itched and blistered from the coarse material.

"Ye think yer better than me?" Spittle flew from the man's mouth. "How about I garnish yer mither's wages too?"

"No." The word quivered off Félip's parched tongue.

The man sneered. "Yer mither should 'ave left ye in The Wilds as a wee bairn fer the wolves to find. The selfish cow. Aisling should shun her ugly face too."

"No." Rage billowed in his belly and curled out to each limb.

The wash women laughed louder, their programmed smiles growing even more twisted and beautiful.

Félip . . .

The raspy wind no longer beckoned but cooed his name in dark pleasure. Shadows writhed across his face and down his body—new shadows separate from the winged creatures overhead. Tears continued to sting his eyes. The ghost of Aroreh's touch traced along his frostbite scar and he shivered. He could almost hear her whisper to him, her song-touched voice speaking to his grieving heart. *You survived, when many had not.* The sunlit words chased at the carrion shadows clinging to his shame. *Survive again, lost prince.*

"She doesn't know her own mind."

Félip spun toward the voice. A pale elf with pupiless black eyes grinned at him. Raven feathers formed the sleeves of his obsidian robe and tufted from his oily midnight hair.

"The princess is programmed with gentleness, good cheer, and the wit of an angel," the male continued. His voice was eerie, as if his rustling words were formed by the rushing flap of many wings in flight. "She isn't capable of being cruel to your kind."

"She's capable of anything, ye rank flap-dragon."

The male threw his head back and laughed. Félip shuddered at the rotting darkness inside the sluagh's mouth, darker than the lips spread wide in humor. "You are a desperate, delusional fool." The decaying Malfae Underfolk stepped closer, his sharp fangs bared. Félip's eyes darted around for an escape and froze. The factories, they were gone. The muted-hued forest surrounded them once more. Mist swirled around their legs as if the very breath of the dead. "We have come for your blighted soul, Félip Batten of Glenashlen."

A dark cloud of ravens swooped in from the west and swarmed the neighboring grove of trees. Limbs rattled and charcoal-colored leaves shook free, dropping into the mist like black tears. Weeping, anguished caws screeched over the landscape and called to the shadows still writhing over Félip's body. Was this his shadow-self surfacing? For thirteen rotations he had known only hopeless misery, until he returned to Dúnælven. Until he touched the light Aroreh captured from the sun. She was beauty personified, a dream—inside and out. And he the nightmare.

"You were selected by the goddess to pay for the sins of your dusted ancestors," the sluagh crowed in delight.

"All lies, ye maggot filled corpse." Félip balled his hands into fists. "The Dúnælven spared me from the Cold Winds. I scarred from the magic. No more."

"So, you were just told by the Death Talker." The male angled his head, similar to the other blackbirds around them. "The Kingdom of Ealdspell feeds off the dreams of children. Of course, the faeries wanted to keep you alive. The Dúnælven don't really care about you or your foster parents. Only their own survival and the eternal balance of life and death." The male angled his head the other direction. "And those who can harness the dreams of children for themselves? They possess a magic unlike any other. Powerful magic. Shadow magic."

Félip's breathing grew shallow as he listened. Did the male speak of the queen? Did she work for the sluagh? He knew the answers. Still he asked.

"Were ye once Malfae, dark elf?"

"You can either join us of your own free will," the male said, ignoring Félip's last question, "or we'll eat you until your unforgiven soul is consumed." The ravens broke into excited chatter and Félip covered his ears at the piercing sound. A black grin stretched across the decaying elf's unnaturally pale face. "You've been lonely and unwanted for so long . . ."

Icicle claws scraped down Félip's spine and the tiny hairs on his arms stood on end. The shadows writhing over his body practically begged him to relent and join the horde of sluagh. What else did he have to live for, anyway? His foster parents were cared for and Aroreh's heart had never belonged to him, despite betrothal contracts and Fate Makers and foolish longings. She had only wanted to play in the wood. Her girlish whimsy and laughter a reaction to their games of hide-and-seek, nothing more. Every touch was a caress of pity, every smile flashed his way naught but feminine programming to stroke his masculine pride. Another bitter laugh left his knotted throat. He didn't have any pride for her to please. Only stories of what he should have become. Though, if he were honest, it was those very origin stories that had sparked a tiny ember of empowerment all those wretched years in Rothlín. A speck of light all his own in a world of cold shadows. "Light," he whispered under his breath. *Lad, ye horse-kicked eejit.*

"What is your choice, Félip Batten?"

"MacKinley, ye ken?" He lifted his head and glared at the male. "My name is Félip Batten MacKinley."

The sluagh cocked his head again. "Your name is meaningless. Like you."

"My name is all the light I have left."

"A despicable name only whispered in shadow."

You survived, when many had not.

Anger re-stoked in his belly and billowed out into his raging pulse. "I am Félip Batten MacKinley, lost Prince of Glenashlen and Dúnælven, fostered son of Rothlínian Castoffs. My name holds the light of three realms."

"You are nothing and no one has or will mourn your death."

"The Dúnælven planted light inside of me, to thaw the frozen world I was born into."

The male's black eyes glittered. "You can't even thaw yourself, Shadowling Prince."

Félip's lips curled into a mocking grin. "And I suppose ye can? With yer glorious promises of eternal decay and torment? Tempting. But ye'll have to eat my manufactured goddess forsaken soul, if ye want it."

Wickedness curled the dark elf's lips.

A raven shrouded in dark mist flew down from a nearby tree and landed at Félip's feet. A stab of pain shot up through his foot. Then another stab. Félip watched in horror as the bird pecked at his shoes, its bill piercing the leather to his flesh. Scenting his injuries—and his fear—more ravens alighted into the air and circled him. Some pecking at his ears and eyes, others his back, arms, and legs. He screamed as he crouched and covered his head. Curse his hot-blooded ego and the never-ending restless need of his to pick fights! The male sluagh cawed loud with laughter, cawing louder whenever Félip screamed in terror.

Survive again, lost prince.

Félip pulled inward and focused on that tiny speck of light. The way the warm beam illuminated happy memories. How motes of dust from rarely used areas of his heart and mind twinkled and glinted to life in the golden glow. He didn't need a faerie-made cloak to walk the light and shadows of his life. No, he slipped into the wee sliver of light on shaking legs and an even shakier mental grasp. The sluagh pecked at him, taking chunks of dignity and pieces of his soul. The pain was unbearable. But he wanted to live. He wanted to wake Rothlín from the nightmare they called a Dream. And he wanted to know the feel of Aroreh's lips on his. Stars, the very thought swooned heady circles in his mind.

Warmth trickled down his icy arms and legs before blooming bright in his chest. He was a man half-starved for warmth and hungrily reached for more, for whatever the light inside could spare him. His skin burned hotter, brighter as droplets of illuminated gold rolled down his body. A sluagh on his back screeched and flew off him. More frantic caws echoed in his ears. The liquid light coated his clothing and bare skin, forming an armor of sorts. The ground beneath him shook violently and then he felt himself yanked back, as if an invisible string was wrapped around his waist. Ravens alighted from his body in a thundering cloud of black feathers.

"What are you?" the dark elf asked him.

Félip rolled his eyes. "Were ye not listening? I told ye, I hold the light of three realms." His body was yanked back again, like how Gellynor was pulled back. "How else do ye combat the dark power of the Cold Winds? Didnae ken how to walk this inner shade of light until now, though. I'll give ye that one." Félip looked over his golden armor with a self-satisfied smirk. "Och aye, a rather convenient trick, if ye ask me."

The sluagh's eyes widened before he misted into a raven and flew off to join his fellow Underfolk.

Félip started to laugh, a ready taunt on his tongue, when he was yanked back again. This time, the invisible string pulled him through the Land of Mist, through Leaf Curl, over palace guards and Dúnælven warriors, into a gilded room, and kept pulling until his soul collided with his rapidly thawing body.

CHAPTER 21

AROREH

Aroreh hid behind a tree's shadow in the outskirts of the village. The smoke, the screams, and the shrill and clank of steel hitting steel tore at her tattered heart. Palace guards streamed by in a uniformed march. Children kicked at their assailants and sobbed, but nothing deterred the guards. Not even when a faerie child sunk her fangs into one's forearm—twice. The man only marched to the booted rhythm of his fellows, his shoulders straight, his gaze fixed toward Rothlín.

Rune whispered, she realized with growing horror. The palace guards were all rune whispered.

Hot tears dripped down Aroreh's cheeks. She pressed a hand to her midsection, but the souring nausea in her middle persisted.

More children were carted by, their little hands bound and tethered to others in row after row of vacant-eyed guards. Mothers wailed their children's names. The erosive sound tore at Aroreh's ears akin to rocks that wept a winter's snow melt. She allowed the tears to carve themselves into her memory—each name, each shattered scream of grief.

A gurgle caught Aroreh's sensitive ears—one far too close to where she crouched—and she whipped her head the other direction. Not ten paces away, blood dripped from a fae's mouth. A palace guard slowly withdrew his sword from the warrior's chest and then wiped the blood on the wild grass. Aroreh sucked in a sharp breath and bit back the scream worming its way up from her churning gut.

What if the guard spotted her? She needed to keep moving—

A zap struck her mind. The ache in her chest blissfully eased into numbness. Her shoulders rolled back, her chin lifted, a kind smile warming her lips. She softly blinked and considered the clear sky up above. Around her, mortal and fae fought as though mountain ogres before a feast of fresh kills. The scene was entirely undignified and Aroreh averted her gaze to more happy images befitting a lady—the ladybug crawling along a single blade of grass; the bird trilling a proud song of triumph; the red-capped mushroom at her feet, poking through a pile of brittle, gold leaves. A woman didn't belong in battle, but in the home caring for her children. For children were a gift from Aisling, their dreams her blessing to the realms of Ealdspell. Aroreh smiled wider as the little bodies were carried off to learn the ways of her goddess. Their tears of joy swelled her heart with gladness. She should go to them and sing lullabies until their minds quieted and their souls opened to the ways of Aisling.

The sounds of battle snapped her back to attention and Aroreh gasped in pain. The headache behind her eyes throbbed as hazy thoughts swam mercilessly around her head. The landscape faded into focus. In the distance, elven warriors struck steel with palace guards. Around her, the forest sang melody after melody. The haunting notes of leaves fell from trees to their forest-littered graves. Her body drowned in sensation, in everything and nothing, the sensations gaining strength as the world around her spun in a blur of light and shadow, earth and sky—and then stilled. Abruptly.

A roaring whoosh filled her ears and she squinted curiously at the strange dark streaks flying through the air in her direction. Had the guards seen her? They must have and thought her fae. Aroreh leapt out from behind the tree and ran, zigzagging in and out of shadows. Metallic rain hit the ground around her and pierced nearby trees. Footsteps clattered across leaves and over logs behind her. Terror nipped at her heels and blood pounded in her ears—blood she feared would spill at any moment.

Golden light moved through the trees and swayed across the ground. She could almost hear the scintillating aria floating down from the heavenlies. The shadows hummed, a low tune that lilted on the edge of a leaf's underside and grew in volume around fallen logs, large rocks, and from the side of trees hidden from the sun. This was her song of survival. And her feet itched to move to the rhythmic melody.

Then she noticed her error. The shadows had shifted and she had failed to angle her body within their protective folds. She started to adjust Félip's cloak but it was too late.

"Halt!" A man shouted and Aroreh peered over her shoulder. A palace guard raced toward her, sword raised.

In that same moment, a zap tingled in her brain and her body stiffened into a more regal bearing. "No," Aroreh gritted. The beginnings of a smile shook the muscles around her mouth. "No," she whispered harshly to herself. It felt as if iron poured into her body and shackled her into place. Each foot was heavy. But she stepped backward. Then stumbled back another step, her eyes riveted onto the guard who was ready to slay an unarmed woman—his future queen. She forced another step backward, the movement lighter, and adjusted her cloak to absorb the shadows and reflect the light of her present surroundings. Darkness quickly embraced her entire form and cooled her heated pulse. The guard slid to a stop and frantically looked around, a bewildered expression breaking through the programmed stoicism.

Aroreh drew in a ragged breath, spun on her heel, and ran. She was a wild hart all over again—leaping over rocks, gliding from one shadow and into the next—but this wasn't a mere game of hide-and-seek. Palace guards burst from the underbrush toward Leaf Curl, a war cry on their tongues. Aroreh nearly yelped but angled past a sliver of light and remained unseen. She could slip through shades of light but didn't want to risk being seen. Light, it seemed, was drawn to her, and she didn't know when The Dream would sink its claws into her mind again and force her into a happiness she didn't genuinely feel, despite her faerie blessings.

She skirted the meadow and past guards with children in their arms. Tears blurred her vision at their terrified faces. But she kept running. Rothlín and the Dúnælven both depended on her to reach the castle tower and stop the queen. Her breath came in short pants; the muscles in her legs burned. Sweat dripped down her forehead and into her eyes. But she kept going, only stopping to blend in with the marching guards at the Veil.

The faerie programmed gate into Leaf Curl lay shattered like glittering dark stars among the golden corkscrew leaves. Aroreh tried her best not to step on the glass-like purple substance, or whimper as she carefully stepped over human and fae corpses strewn across both sides of the Veil. Streams of blood drenched the forest floor and seeped into her boots, and Aroreh gagged, followed by an undulating wave of dizziness.

The Wilds spun all around her—golden trees, purple glass, the black and red of palace uniforms, the pale, lithe elven forms, their silvered steel. She staggered toward a nearby bush and bent at the waist as the contents of her stomach emptied. The humming melody of shadows grew louder in her ears, ruffling ever so slightly with the breeze. It was almost as if the shadows sang her name, a light, airy call to keep moving forward.

A zap sparked in her brain and tingled down her bone-weary body. The muscles flinched before straightening her back, squaring her shoulders and lifting her chin. *No, no, no!* Her hands balled into fists. She grimaced, trying to mentally shove The Dream away. But she was slipping. A numbing warmth trickled down her body and her lips curved into a smile.

Aroreh, her mother's voice soothed in her mind. *I'm waiting for you, Daughter.*

Happiness bloomed bright in Aroreh's chest and erased every ache and twinge of pain in her body. Her mother—she was waiting for Aroreh's return. Even though Aroreh failed to bring the prince to the temple.

The prince.

Aroreh felt her smile melting away. "Félip . . ." How did she know this name? Who was he? And yet, she couldn't deny the knowing pull in her stomach at the hazy memory of a handsome young man with a freckled nose and dark, earthen eyes.

Daughter, her mother spoke to her mind once more. *I need you. Come to me.*

An unseen force tugged at her body and pulled her forward. Then her legs obeyed the nudge and stepped around a fallen guard toward a copse of trees along the leaf-littered path. A woman, after all, should always remain subservient to her betters. Aroreh nearly skipped at the rush of giddiness bubbling up in her chest. Her mother was pleased with her.

Yes, come to me, her mother hissed in excitement. *I am waiting for you.*

Aroreh lowered the cloak's hood and lifted her face to a glittering shaft of sunlight. Melodious giggles escaped from a cage inside her chest to flutter free to the chirping birds above. The song twirled in her veins, a contented tune like the lyrical sway of buttercups and the chiming notes of a rainbow. Her mother needed her and Rothlín would soon be filled with magical children for the goddess.

The grin stretching across her face faltered. Something didn't feel right. *She* didn't feel right. Shadows hummed her name louder, almost a crescendoing wail. The songbirds above her head faded into the loud caw of a raven. Bodies blurred in her mind's periphery. Pale faces with blood. So much blood. Carrion birds hopped across the forest floor from one meal to another. Did Aisling rejoice in the willing blood sacrifices? And there were so many!

The screaming wails of mothers scraped at her warbling thoughts. Mothers, children, and unwed maidens were only protected when Aroreh obeyed. She understood now. Her obedience secured Aisling's blessings for others. The knotted sob clutching her throat broke free. Those poor faerie children and their frightened parents. To be separated so violently. How their hearts must tremble and ache. And it was all her fault.

Daughter, her mother's voice cooed in her head and Aroreh wiped at a tear. *I will purify you. Forgive you . . .*

She yearned to absolve her sins and bring others joy. No more pain. No more sorrow. Humanity's imperfections should remain asleep.

I'm coming, Mother.

"Princess?"

Aroreh lifted her gaze toward the voice. A white-haired elf with startling blue eyes strode her way. He stepped over fallen guards and warriors, worry creasing his brow. Bleating pain throbbed behind her eyes. Nausea hit her gut in sickening waves. And then the landscape around her came into sharp focus. Vacant eyes judged her from the forest floor, the warriors fallen like autumn leaves to their graves. Aroreh sucked in a sharp breath, eyes wide. A hand clapped over her mouth just as she screamed.

"Shhhhh!" Dalbréath hissed in her ear. "The palace guards will hear you, mortal."

Slowly he released his hold and she sputtered out, "Don't leave me. Please don't leave me."

"Why are you shadow walking?"

She wiped at a tear with a trembling hand, looking anywhere but at the blood-soaked forest floor. "To reach the castle tower unseen and block magic."

Dalbréath tilted his head. "Then I'll ensure your safety."

"Thank you." She drew in another ragged breath. "I fear my mind isn't strong enough to resist The Dream."

A soft smile touched the corners of the elf's mouth. "Oh, but it is, little queen. And that's why your mother is so terrified of you."

CHAPTER 22

FÉLIP

Félip's eyes snapped open to the gilded room and Gellynor, who hunched over spectral runes in the air, weaving spells. His body shook violently as he curled into himself. *Cold.* He was so cold. Glacial drips of water ran down his face and soaked his clothing.

"Welcome back to the living, nephew." Gellynor was by his side in a flash, then cradled his shivering body by placing an arm underneath his knees and his shoulders. "We need to quickly change you into dry clothes. I'm going to ease you up. The quicker you begin using your muscles, the better."

He couldn't speak from the clattering of his teeth. The room tilted and his stomach nearly heaved. Every stiff, convulsing muscle in his body screamed with the movements.

"There," Gellynor spoke softly. "I'm going to undress you. Don't fight me. Understand?"

"A-aye."

Carefully, she peeled away his layers of thawed clothing. He would feel shame, but he was too damn cold to feel anything else but the ice still coating parts of his burning skin. Nor could he move his limbs without assistance. Once bare, his body took on an entirely new type of shiver. The room's warm air brushed against him with each of her movements, and his body chilled into fresh goosebumps every time. From a cabinet a few steps away, Gellynor retrieved several cloths, a fresh tunic, breeches, and boots.

"Not sure these boots will fit." She tossed all but a large cloth onto the bed beside where he sat. "Hold still. This is going to—"

"Ow!" He flinched away from her touch and scowled.

"Need to get circulation flowing."

"I'm n-n-not used to another's t-touch, ye k-ken?" Félip angled his head away, embarrassed. For some eejit, head-kicked reason, admitting his sensitivity to skin-on-skin touch felt more shameful than sitting before her undressed.

"I know." Gellynor's voice was soft, sad even. "But we need to get your blood pumping out to each limb or you'll start losing body parts."

"Aye, th-then."

She continued rubbing his legs, feet, then chest and back—vigorously. Each stroke like sand used for smoothing out planks of wood. Gellynor grabbed an arm next and began kneading the rough-spun cloth into his shaking muscles. Time blurred by in a haze of clattering teeth and full-body chills then scalding warmth followed by sharp, pin-prick sensations in his limbs. But slowly his muscles relaxed as his circulation returned and body temperature rose. And he found that his ability to focus began to thaw too.

"Lift your arms up." He obeyed and she slipped a soft Elven-styled tunic over his head in shades of dark green with cinnamon-hued trim. The fabric felt heavenly on his snow-touched skin. A finger lightly tapped his lower, right calf. "Lift this leg." He did—swearing under his breath—and Gellynor maneuvered the breeches over his foot. She repeated the process on the other leg and then pulled up on the material until he was properly covered. "You can lace your own breeches, prince." She winked at him and a flush wormed its way up his neck and heated his face—again. As she swaggered away to a nearby stool, she said, "Frost may come and go on your fingertips and toes for the next few hours. Maybe even for a day or two. Runic magic can take longer to thaw than a body, depending on the nanotech."

"Aye, thanks. Where's Aroreh?" he asked while fumbling with

the laces. "I'm in her bed."

"Three things you should know." She paused a beat. "First, Leaf Curl is under attack. Second, the cottage is cloaked, but we think Cerwyn has shifted into this room to spy. Like how she rune walked Aroreh's system when the princess was in hibernation."

"What?" Félip's head snapped up. He leaned forward, his gaze sweeping about the room, and whispered, "She saw me . . . *naked* . . . just now?"

Gellynor snorted. "Maybe. Probably." Mischief twinkled in her marigold eyes. "Definitely."

"Feck," he muttered, his head falling back on his shoulders with a mortified groan. He didn't think he would want to plane walk again— ever. But there it was. He was almost ready to beg the Death Talker to make it so. Why was facing sluagh less terrifying than another faerie female seeing his frosted arse?

"I'll deal with her." The black-haired elf spun a purple rune in the palm of her hand, a smirk taunting the corners of her lips. With a flick of her finger, the rune disappeared into the air. "I've already hacked her code."

Félip yanked a boot on and busied with tying the laces, silently cursing the blush he knew still reddened his face. "Ye said three things I should know," he said to think on other things. "What's the third?"

"Aroreh grabbed your cloak, a handful of sweet briar roses, and left . . . without a guard."

His hands stilled. "She *left*? To hide in Leaf Curl?"

"No." Gellynor let out a slow breath. "She plans to free Rothlín."

"And ye just let her leave? *Alone?*" Félip grabbed the other boot and shoved it on, furiously tying the laces. He needed to track Aroreh's trail before the hag caged her daughter's mind once again.

"She's shadow walking!" Gellynor rolled her eyes. "Because *you* taught her."

"Aye, and I will not apologize. Might be the only thing that keeps her safe." Félip hopped off the bed and strode toward the door on stiff legs. "And I might be the only one who can find the lass."

Gellynor leaned her hip against the bed. "If Aroreh falls asleep to dream weave, which I think is her plan, she'll block all magic. You won't survive another freezing, prince."

"I have inner armor now. Dinnae fash yerself, ye fussy hen." He winked and Tyllie hooted. "Yer the spotted chicken. She's a fussy hen."

"Hoot!"

Félip grinned as he opened the door, "Och aye, Brandu is a featherless goose."

Tyllie chuffed a hoot and fluffed her feathers, as if pleased with herself.

"Earth, water, and sky be with you, Félip Batten MacKinley."

And with Gellynor's parting words, he slipped out of the cottage. Pride swelled in his chest over Aroreh's cunning bravery. Though, he still thought her a fool lass for running off without a shieldman at her side. Or someone to anchor her mind from The Dream.

Elves in leathers and palace guards in metal plating struck steel in nearly every patch of light and nearly in every shadow. Félip swore under his breath. He didn't have his cloak. He didn't have anything. Crouching as he moved, he dashed behind one cottage to another.

Mothers wept and pleaded the old gods for their wee bairns. Were the faerie children taken? Fury curled through his body at the thought and he clenched his jaw. That bloody hag should die a thousand deaths. And that would be a kindness compared to what Félip really wanted.

Spell weavers hid behind runic shields. Electricity crackled from their fingertips and discharged onto unsuspecting guards. Metal plating sparked like a lightning strike before dropping the guards to the ground in writhing convulsions.

Elven warriors carved the air with their weapons and filled the sky with their war cries. Across the village, Gedlen jumped from the training ring's wall onto the back of a palace guard, biting the man's neck from behind while plunging a dagger into the guard's gut. Blood dripped from Gedlen's mouth in a battle-frenzied grin as he moved onto his next victim.

Félip shuddered. He needed to cross through the fray to the training ring. A cold sweat broke out over his face. His heart thundered behind his ribs. His leg muscles bunched and then he sprang from behind cover and out into the open. Bodies moved in constant motion. Félip ducked as a sword swung over his head. Then he angled left when a palace guard lunged right. Spinning out of reach, he sprinted several steps farther. An elven warrior noted his presence and slid to his side to block an unseen blow. The training ring grew close. And miraculously, Félip slipped inside the gates unharmed. Arms and legs shaking from adrenaline, sure. But unharmed.

Crawling on hands and knees along the short wall, he reached the pile of practice leathers and weapons. He darted panic-stricken eyes over his shoulders while fastening on braces, guards, and a chestplate. Next, he found a sword belt and the sharpest practice sword in the dull and somewhat blunted lot. His shoulders slumped.

"Blight!"

Félip's head whipped up toward the cry. Really? The palace guards were eejits. "I'm blighted, not deaf, ye mewling dung minnow." Then he was on his feet and grabbed the man by his face to shove him back. The guard screamed something about an unnatural cold touch and dropped his sword. Félip released his face and glanced at his frost-tipped fingers. Huh. Seizing the moment, he said, "Ye might survive this fight, laddie, but ye'll not survive Blight Rot," ending with a grin.

Lifting his sword, Félip hopped over the short wall and paused to get his bearings. A different guard charged toward him. But instead of readying his sword, Félip lifted his hand and shouted, "I'll curse yer home! Blight Rot on yer life, on yer family!"

The guard froze in place, which Félip found ironically amusing. But he forced his lips to curl into a scowl instead of another humored grin. Then he took one quick step forward in a mock lunge. The guard staggered back, eyes large, a high-pitched, squeal escaping his barreled chest. Now Félip did laugh. The guard regained his balance and ran, screaming warnings to others of the "Blight Mage."

Gedlen caught his eye over the skirmish, dark brow arched. Félip wiggled his ice-tinged fingers at the elf, a crooked smile inching up his face. The Fate Maker replied with a toothy grin and a curt nod before jumping back into the battle.

Félip wanted to stick around and see the chaos unfold, now that a rare and legendary Blight Mage had joined the fight. But he needed to reach Rothlín and with haste. Aroreh was returning without the blighted Prince of Glenashlen. And the hag wanted a sacrifice for her temple.

Immediately upon the faerie touching the palace servants, they all fell asleep, that they might not awake before their mistress, and that they might be ready to wait upon her when she wanted them.

. . . the prince approached with trembling and admiration, and fell down before the princess upon his knees . . . And now, as the enchantment was at an end, the Princess awaked, and looking on him with eyes more tender than the first view might seem to admit of: "Is it you, my Prince," said she to him, "you have tarried long."

The Prince, charmed with these words, and much more with the manner in which they were spoken, knew not how to shew his joy and grati-tude; he assured her, that he loved her better than he did himself . . .

"The Sleeping Beauty in the Wood" by Charles Perrault, *Tales of Mother Goose*, 1697

CHAPTER 23

AROREH

Smoke and dust coated Aroreh's parched throat. The burn fields, left unattended in battle, now hungrily licked at the gold, orange, and red trees inside The Wilds. White ash covered every leaf in the spindle orchard and snowed over the smoke-stacked textile factories in Rothlín proper. Until this day, Aroreh thought the textile factories were crafted from rose gold. Seeing their actual condition, and not in a dream, ripped fresh horror through her tender mind. Condensation wept down the rusted walls to orange-red pools along the rutted industrial spokes as though tears made of blood. Aroreh stumbled down one such spoke as she wended her way through Rothlín toward the castle grounds, Dalbréath by her side.

Garments in blues, reds, greens, and purples fluttered like pennants in a sooty breeze. Children wailed and coughed. Dust- and ash-coated women smiled while stirring linens in large dye vats. Upon seeing her, they cried out praises and fell to their knees, pressing sweat-streaked foreheads to the street. Then Aroreh would remember the Cloak of Light and Shadows and slip away to remain hidden. Her heart simply couldn't handle their acts of adoration. Is this what she looked like to the Dúnælven and to those who couldn't afford Aisling's blessings? All smiles without care or concern? Without awareness of her own suffering or the suffering of others? What good are humanity's perfections if they fail to heal or bring prosperity?—

A tell-tale zap sparked her reeling mind and her body flinched out from a shadow and into the light. The muscles around her mouth trembled as her lips stretched into warmth and cheer. For the women before her worked hard to restore glory to Rothlín. Aroreh wanted to grab their hands and spin them in a celebratory dance, singing songs of thanksgiving. She took a giddy step forward when a handsome white-haired elf cupped her face and blocked her motion.

"Aroreh, resist," he whispered, lowering his hands. "You are stronger than the broken system that raised you."

"I am needed in Rothlín, kind sir." She attempted to politely side-step him, but the elf grabbed her arm.

"Not without me." The elf released his hold. "Let's get moving. Time to jump into the safety of another shadow, princess."

Aroreh didn't move, though, despite the elf's gentle tug. The word "shadow" jolted her mind and the rosy light haloing around her thoughts faded into yellows and browns. Confused, Aroreh studied the wash women. Blisters covered their hands from endless stirring. Their faces flushed over the steam. The screech of metal wailed in her ears, not the humming lullaby of softly clanking looms and whirring spinning machines.

Then she remembered: they were on their way to the castle tower.

Relief rushed through her. The forced smile plastered on her face relaxed and she loosed a trembling breath.

A corner of Dalbréath's mouth hitched up. "Ready?"

She continued to slip unseen through shadows while Dalbréath scaled factory walls nearby. They didn't meet much resistance as they worked their way down another spoke or even when passing the temple. The white, gleaming building now seemed oddly out of place in Rothlín's dust- and factory-smoke filled town square. Aroreh's disgust was bottomless, every new sight heralding another layer of grief and anger.

The castle's blue stone eventually moved into view. The tower's point could be seen, but most of the slated tiles were hidden behind swirling mist. She and Dalbréath jogged around the side, away from the main entrance to the garden.

"Do the briar bushes require a password?" Dalbréath asked as they approached the arched wrought iron gate.

Aroreh tilted her head. "I surely hope not—"

Before she could finish her thought, the soft crackling groan of a brambling limb skipped in her ears, as though the sweet briar rose bushes smiled. She had never thought to pair such a gnarled sound with smiling and the discovery elicited one of her own. Dalbréath watched her closely and she shook her head.

"I'm not addled. Simply smiling back at the briar roses."

"Right." He studied the thorn bushes dubiously. "They're smiling?"

"I do believe they like me."

The branches stretched and wrapped fingerling limbs around the wrought iron bars and pulled. The gate creaked open and Aroreh slipped into the gardens, waving Dalbréath inside. No guards in sight, they jogged toward the stone staircase at the far end, but Aroreh couldn't help but slow long enough to appreciate the large stone circle. Did they truly protect her mind? Just in case, she dipped her head into a bow, and then continued on.

"Halt!"

Aroreh spun on her heel toward the unexpected sound. Two palace guards marched out from behind apple trees, swords raised. Lifting the hood on Félip's cloak, she melted into a nearby shadow, almost afraid to breathe. Dalbréath didn't have the luxury of shadow walking, like her. The white-haired elf slid behind a pear tree, then a cherry. The palace guards turned in circles, brows pinched and clearly spooked. Did the guard search for her or Dalbréath? She wasn't sure, thankful that her companion remained unnoticed. Especially when he crept behind the guards, his footsteps softer than a whisper. Creeping closer and closer until his fingers could touch both guards' temples simultaneously. Dalbréath's mouth moved and blue sparked from his fingertips. Then the guards crumpled to the ground.

"Did . . . did you kill them?" she asked stepping into the light. The images of corpses strewn across the blood-soaked forest floor haunted her still and probably would all the days of her life.

"They're asleep." Dalbréath took the guards' swords and threw them into a nearby rose hedge. "You'll need soldiers and servants, little queen. We can't dispatch them all."

"Thank you." Tears blurred her vision. "Thank you for sparing their lives."

"I shall spare others too."

Grateful, she lifted a wobbly smile before facing the stone staircase and freezing. A strange sound came from the slitted windows. Almost as though despair weighted down the air pouring out from inside the castle, making it whimper. Trepidations spurred her pulse into a gallop once more though she approached in quiet, wary strides. Dalbréath slinked up the steps first and she quickly followed.

"Halt!"

Dalbréath rolled his eyes. "They need to stop announcing themselves," he muttered. Then he ran up the stairs toward the guard before the man could brandish his sword. A heartbeat later, the guard fell to the top landing in a clanking thud much like the ones they had left behind in the gardens.

Aroreh turned toward the narrow opening in the stone wall and flinched. A zap tingled in her head and spilled glittering warmth down her arms and legs. The ache in her muscles eased. Yet she clenched every single one she could still feel, clenching harder and gritting her teeth. Her lips wanted to smile, her shoulders wanted to roll back, and her spine wanted to straighten. But *she* wanted to resist even more. To anchor her mind, she moved toward the slitted window and peered inside.

Around a hundred mortal and faerie children were forced onto their knees. Three male and two female faeries walked among them, touching the sides of their heads before the little bodies slumped to the floor.

"The older children," a palace guard began, "would you like them placed in the cells beneath the temple with the others or in the dungeon?"

"Dungeon," a female answered.

More guards stepped forward and scooped up what appeared to be sleeping children and carried them to a cart.

Anger pinched the corners of Dalbréath's eyes. "Come, mortal. Let's hurry before the Malfae sense us."

As nimbly as possible, she and Dalbréath quickly climbed the stairs and entered a service loft above the Great Hall. Aroreh peered over her shoulder toward the children, then disappeared into the servant's hallway, keeping to the shadows. They crept down hallway after hallway. Dashed across one open room to the next.

Along the way, Dalbréath rune whispered palace guards and servants into a slumber, dragging them to corners or into side rooms. A drip of blood appeared from his nose and the pallor of his skin grew more pale and sickly each time he exerted magic. Even his steps grew fainter. She couldn't understand the ancient runic language he spoke. Strangely Félip understood runic and spoke Owl and Raven too. She peered over at Dalbréath curiously, who had stopped to assess activity in a nexus room of sorts.

"Did you teach Félip to shadow walk?"

"Yes," he whispered back. Two palace guards marched across the open room near the tower stairs before disappearing down a corridor. "My mother found him in Glenashlen's remains when searching for survivors. The prince was raised in my home until age five and then I was charged with his care while he lived in Rothlín. You wear my cloak, princess. The one I gifted to Félip a few rotations back."

"You didn't get a new cloak?"

"They're made from rare materials in a dimension not our own. Shadow walkers are chosen carefully."

She considered the handsome elf. "I don't recall meeting your mother."

"You haven't. She lives in the mountains near Clifstán now, caring for another lost royal. Princess Eirwen." He looked at her then, taking her hand in his. "The hallway is clear."

Another lost royal? She had never heard of a Princess Eirwen before. Even more strange, the name, Eirwen, came from a Rothlínian word for "white as snow." Before she could contemplate any further, Dalbréath tugged on her hand.

They dashed out into the open toward the tower stairs.

"Halt!"

The shrill of metal screeched in Aroreh's ears, as though a hawk hunting for prey. Four palace guards, swords raised, ran toward where they perched on the bottom steps. A fifth disappeared down a hallway, shouting "Intruder."

"Run," Dalbréath said. "And don't stop. Stay in the shadows." He tugged the hood farther over her head.

"Don't leave me—"

"GO!"

Dalbréath shoved her away from him before weakly jogging into a patch of torchlight. The palace guards paused only a blink before storming toward the white-haired elf. A sob quivered on Aroreh's bottom lip, a tear slipping through when Dalbréath whispered, "Run. Now," before angling past the guards and into a dark hallway.

She didn't move. Couldn't move, paralyzed by indecision and shock. Her eyes darted around, fear clutching at her throat until she grew lightheaded. Now alone, every shadow seemed to crawl and the flickering torchlight grew hypnotic.

Come to me, her mother's voice beckoned. *I will purify you.*

No, Mother.

She refused to listen to this traitorous voice. Peering up the long, winding staircase, she took in her surroundings as quickly as she could and then began climbing. Up and up and up. Her steps quick and soft, her chest gulping lungfuls of breath. The muscles in her legs burned and grew shaky. The stairway continued to wind up into the sky, a seemingly endless journey. Torches dotted the curving stone wall and brightened into larger flame with chanting commands to descend and retrace her steps back toward the temple. The crackling, hypnotic melody burned her ears. But she pushed onward, past the dizziness and past the fatigue.

Daughter, her mother's voice cooed in her mind. *Don't you want forgiveness?*

Aroreh pushed open a large hewn wood door at the top and stumbled inside the small room. Unable to walk another step, her knees gave out and she collapsed to the floor. Nothing occupied the space but the cobwebs stretched over the vaulted ceiling and draped along the splintered floor. The fiery sunset outside her window spilled pink, gold, and orange light across the stone walls. It was beautiful and she drank her fill, knowing this may very well be the last sunset she ever saw. But she couldn't tarry. Every heartbeat counted.

Dragging her legs behind her, she clawed her way toward the room's center. Tomorrow she would have turned sixteen. But she didn't cling to a tomorrow. Only this moment and the sacrifice she must make for Rothlín. And she hoped the korrigan was right and that her sacrifice would illuminate a new era for her realm.

Aroreh! her mother's voice screamed. *If you ever loved me, you'll obey me!*

A zap sent fire spiraling through her body and she flinched with a whimper. A pleasant warmth lapped over her tired, trembling muscles and eased the discomfort. She forced her arm to move. The muscles in her hand and forearm cramped. She grit her teeth and pushed harder. Her mother's Dream would win, she knew. Her mind was simply too tired. A smile crept up her face. A woman's beauty was more serviceable when she smiled, a familiar voice soothed in her ragged mind. More of her muscles relaxed and caved to the system taking over. But her fingers, stiff and quaking, fisted the briar rose petals in the cloak's pockets and brought the magical petals to her nose as her eyelids gave into the exhaustion.

Gnarled groans quaked the room, growing louder and louder. As though brambling thorn bushes crept through the slitted windows and along the floor and walls. Shouts rang from outside her door. Then the door shattered open. Metal shrilled and screeched.

"Where is she?" A voice called out.

"She's up here," another responded. "The thorns were enchanted to protect her."

The gnarled groans grew louder still, followed by a scream. Aroreh's eyes fluttered open just long enough to see a thorned bramble coiling around a faerie with scarlet hair and tightening until the screaming stopped. Then Leaves unfurled over her head and smiling roses bloomed around where she lay.

The fingers clutching the bouquet of bruised, wilted sweet briar roses relaxed on her chest and her heavy eyes drifted closed.

CHAPTER 24

FÉLIP

Félip squinted his eyes as they adjusted to the darkness and slowly, ever so slowly, he inched inside the temple. He could hear voices up ahead. Several voices, actually—male and female. But he couldn't see anyone. The Great Spindle Tree captured most of his view, as though the tree itself were the sun bidding the sky goodnight in a brilliance of dusty rose, garnet, and burnt orange leaves. Beneath the leaf litter, large, thick roots tangled over the mossy mound to dip into the pristine faerie pool. A truly beautiful sight, but he needed to inventory possible dangers while creeping forward.

Purple-hued runes scrawled across the ancient stone walls framing in the temple. Félip passed beneath the faerie code, cringing each time a hazy mist of lavender light brushed over his body. Without his Cloak of Light and Shadows, he had to rely solely on instinctual stealth.

Machines rumbled softly up ahead. Wires knotted up the wall and were strung along the ceiling to dangle down to the Great Spindle Tree and port into the trunk and various limbs. This is what he needed to destroy, not unplug like last time. Whatever Aroreh had planned, maybe this would grant her more time.

The voices hushed as he crept closer to the largest machine. His hand strayed to the hilt of his sword while he scanned the shadows for movement. Leaning forward to peer around the queen's manufactured goddess, he made out the outlines of a dozen shapes—mostly hulking frames. His sword skills were shamefully dull. He would need to act quick and leave even quicker.

"Aisling is pleased," the queen practically purred. "How many more children remain in the castle?"

"Forty, Yer Majesty," a palace guard replied. "We'll transfer them to the temple cells."

"All younger children?"

"Aye, Yer Majesty. The older children are in the dungeons."

The queen laughed low, a throaty sound that made the hair on Félip's neck stand on end. "Spread your men out, Captain. Finding the princess is now your top priority. She's probably with Milfae escorts. Kill her elven guards and then bring her to me for purification."

The guard shuffled on his feet. "And the remaining children?"

"Let sleeping children lie, captain. Finish moving them once the princess is found."

"Aye, My Queen."

Félip toed out of the shadow a smidgen more to better see the silhouettes near the machines. How did the queen know Aroreh was in Rothlín? Was she spell woven with tracking runes? Or did the queen use more sophisticated magic?

The captain of the guard bowed and marched toward the exit, all but one guard on his heel. Félip pressed himself to the wall and held his breath. Metal plating gleamed purple beneath the glowing runes as they passed. When the last of their footsteps could be heard from the exit, Félip tiptoed closer to the machines. One guard he could handle—maybe. Either way, it was far better odds than before.

"Prepare the ceremonial bowl," the queen said to the priestess. "Princess Aroreh is defective and no longer in service to the New Dawn Era."

"But the korrigan—"

"The people will believe whatever I tell them!" the queen roared, slamming the palm of her hand onto a machine. "Weave a new message for the faithful. Princess Aroreh has turned her back on their beloved goddess and spies for Dúnælven. Any act of contrition is a lie. And the price for desecrating the temple with lies is death."

"Yes, Your Majesty."

"And weave another message for the princess. Beckon her to the temple. Promise forgiveness if she obeys me."

The priestess bowed her head and then moved to the machine closest to where Félip crouched. Disgust coated every emotion blazing through him. Turning back to the large runic machines nearby, he studied the exposed motors and circuitry. Most of the parts were hidden behind a case, however. If he struck the machine with his sword, he risked electrocution. His gaze flit to the Great Spindle Tree. Most of the limbs were far too thick to break off and too high off the ground too. Still, he would try.

The temple wall remained shadowed beside the machines and priestess and curved behind the Mother Tree. Gradually, he stood from his crouch and began to scale the shadows along the ancient wall. The priestess busied with spell weaving messages to broadcast through The Dream. Sucking in his stomach and holding his breath, he slipped by the older woman unnoticed. The darker shadows were only a few paces ahead. He could do this. The guard stood sentry in the center aisle before the faerie pool. And the hag—

Where was the hag?

Félip whipped his head the other direction and sucked in a sharp breath. Gleaming, predatory blue eyes locked onto his, her body half an arm's length away. She smiled at him then, a grin both wicked and delighted. How did she move so fast from across the room? Only heartbeats before, she paced by the guard.

"Prince Félip Batten," she cooed.

A chill frosted his blood despite the wildfire blazing through him. His fingers curled around the hilt of his sword and pulled. Electricity sparked from her fingers and slammed his hand onto the wall. Then his other hand. His heart leapt to his throat and he cried out in fury. She was a spell weaver, he realized. *Of course, she is eejit!*

"How kind of you to offer yourself up as a willing sacrifice. I've been waiting for you."

"I've come to wake Rothlín from the nightmare ye dare call a Dream!"

Sharp pain ran through his palms, as if his hands were being nailed to the very stone. He yanked and yanked, a cold sweat breaking out over his face. The queen laughed as she waved over the remaining palace guard.

"You're a hotheaded fool, much like your mother."

His mither? She was a fiery lass? Pride flushed through his veins and he spat, "Ye mean, not a blood-leaching ogress, like ye?"

The man removed the practice sword at his hip and tossed it to the floor. Félip watched helplessly as his useless blade clanked across the stone. Satisfied, the guard's face split into a sneer, right before he struck Félip in the gut. Followed by another punch. Air exploded from Félip's lungs and he couldn't draw breath. Then he curled into the nauseating pain and cinched his eyes closed. Air finally hissed through his clenched teeth.

"I've come to wake Rothlín from the nightmare you dare call a Dream!" He raised his head, eyes narrowed.

The hag circled closer to him, head cocked. "Repeating yourself won't add power to your weak threat." her gaze sharpened onto his scar. "You are filth."

"Ye ken what I am," he heaved through ragged breaths.

"Yes, Milfae prince. And you served your purpose, for the Dúnælven and for me." Another wicked smile curled her lips. "Now you'll serve another."

Félip fought the hold, gritting his teeth. She watched him struggle for a heartbeat, then turned away with a throaty laugh.

"String him up."

Ice spiked up his spine to his fingertips. He could feel the blizzard gaining strength in his pounding pulse. Fisting his pinned hands, he yanked again, grunting. Every muscle in his body shook. Cold sweat continued to dew over his forehead and dripped into his eyes. The guard postured to swing another punch at his gut. Lightning fast, one of Félip's hands freed from the stone wall and he grabbed the man by the face before he could consider how he broke the spell.

"Yer now blighted," Félip seethed. And he swore frost formed in the air with his words. "Rot with the sluagh, ye worm-infested dog's arse!"

The man screamed and clawed at Félip's hands. Félip shoved his head then kicked the man in the groin with all the surging energy ripping through him. The guard flew back and smacked into the largest machine. The loud clatter of metal hitting metal echoed through the stone chamber followed by a thunderous crack. The priestess jumped back and gaped, the whites of her eyes growing wider. Sparks crackled and lit up the guard's metal armor. Then a miracle of miracles happened. A fire. Félip grinned as the machine burst into flame.

"No!" the queen screamed.

She rushed to the other two machines and pulled out cords ported into the Great Spindle Tree. The priestess joined her and together they started to push the metal structures away. But it was too late. The fire traveled down a wire from the large machine to one of the smaller two. A wire the queen had not unplugged. The machines exploded into blue sparks and purple magic. A scream—ripe with agony—scorched the temple walls. Fire licked at the priestess's ceremonial robes. The woman's screams writhed through Félip's tender gut and he flinched with the splash and hiss of water. Clenching his jaw, he tried to free his other hand again, before he caught flame too. The roaring heat already felt like it was burning his exposed skin.

The queen seethed, her chest rising and falling with angry breaths. "What have you done?" The words were a growl, and goosebumps fleshed across his arms and torso despite the searing heat. "What. Have you. Done?"

He rolled his eyes. "Ye want me to repeat my words to ye? Again?"

In two unnaturally fast steps, the queen was before him and struck his face. His head snapped to the side, one cheek scraping against the stone, the other stinging from the force of her slap. "Your death will be slow and I'll ensure Aroreh sees your mutilated body before I feed her to the crows!"

She laughed then, a cackling sound that made the fire leap and dance behind her. His head slammed to the temple wall. A starburst of pain bloomed from behind his head and spread outward down his jaw, neck, and shoulders. Ice surged in his veins and clawed down his spine. The hag had forgotten his free hand in her demented fury. A smirk darkened the corners of his mouth. He lifted his hand to squeeze her throat, hoping his frost-tipped fingers froze her windpipe shut—and halted. She staggered back a step, her own hands clutching at her throat.

Félip looked at his hand, confused. The frost was receding.

Flickering orange light caught his eye through a gap in his fingers. "Shite!" An ember had landed on his breeches and smoldered. He saw the flash of yellow before he felt the searing pain. The hag continued to grip her throat and gasp for breath. Félip tried to put out the small flame with his fingers, then started slapping his thigh. The wee flame winked out, thankfully. His shoulders slumped for a mere beat of his heart. But no time to rest. How did his other hand break free? He didn't know nor did he know how to summon ice at will. So, he yanked again, groaning with every quivering strain of muscle.

The queen screeched in runic, as though a wailing banshee. A strange ripple in the air breezed through the temple following the sound. The feeling was gentle, almost a caress. This couldn't be from the queen. The sensation was far too . . . pure. Weight fell off his body and his mind grew lighter—clearer—while a stardust of twinkling light seemed to coat his skin. But he saw nothing, not like when light armored his corporeal body in the Land of Mist. Still, afraid of what the queen might have summoned, he chanced a look her way. His mouth fell open and his heart spurred into a fresh gallop. Panic shuddered through his system so fast, he almost didn't register how his other hand had finally released and was now dangling at his side.

Was this Aroreh's doing?

The buoyant feeling in the air . . .

Magic had ceased. All the lies, the glamours—they shadowed before his eyes.

The bright colors once painting each leaf on the Great Spindle Tree deadened and curled. A green film billowed through the faerie pool like thunder clouds rolling across the sky. But it was the queen who captured all his attention, and all his current fear.

Long golden hair brittled into frizzy white. Patches fell off her scalp and clumped on the floor around the hem of her dress. Skin, once smooth and radiant, shriveled into wrinkles and spotted with age. Her once intense, glimmering blue eyes dulled and a sheen of milky white coated her pupils. She was now a hag—his insults proving prophetic. But it was the tapered, pointed ears that stilled the dusted air in his lungs.

She was a faerie. Ancient and malevolent.

Gellynor's speculation was true.

And he was pissed. No, enraged. Countless people had suffered from her glamoured lies. Countless children.

Grabbing his discarded sword, he marched over to the hag, prepared to run her through. But that would be too good a death for the likes of her. She lifted her hunched over, milky gaze at his approach. And instead of piercing the hag through her black heart, he dragged the blade's blunted tip across the fragile skin of her face. Blood trailed over her cheek and dripped down her face. She hissed and tried to move away, but he fisted her by the hair and held her in place.

"That was fer all the Blights ye tormented." Félip raked the blade's tip across the other cheek. "And this is fer the people of Rothlín."

"Félip!" a voice shouted. "Félip!"

Dark silhouettes appeared in the writhing smoke. Félip angled his head and squinted his eyes, his sword arm slowly dropping. Was this Gedlen? And an elven cavalcade? Relief flooded him and his sword arm dropped lower. The faerie general would know what to do with the queen.

His name was frantically shouted once more.

"Behind the fire!" he shouted back.

He was so happy to see Gedlen and an army of Dúnælven warriors, that he didn't feel the queen wiggle free of his hold or see how she was now quickly hobbling away until one of Gedlen's warriors caught her arm and swung her around.

"Mercy on an old priestess," she begged. "The prince gave me leave."

"No—" Félip began and was cut off.

"You live!" Gedlen clapped his back and flashed a canined smile. Dúnælven warriors poured into the chamber, weapons raised.

"The queen," Félip yelled over the fire's roar and pointed. "That way! She withered into an old hag!"

Gedlen's eyes darkened and he clenched his teeth. "Mælfallyn Galanmiel."

"Who?" Félip asked.

The general's eyes closed for a half a heartbeat. "She must have Rònan."

"Who the feck is Mælfallyn?"

"The Malfae hag, Queen of the Underworld." Gedlen drew in a tight breath. "The Druid and I had mistakenly believed her dead. You"—the general gestured with his head for two warriors to follow in the direction Félip indicated. "Bring the hag back you released."

Brandu leapt into the air with a caw and followed the elves.

A smile ghosted Gedlen's lips as his eyes wandered over the charred guard, the machines, the priestess floating face down in the slime-ridden faerie moat, and the dying Mother Tree.

"Where's Aroreh?" Félip asked.

"The castle tower, My King." The Fate Maker bowed and Félip

shivered at the title. "Follow the sweet briar thorns and you'll find your slumbering queen."

"General!" A warrior called out. "There are hundreds of children in cells beneath the temple and they're waking up."

"More children are held in the castle dungeons," Félip added.

Gedlen shifted on his feet. "And the hag Mælfallyn?"

"Gone," the warrior said. "We can't find a trail and with magic blocked . . ."

"Send half a dozen warriors to search for Mælfallyn's hag form, not Queen Líeh. I want you to focus on the children," Gedlen said. "Bring them up to the town square to be reunited with their families. Assign escorts to return our faerie children to Leaf Curl." The warrior turned and Gedlen grasped the female's forearm. "Dispatch a message to Dalbrenna. Princess Eirwen is in possible danger."

Félip paused at the sound of his faerie mother's name—foster mother, that is. The one who had found him as a wee babe. And the one who had raised him until the age of five. But who was Princess Eirwen?

"Go, Your Majesty." Gedlen leaned in close and whispered, "Faeries will grow sick without magic. Wake your queen."

Félip didn't waste another breath and sprinted out of the temple and toward the castle.

CHAPTER 25

ARÓREH

Clover cushioned the soles of her bare feet. The stone circle surrounded Aróreh and she drew in a comforting breath at the protective sight within her dreamscape. A breeze skipped through the gardens and ruffled Aróreh's long strands and braids woven with honeysuckle vines and violets. Her plum, asymmetrical gown flapped against her legs. One gentle touch of a stone is all it took and purple magic seeped from the base of the largest Menhir and twirled around her outstretched arms.

She was ready to find her mother now.

And she was ready to weave a new dream.

The sweet briar roses continued to creep over the castle grounds and up the stone walls. But they opened the gate for her as she approached. With a dip of her head at the enchanted thorn bushes, she stepped through the gate and ambled toward Rothlín.

Ash dusted beneath her feet. Rusted factories flanked her sides as though a walled fortress. The industrial alley clouded with steam, but she could make out feminine shapes in the silvered vapor, and she moved toward the wash women. They smiled while they worked, as she had seen before. Their hands blistered and children clutched their skirts. But a strange, blurry image wavered across their faces. A spectral double with eyes closed and heads lolled onto a shoulder as if asleep. Was this their slumbering mind? She stepped closer toward one, close enough until she could see each crack of dirt over the woman's sweat-caked face. Aroreh angled her head in wary curiosity.

Why did they not wake? Aroreh thought if she dreamed, she would slay the goddess and magic would cease. Light swirled around Aroreh's fingertip, a soft corded ribbon of sun, moon, and starshine. And then she understood. The Dream was no more, but Aroreh needed to illuminate the minds that only knew how to sleep.

Reaching out, she touched the woman's temple. "Wake up."

The wash woman blinked and her body slumped. Aroreh caught her beneath the arm and eased her to the ground. The smile on the woman's lips faltered, then disappeared into a frown. A little girl climbed into the woman's lap and nestled against the woman's chest saying, "Mither, mither," through hiccupped sobs.

"Thank ye," the woman said to Aroreh.

Tears lined the edges of Aroreh's eyes. "You are free, mistress. Go home to your family and heal."

"Me wee ones, they're hungry, Yer Highness," she said, weeping into her child's hair. "How will I feed me family?"

Aroreh considered the crates of rotting vegetables. Magic danced along her arms and fingers in twinkling wisps. As she had with the wash woman, Aroreh touched the crate of food and whispered, "Wake up." Leaves lifted toward the light and unfurled in healthy shades of green. Fruit plumped and shone in jewel tones. Rot blew away off the root vegetables and bundled herbs.

The little girl sprang from her mother's lap toward the food and snatched a red apple.

"Thank ye! Och, thank ye!" The woman wept into her hands.

"Take your fill of the food," Aroreh said before moving onto the other wash woman and releasing her from the spell as well.

She continued down the spoke, waking the minds of other women with the power of her own. Each time, she would heal the crates of food and sometimes even heal a hunger-sick child.

Inside a factory, Aroreh touched each woman, even if their minds weren't sleeping. She even touched the foremen and broom-sweeping Blights. As with the wash women, the people would slump over. Some collapsed to the floor with weakness. Some even fainted. Her message was always the same. "You are free. Take your fill of the food. Go home to your family and heal."

In the corner, children sat sorting, washing, and combing through wool to process. Their wiry frames shook with each cough. Sweat beaded on flushed faces, some already covered in boils. Aroreh approached, her heart weeping for their pain. Magic continued to swirl around her arms and fingers, though the twinkling runes grew dimmer.

"Are ye sick, lady?" a little boy asked her through wet coughs. "Yer lips are turning blue."

"No, little one." She brushed a lock of limp brown hair from his eyes. The magic on her fingertips caressed his fevering face. "I shall find healers for you, though. The best in Ealdspell."

"Fer me?" The little boy's eyes rounded. "What about me friends?" He pointed at the other children.

"For them too." Aroreh didn't smile, not wanting to mock his pain. "You and your friends are free. Go home to your mothers and fathers. They have food waiting."

"Food?" His eyes grew even rounder. "Thank ye, lady!"

Aroreh watched as the children abandoned the wool and followed the men and women out of the factory. Dizziness flooded her head until her body swam in the lightheaded haze. But she forced herself to stand on weakened legs and leave the factory. Guilt tore at every beat of her shredded heart. The pain, the sickness, the suffering in Rothlín was far too much for her to wake. She would need help. Perhaps Gedlen or Gellynor would take over once Aroreh passed on to The Beyond. But Aroreh couldn't die just yet. She still had one more task and needed all her remaining strength.

She stumbled along the streets, heaving in lungfuls of dusted air. The temple gleamed up ahead and anger boiled in her gut at the sight. Another dizzy spell rushed her head and she started to lose her balance. Lowering herself onto a bench in the town square, she focused on regaining her strength. Melodies drifted to her ears. The sliding notes of worms crawling through the earth beneath her feet. The tinkling chimes of steam. The airy chortles of a happy blue sky.

Earth, water, and sky . . .

The songs of nature lifted the beat of her fading pulse and warmed the cooling blood in her veins. More sounds joined the rest and she moved her head toward the nearest factory. Men and women streamed out the doors in steady currents, weeping and embracing one another. Then another factory. And another. Freedom hummed from every shadow and laughed from every shade of light. They were waking each other now.

Aroreh pushed off the bench and staggered toward the temple. She could finish now that she knew her people were safe. How they woke each other? She couldn't say. But it mattered not. All she knew was that she needed to find her mother. Not for forgiveness or purification, but to end any possibility of The Dream starting up again.

Wheezing, Aroreh stepped into the temple and shuddered. Black smoke billowed past her, whispering for her to run. The ancient stone walls lay bare and dark. A memory surfaced. The morn of Spindle Day, when she had attended the Great Spindle Tree with song and a handsome young man had disrupted The Dream and awakened her mind. The runes had faded into the walls, like now.

She moved through the soot and smoke, her breath ragged and tight. Up ahead, the machines lay in charred piles. Embers winked and glared from crevices. A few small flames remained. But her mother was nowhere in sight. The entire chamber was empty and the hair on her arms lifted as she looked around.

The faerie pool now resembled a stagnant pond. The decaying stench was overwhelming too. The greened water retched over and over again, and Aroreh's stomach clenched with growing nausea. The faerie pool was poisoned all along. What did the waters actually do to a person? And how could the vomitous grime purify one's soul?

Her horror only grew when she took in the Great Spindle Tree.

The bark peeled and molded. The leaves, once vibrant and containing the sunset's fire, now brittled and curled, the colors browning. Rothlín needed this tree. A gift from the Dúnælven to help Rothlín recover after the Cold Winds, spindle production now depended on seeds gifted from the Mother Tree's dryad. Closing her eyes, Aroreh centered her mind on The Wilds, and on the haunting notes of falling leaves to their earthen graves. Perhaps the Mother Tree needed to grieve after the queen tormented it for so long. How could a tree spirit thrive if sick and fed poisoned waters?

A song simmered up from her soul. A song she wanted to sing several weeks ago but didn't know how. Opening her eyes, she drew in as deep of a breath as her dying lungs would allow and let the sorrowful notes pour from her body. Tears slipped down her cheeks. Her legs trembled with grief. But she moved closer to the Mother Tree, toward the tiny foot bridge near the far wall. The limbs began to sway and the leaves shook. So she sang louder, shoving every emotion she felt into every note quavering free from her cold lips. The magic spinning around her arms and fingers grew even fainter until she could only see the occasional flash of lavender-hued sparkles. She stepped off the bridge and over a rambling root. But she didn't get far.

Aroreh's legs crumpled beneath her, her feet unable to take another step. The haunting notes escaped her lungs in a melodious death rattle. She was a leaf, falling toward her earthen grave. A sad smile flitted across her lips as The Wilds filled her mind.

Songbird, a tear-stained voice called out to her. *Wake up!*

"Come find me, Félip Batten MacKinley," she whispered to the black smoke.

Then she hit the ground, hard. Fiery pain shot through her limp body, as if her nerves were on fire. A flash of golden-white light dotted by twinkling purple runes wreathed her curled-up form and she blinked. Magic flowed from a blue-tinged hand resting on the trunk of the Great Spindle Tree. Was this her hand? The world around her was fading along the edges of her vision. But what a sight to see as one died. The trunk, limbs, and leaves shimmied into a golden light that illuminated into every shadow and spilled into the faerie pool. The green evaporated almost instantly until only clear, sparkling water remained.

"Little queen spun of sunlight," said a gentle voice, like the soft rustle of leaves.

She slowly blinked again and tried to focus on a faerie with tree-barked skin and vined leaves for hair. The dryad in her dream took her hand in hers and began singing a beauteous melody. Pain and sorrow floated free from Aroreh's body to be cradled by the golden leaves and glimmering light. She wouldn't wake. But hopefully her sacrifice had illuminated a new era in Rothlín.

They were free.

Aroreh smiled as the song carried her into peaceful slumber.

CHAPTER 26

FÉLIP

Félip sprinted into the castle, sweet briar roses snagging his leathers and ripping his breeches. He darted past armored palace guards, who turned and gave chase. But he didn't slow to fight. The clogging streets of Rothlín had slowed him down enough. The people were free from the hag's mental claws. And they claimed visions of a beautiful woman before tasting freedom. Félip reveled in the swell of pride he felt for Aroreh. But if she continued to sleep, the Dúnælven would sicken and possibly even die without their magic. And how long could Félip's inner-armor last too? He better not find out.

Frightened children cried from the Great Hall. How their wee hearts must tremble. Gedlen's warriors would arrive soon and escort the lads and lassies to the town square. Already, mithers and faithers were weeping for their bairns around the temple and calling out their names. Would they storm the castle?

Félip skidded into a service lobby and slowed his steps. He turned and considered each hallway. Thorn vines slithered down each path, further confusing him. In a high sing-song voice, he said, "Wake yer queen, Félip Batten MacKinley," ending with a roll of his eyes. "Bloody faeries."

"Caw!"

"Och aye, go down that one ye say? *Which one?* There's four hallways!"

210

"Caw!"

Wait. He was talking to a raven. Félip twisted toward the window. Brandu perched on the stone sill and cawed again. And for the first time, Félip could honestly say he was glad to see the fae demon's featherless goose. "Lead the way, then," he encouraged the bird.

Brandu leapt off the windowsill and swooped down a hallway to Félip's left. Sword lifted, Félip followed, swearing at every thorned snag and cut. His legs would be riddled with injuries if every hallway was crowded with sweet briar roses like this one.

Down hallways and through other service lobbies, they passed what appeared to be sleeping servants and palace guards tucked into shadowed corners. Why did they sleep but not others? He brushed off the disturbing thoughts as he wound down yet another hallway and into a torch-lit corridor.

"Caw!"

Félip pivoted on his heel and blocked a thorned strike. Another vine lifted and swung his way. He ducked, then tumbled away from another sweeping vine. Scrabbling to his feet, he carved the air with his blade and lopped off a flowered head. The bramble creaked in pain and curled around its injury. Brandu flapped in Félip's face then flew down an adjoining corridor. Félip didn't need any further encouragement.

They continued in this pattern, winding through the castle and dodging thorned vines. Until they reached the tower stairs and horror halted his steps. Bloodied faeries and palace guards hung from vines coiled around their broken bodies. Félip's eyes darted around the shadowed corners. Spindly sweet briar rose brambles groaned and creaked, slithering across the stone floor and lifting as though a snake ready to strike. Shouts echoed behind him and his muscled tensed. The palace guards were still giving chase. Brandu cawed for him to run and hide. But Félip knew it was pointless. The vines would still see him without his Cloak of Light and Shadows.

Slowly, Félip laid down his sword at his feet and lifted his hands above his shoulders. A thorned limb coiled around his ankle and he swallowed painfully against the thundering pulse knotting his throat.

"I dinnae wish Queen Aroreh Rosen harm," Félip entreated. "Gedlen Fate Maker sent me to wake her."

Another vine slid up his leg and he sucked in a shaky breath. The thunderous clomp of boots ricocheted off the stone walls joined by a chorus of voices shouting "Halt!"

"I'm Félip Batten MacKinley, lost Prince of Glenashlen and the . . . Dúnælven King. I'll show ye." He closed his eyes and pictured the golden light that once armored his body. He could still feel the glittering warmth in his veins despite the dampened magic from Aroreh's slumber. The vines loosened around his body. Félip opened his eyes, nearly weeping in relief when the brambles retreated into the shadows. Roses opened and bloomed on the exposed vines trailing up the stairs. "Thank ye." Félip bowed. "Queen Aroreh's protection will not be forgotten." A limb nodded its flowered head at Félip before pushing him toward the staircase while another limb thrust his discarded sword back into his hand.

Strange how the limbs remained enchanted despite Aroreh's rules of magic. Perhaps they carried inner armor that was tied to her survival, regardless if she were awake or asleep. With another gentle nudge from the flower head, Félip dashed up the first tower spiral. Behind him, boots skidded to a stop and the screams of men reverberated off the stones, followed by the crunch of bones. Félip shuddered and pushed down the bile worming its way up from his gut.

The spiraling staircase seemed endless. Brandu continued to fly ahead as Félip followed the flowering vine. The more flowers that bloomed, the sleepier he felt. Perhaps he fatigued from the dampened magic. He wanted to rest a spell but knew that would be dangerous. So, he continued forward.

Up ahead, Gedlen's familiar swooped down and landed on a strange lump in leathered armor. Faerie armor. Félip slowed his steps and crept up, his chest panting for air and sword at the ready. Disheveled white hair draped over the elf's face. Blood had dripped from the male's nose and pooled onto the step. But the sweet briar roses had oddly left him intact. Félip knelt before the faerie and brushed the hair from the male's face.

Dalbréath.

Did he live? Félip felt for a pulse, relieved when a steady rhythm pushed back against the two fingers he pressed to Dalbréath's neck. At the touch, the elf's blue eyes peeked open into heavy-lidded slits.

"I'm fine," the elf rasped. "Wake the little queen."

"Ye make an ugly sleeping maiden." Félip pretended to shudder.

The elf weakly lifted his hand in a rude gesture. "No one is as beautiful as me, arsehole."

Félip laughed, then peered at a large briar rose. "Protect Dalbréath. He's a brother to me." The flower head dipped in understanding.

In a teasing voice, Dalbréath asked, "Do you actually care for me?"

"Aye, Dog Breath. I suppose I do." Félip grinned, patting the elf on the cheek.

Dalbréath closed his eyes. "The blooms keep her asleep . . ."

Félip waited for more, but the elf had blacked out. Would the briar roses make Félip sleep too?

"Let's go," he said to Brandu.

Leaping over the white-haired elf, Félip continued his journey upward. He could see a partially opened large door from where Dalbréath rested. And he kept his yawning gaze fastened to the splintered hewn wood with every step until he could touch the iron ringed handle. Félip pushed against the door's broken hinges, his heart galloping anew. The heady sweetness of flowering vines was thick, the brambles even thicker. Nearly every inch of stone was covered in red and pink roses, every flower dusted in golds by the waning sunlight.

"Please," Félip said to the vines, "Leave this room so the queen may wake. She is needed, ye ken?"

He didn't expect the enchanted roses to listen to the likes of him. But the wooden floor beneath his feet began to rumble. Groans and creaks roared in his ears, growing only louder. Brandu cawed and circled the tower rafters while Félip anchored himself in the doorway. Flowers disappeared into the thorned limbs before the very vines crept out the narrow windows. The air cleared and Félip felt like he could breathe again. Even his mind cleared from the sleepy haze. But in the retreat, he still couldn't see Aroreh.

"Wait!" The vines stopped moving. "I need petals. A good handful."

The brambles continued slithering out the window. A stone dropped in his stomach and his shoulders dropped. They wouldn't help him. Félip began unbuckling his leather armor. If they wouldn't spare petals, he would use his tunic to find Aroreh. He feared stepping on her and harming the lass. His chest plate fell to the tower landing in a clank. Then his forearm braces. He started to remove his neck guard when the last vine creeping out the window stopped. Félip bowed his head in thanks and continued unfastening his neck guard. But the vine remained. Dropping his neck guard, Félip lifted an eyebrow at the bramble. The enchanted plant shuddered, then several roses bloomed and burst into a spray of petals. With a final shudder, the vine disappeared over the windowsill, Brandu angling through the window behind it.

"Thank ye!" Félip inched along the edge of the curved wall, careful to test his steps before moving forward. He reached the petals and scooped them up. "I will find ye, lass," he whispered and tossed the petals in front of him. They fluttered flush to the floor. He scooped them up again and repeated the process as he shuffled slowly toward the center. He released the petals again and watched as they landed in the shape of a bundled body. "Found ye," he whispered, falling to his knees before her.

Brushing along the form, he found the cloak's hood and pulled back until Aroreh's white-blonde hair and pale skin moved into view. "Wake up . . ." He caressed her cheek, pulling down more of the cloak and stilled. Her lips were blue. A mountain of fear rumbled and quaked inside his heart. Then his fingers found the cloak's ties and unlaced the wool, sliding the garment from her body. "Please live," he choked out. "Please, lass. Dinnae leave me." He checked her pulse and heaved a sharp breath. She wasn't dead. Her pulse was weak, but she wasn't dead.

Félip gathered her into his arms and cradled her in his lap. "Songbird, wake up!" Still she remained limp. He tapped her cheek. Nothing. So, he lifted her hand and slapped her palm. Still nothing. "Aroreh," he wept into her hair. "Sing fer me again. Please." Fear scraped down his spine and grief owned every sob-filled breath. She was dying in his arms. "Wake up!" He shook her shoulders so hard his gritted teeth clacked. "I found ye! Wake up!" She slumbered still.

His grip loosened and he studied her face. The world could be shattering like glass all around him, each shard tearing into his body, but he could feel or see nothing but the broken and fading girl in his arms. Quiet fury settled in his bones. And guilt. He should have run the hag through. She lived but her daughter was dying. His fingers tucked a stray strand of hair behind her ears. His gaze drank in her soft lashes, the curve of her cheeks, the fair line of her nose, and her parted lips. Even tinged blue, her mouth held the beauty of a song yet sung. And he wanted to set that song free.

"I dinnae live to take yer throne," he whispered across her skin. "Rothlín needs your keen mind and yer gentleness." Tears slipped down his cheeks. "Ye give me joy, Aroreh Rosen. I need yer laughter."

Out the window, a bright flash of white-gold light lit up the sky and beamed through the tower's east window. Félip threw an arm over his eyes. The light was far too intense. Did it come from the temple? The brightness strobed and then waned, and Félip lowered his arm to find a shaft of golden light trailing across the floor as if searching for something. But Félip knew what and his pulse flushed with hope. She was happy. Even in near death, the sun was drawn to her radiance.

The gilded beam rested over where he sat holding his queen, Rothlín's future.

"I want new beginnings with ye," he whispered to Aroreh. "But first ye need to find me."

Twinkling purple runes glittered from the golden light and danced across her limp body.

"That's it," he said, unable to stop the stupid grin. Aye, he was a fool lad for her. "Find me, lass. Chase after me in the shadows toward the light."

The purple magic spun around Aroreh faster than a spinning wheel. Her fair hair danced and her dress rippled over his arms. Rose petals and golden leaves twirled through the air and rained down on their bodies. Where did the gold leaves come from? He didn't have long to think on such oddities.

Blue eyes blinked open and Félip's tears dried into laughter.

CHAPTER 27

AROREH

Air rushed into Aroreh's lungs. Then her eyes fluttered open to a face she found more beautiful than any in all Ealdspell.

"You live," she said, unable to stop her laughter. "I feared I had lost you."

"I'm too stubborn to die, ye ken?"

"I hid and you found me." Mesmerized by his handsome smile, Aroreh reached up and traced a finger along his scar.

His smile faded into a shiver as his lashes lowered under her touch. "Aye," he breathed. "I would fight armies, monsters, and hack through the thickest thorn bushes just to find ye again."

"Félip—"

His kiss silenced every word forming on her tongue. And, she swore, she had never known magic until this moment. His fingers slid into her hair and his palms cradled her face. Lips, warm and soft, danced across her mouth and invited hers to play. But before she could, he gently lowered her to the petals and leaves strewn across the wooden floor and leaned over her body, his gaze caressing her face and his fingers entwining with hers.

"I want to kiss ye until I cannae think straight. But we need to talk first."

Aroreh touched her mouth in wonder, taken with the way his hair fell over his eyes and the flush of his lips. She was unsure how she would focus on anything but him but nodded her head for him to speak anyway.

"Rothlín no longer slumbers," he whispered. "The Dream is no more and yer mither disappeared."

The music of his voice carried away her heart and she melted into his song of freedom.

"Without magic," he continued, "The queen turned into an old Malfae hag."

Aroreh's brows wrinkled. "An old hag?"

"Aye. Named Mælfallyn."

"My mother is a Malfae hag?" her heart sank.

"She escaped," he continued, and she was grateful that he pressed on. There was simply too much to process. "Gedlen believes she's on her way to Clifstán, for a Princess Eirwen."

"Dalbréath mentioned the lost Princess Eirwen. Who is she?"

Félip simply shook his head and lifted a shoulder in a shrug.

"And the children?"

"All free, lass. They're reuniting with their mithers and faithers in the town square. The faerie children are on their way back to Leaf Curl too."

Tears blurred her vision. "My heart can rest now."

"I saw a light from the temple," Félip said. "The machines were already destroyed. Was that ye?"

Aroreh smiled again. "While dreaming, I freed a dryad imprisoned within the Great Spindle Tree by my mother. Oh Félip, she was beautiful! Her magic was oddly unaffected by my slumber."

"The sweet briar roses too," Félip added. "They must have inner-armor."

"I would have died if not for the dryad," Aroreh continued. "As thanks, she healed me and I gifted her all my programmed faerie blessings save my sunny disposition. She told me I must keep that one." Aroreh cupped his cheek, butterfly wings softly fluttering in her middle. "I can sleep now without harm to myself or others. Isn't that wonderful?"

He leaned into her touch, then his eyes dipped down to her mouth and lingered. "Ye shadow walked through battle, fought yer program‐ming, and risked yer life fer Rothlín, fer Dúnælven. Ye are the stron‐gest and bravest woman I know."

She flushed under his praise. "Dalbréath helped me."

Félip's face twisted up humorously. "No speak of Dog Breath, lassie. That's twice now."

She laughed and the sunset's lavender and pink light brightened the room. Dust motes glinted and sparkled gold and fell around where they lay. Félip watched everything with a sharp eye—the light, the dust motes . . . *her*. Warmth trickled down her body in a pleasurable rush. The butterfly wings fluttered faster. And the light pulsed even brighter. Félip's attention drifted away from her toward the window, his brow furrowed curiously as he watched a beam of warm light slide across the floor toward them. Biting back another laugh, her fingers felt for the petals and leaves at her side and clutched a handful.

"What's this?" Félip asked, staring at her fist, his eyes narrowed playfully.

A delighted giggle sprang free and she blew the petals and leaves into his face.

"Och!" Félip batted at the leaves. "Ye wee imp!"

"I—"

Once more her words were lost to his lips upon hers. She still sputtered with laughter, making him smile. Then her happiness deep‐ened into an emotion she couldn't name. One she had never felt before until now. Was this love? A heady, whirlwind feeling as though one might fly away to live among the moon and stars? His kiss slowed to an achingly beautiful melody that drew the very breath from her soul and rewrote the beating rhythm of her heart. He leaned in closer to her body, but he still wasn't close enough. She remembered the feel of him when they tumbled in the meadow and how she yearned to touch him in the forest. Not caring if she were ladylike or if he thought her too forward, she rolled him onto his back until all of her pressed into all of him. Wild strands of russet-brown hair fell over his dark eyes, and the air fairly crackled when his gaze locked onto hers. She brushed the tip of her finger along the freckles on his nose, down his cheek, across his lips flushed from their kisses, to settle on the slight cleft in his chin. His eyes closed and he drew in a long, ragged breath.

"Yer killing me." His eyes slowly opened.

She frowned. "Forgive me, I didn't mean—"

"Aroreh . . ." Her name became a caress, a secret delight on his lips. And she wanted those lips to find hers again. And again. And again. "Ye're not harming me."

"Then why do I kill you?"

A lopsided smile appeared. "I die with want."

"Oh." Her pulse quickened with his confession. "Then kiss me, prince."

"Are ye begging me?"

She tried to bite back more laughter and failed. "Do you find my request not to your liking?"

"Nae, My Queen." He tangled his fingers into her hair and pulled her toward him. "If ye beg of me then . . ."

"I can see an open door!" Gedlen shouted from the stairs.

Félip's hands flopped to the stone floor with an annoyed sigh. "Kind of him to announce himself."

Aroreh stilled on top of Félip, eyes wide.

"Beg me another time," Félip whispered, ending with a wink. Stealing a quick kiss first, he gently settled her beside him on the floor and pushed up to a seat.

Brandu flew into the tower and softly landed beside Aroreh and cawed at Félip, who stuck his tongue out at the black bird. Gedlen and a few of his warriors spilled into the small room soon after. Both she and Félip looked up at the faerie with what she hoped was innocence in their eyes.

"Hail Queen Aroreh Rosen!" Gedlen knelt on one knee and lowered his head in a bow. "Long live the queen!"

"Long live the queen!" the warriors chanted in reply, including Félip.

"Rise," Aroreh quietly said.

Gedlen's gaze combed over her. "Are you well, Your Majesty?"

"Yes, I am well. Thank you."

Gedlen slid a sly look Félip's direction. "Yes, quite well from the looks of it."

The young man at her side rolled his eyes and Aroreh felt her face burst into flame. Did her eyes share of her moon-spun affection? But how could they not? She was fairly drunk on every look and touch shared with Félip. Mortified, she studied her hands to gather her thoughts and regain composure.

"Thank you for your service to Dúnælven, My King."

Aroreh's brows pinched together. "Service? King?"

Gedlen nodded. "He's the heir to the Dúnælven throne."

Her mouth fell open and she studied Félip as if for the first time. "Forgive me," Aroreh began, rising to her feet. "He is Milfae, then?"

Gedlen simply nodded his head. "And I am Malfae."

"Yes, little queen spun sunlight. Your mother is Mælfallyn Galan-miel, Queen of the Underworld, and you are the youngest daughter of the High Druid, Rònan Ó Macbea, and why your magic was so strong."

Aroreh placed a hand to her stomach. "There is far too much to process."

"Indeed," Gedlen simply said. "And I will tell you anything you wish to know about your father when you're ready."

"Thank you." Aroreh offered him a small smile.

"Something else you should know." The faerie lifted his hand for Brandu, who cawed before flying up to perch on the Fate Maker's forearm. "The Prince of Glenashlen was betrothed to a daughter born to House Rosen before your birth, as Fate deemed right. And through a union of light and shadow, a union made from choice, the first threads of balance shall spin to restore the Kingdom of Ealdspell."

She found Félip's dark eyes and held his bashful gaze. "Though Fate wove us together, I am still free to choose my happily ever after?"

"Yes, Your Majesty."

Without breaking their connection, Félip asked, "And I may re-spin Fate's wheel for a new once upon a time? No more hiding or se-crets?"

"Yes, My King."

"I choose him," Aroreh rushed out before Gedlen could leave. Félip drew in a tiny trembling breath at her declaration. "I choose Félip Batten MacKinley to reign by my side."

"I choose her," Félip parroted. "I want to help my queen usher in the New Dawn Era. The true one, ye ken?"

The warriors around them grinned and Aroreh smothered her laughter with her hand.

"We have much to celebrate," Gedlen said. "As will Rothlín. Come, little queen. The people of Rothlín await your return." The male pivoted on his heel and marched through the door, his warriors close behind. But Aroreh didn't move. Neither did Félip. Gedlen peered over his shoulder, a dark eyebrow arched high.

She wasn't ready to leave. So many words were left unsaid be-tween her and Félip. And she knew that once she saw the men, wom-en, and children of Rothlín, she would dedicate all attentions to their welfare, as well as repairing the land, factories, and orchards of her realm. Squaring her shoulders, she lifted her chin a notch, and spoke the language of give and take. Of striking balance within, without per-mission or fear of disapproval.

"I shall be there in a moment," she said to Gedlen. "I wish to speak privately with your king. We will not tarry long." The gener-al bowed with a knowing smile, then continued down the spiraling steps.

Once alone, Aroreh slowly turned toward Félip. The Cloak of Light and Shadows lay crumpled near his feet. He considered the cloak for a long blink. Then his lips twitched. But it was the rascally glint in his eyes that encouraged her to move. And to sing. Soft, sweet notes lilted from her in a slow dance through the night sky of her heart and she spun, the stars firm beneath her feet. The world no longer made music in her ears as before. But her heart more than made up for the melodies lost to The Dream. For now she truly knew Félip's song of freedom and the liberating rhythm of earth, water, and sky.

"I would ask you to dance," she said to Félip, barely managing to contain her happiness. "But I wish to beg you for another lesson." Kissing his cheek in a flurry of laughter, she then lowered and fetched the cloak.

"A shadow walking lesson, Songbird?" He took the cloak from her hands and wrapped it around her shoulders.

She clasped his hands and brought them to her face. "I am in love with you, Félip Batten MacKinley."

Wonder brightened his gaze and his mouth parted in a quiet breath. Before he could reply, she brought the cloak's hood up and slowly walked backward. Until the warmth of his fingers no longer tingled along her skin and until she knew the twinkling pink and lavender light hid her body from his. The moon-dusted notes continued to hum from her lips and sway through the air. Then, she twirled on her heel and dashed out the door, shouting behind her, "Come find me!"

"She knew the power of her own mind
and so programmed it for success"

Carrie Green

APPENIDICES

THANK YOU

I am not going lie . . . writing a funky twist to the *Sleeping Beauty* story is a longtime dream of mine. And I can't wait to add my weird-brain spin on other faerie tales too! If you're curious about the genre of my strange retelling, be sure to read the *Historical Notes* next.

Novels are funny things. We authors agonize over each word written, over our character's journey, over yours. We never seem to have a shortage of agony during the writing and publishing process. And yet, we rise to write again and again and again and . . . you get the point.

So thank you, dear reader. Thank you for giving *Of Dreams and Shadows* a chance. If you are so inclined, this eye-strained, coffee-addicted, keyboard plunking author would sure appreciate a review. Let other readers know of your journey with Aroreh and Félip. *wipes away grateful tear*

Writing a novel is a community event. I'm lucky to be surrounded by so many people who care about my success.

Myles Sundin: I love you. I find your shadows beautiful. Sorry-not-sorry that my lightheartedness makes you squint sometimes. *whispers* Come find me . . .

My children (Myles, Colin, Adrien): Never forget the power of your own mind. You are magic and this dark world needs your light.

MY BETA TEAM

Claire Rootjes: My fellow badass mistress of fiction, boothmate sister, and dear friend . . . I adore you exceedingly. I love your analytical brain, wit, and compassion. And your truth-seeking heart always inspires mine to dig deeper and wider. Who knew sword jokes could be so inspiring? Thanks for always supporting the awkward chaos that is me. To continued Comic Con shenanigans and fantastical stories! *MoonTree powers activate*

Tyffany Hackett: Your many talents never cease to amaze me, Lady. I'm honored to be a part of your incredible journey to authordom. And I'm humbled that you're a big part of mine. Thanks for your beautiful wisdom, lending me your strength when mine is failing, and for all the laughs. Ahem. I still think my blacksmith is bigger than yours *runs away and snickers*

Sarah Saulness: There is no one else I would rather lose my orientation with while walking in a forest than you ;-) *side-eyes Erik* Hee hee! Thanks, heart-sister, for always taking care of me. I love your integrity and authenticity and inappropriate humor and intelligence and . . . dammit, this list could go on forever. Bailey's Irish Cream for life! *lifts my coffee in solute*

So many others I want to name. SO. MANY. I am blessed by an incredibly supportive community of fellow authors, friends, family, and dedicated readers who continually share my work, comment on all my social media posts, and who give me virtual hugs exactly when I need them.

blows kisses and awkwardly winks

Jesikah Sundin

HISTORICAL NOTES

BY JESIKAH SUNDIN

Thanks, dear reader, for giving my Victorian industrial revolution, medieval dystopian faerie world, with a high tech twist story a try! *giggles* What did you just read, you ask? Allow me to extrapolate. Mythpunk: a derivative of cyberpunk that deconstructs a familiar faerie tale, myth, or folklore, mixing the nuts and bolts with unexpected genres/settings, before reconstructing all the story pieces into something "familiar" but "new." Mythpunk sometimes blends several myths and folktales together too. And, it employs postmodern writing styles. Basically, artsy often self-reflective writing styles through poetry, non-linear plotlines, and weirdness. If you've read my other series, *The Biodome Chronicles,* then you already know I revel in story weirdness.

And if you've read either *The Biodome Chronicles* or *The Knights of Caerleon,* then you also know I like to end my stories with historical notes.

clears throat

The Sleeping Maiden, famines, Black Death, and spindle trees . . . oh my!

The story of *Sleeping Beauty* has captivated me since I was a little girl. Not because of the princess and the prince. Well, okay. Yes. I do like them. But *really* because of the faeries. Evil faeries, no less! My first introduction to the idea that faeries aren't all cute and whimsical but *evil*.

I would be remiss, however, if I didn't confess that I adored Prince Phillip in the 1950's Disney animated movie. I mean, he held conversations with his opinionated horse and way before Maximilian arrived on the scene in *Tangled*. And he stood up to his father and said *no*, this is who I want, forget stupid marriage contracts. Which, as a young girl, I found thrilling. You mean a prince might like a simple girl from a simple world? Before he knew of Aurora's royal heritage, he knew he wanted to build dreams with her. So much so, he fought a faerie dragon and enchanted thorned brambles for the girl he danced with in the woods . . . once upon a dream.

And Aurora? Well, even from a young age I understood that she was denied a personal choice in *everything*. People often make fun of her for the crying scene, where she crumples at her vanity in tears. But think about it for a sec. She was raised in a secluded wood by faeries in a small cottage, no contact with anyone else, let alone another human like her. Never knew her parents or that she was even royalty. Then suddenly she's whisked to the castle and offered no adjustment period to even digest her life changes. And after arriving, she's told that she can't love who she wants because even THAT has been chosen for her and by people she had never met until that very moment.

She was *only an object* in a war for power. And yet she held all the power of life and death and Fate's ever spinning threads in the tip of her finger . . .

I was riveted.

And before anyone says she's mindless and boring, or that Aurora has no agency . . . let me remind you: the Disney story was intended for children. And children often feel like they have no say in anything. They're not wrong. Adults decide most things for children and then expect said children to accept all their decisions without any form of reaction. Unlike the adult. Because if someone did that to an adult, they'd have opinions. Cue the teenager! The young adult is discovering their agency, not only in the home but also in The Wilds of adult life. Which includes falling in love. And Aurora is a teenager. A young one too. Only fifteen in most stories.

This tale is probably one of the darkest in all the popular faerie tales too. Disney sanitized the origins CONSIDERABLY. Can't emphasize that enough. The folktale goes back to the Dark Ages and is linked to Norse Icelandic myths. However, the *Sleeping Beauty* tale didn't truly take off until *Perceforest*, a collection of poetry connected to the Arthurian Legend that gained popularity in the 16th century (though comprised in the 1300's) featuring a story about a Scottish knight (Troylus) who quests to wake an extraordinarily beautiful princess (Zellandine), a young woman who never woke up after mysteriously falling asleep while spinning linen. Long story short, bypassing Zellandine's eventual rape, the princess wakes after she gives birth. But only when her child suckles the enchanted sliver of flax from her fingertip. And thus, women are saved through childbirth.

Oh, and Zelladine is Lancelot's great-great-great grandmother.

Two hundred years after *Perceforest*, a 17th century man by the name Giambattista Basile, from Naples, Italy, wrote down what is attributed as the first national collection of faerie tales. *Tale of Tales* is so incredibly dark (inspiring the 2015 movie of the same name), I struggled to read through the *Sleeping Beauty* story, "Sun, Moon, and Talia." It's really rapey, including necrophilia, and just so patriarchy-vomitous that it was hard to stomach, even for research. But if you want a play-by-play commentary on this disturbing version, read this article (https://www.ranker.com/list/details-from-the-original-sleeping-beauty/genevieve-carlton).

Sixty years later, Charles Perrault published the *Tales of Mother Goose* for the French aristocracy. . . for *adults*, not children. Funny how trends cycle *side eyes adult faerie tale reader* And naturally he cleaned up the tale for the adults, because adults apparently can't handle rape like children. *gags at previous two versions* Perrault was a staunch supporter of the Catholic church and lived for the favor of French nobles, especially those who also supported the church. And so he wove in Catholic themes for good Christian women (like the sacrament of baptism and godparents via faerie godmothers christening the infant princess), cleaning up the stories to be safe for female sensibilities, and ended each tale with a "moral of the story" poem . . . to educate women on how to be virtuous. *clears throat and cues the poem at the end of his SB story*

THE MORAL

To get as prize a husband rich and gay.
Of humour sweet, with many years to stay,
Is natural enough, 'tis true;
To wait for him a hundred years,

And all that while asleep, appears
A thing entirely new.
Now at this time of day,
Not one of all the sex we see
Doth sleep with such profound tranquillity:
But yet this Fable seems to let us know
That very often Hymen's blisses sweet,
Altho' some tedious obstacles they meet,
Are not less happy for approaching slow.
'Tis nature's way that ladies fair
Should yearn conjugal joys to share;
And so I've not the heart to preach
A moral that's beyond their reach.

Remember ladies: you're only truly desirable to wealthy, happy men if you spend your entire existence perfecting your feminine graces and protecting your virtue.

PUKE.

Oh, did I mention the cannibalism? Yeah, a queen in both the Basile and Perrault stories want to eat children. In Basile's version the queen is the rapey king's jealous wife. In Perrault's version, she's the prince's mother, who just happens to be an ogress. Yes. You read that correctly. The prince in "Sleeping Beauty in the Wood" is half ogre. *looks at Shrek*

Here's a fantastic article by Tor on cannibalism and other nightmarish things found in the three early versions of *Sleeping Beauty* just discussed (https://www.tor.com/2015/07/02/cannibalism-and-other-nightmarish-things-sleeping-beauty/).

The Brothers Grimm tale, "Little Briar Rose," is FAR

better and closer to the Disney version we know. And unlike previous written versions, the princess wakes with a magical kiss from her prince aaaaaand she doesn't have to later deal with cannibalistic women who hate children. But . . . thank the Mouse Ears for Disney's version! Yes, still not the best representation of women. *Still* . . . the best well-known version yet.

As a side note: Prince Phillip in the Disney version is the first prince to be named in the *Sleeping Beauty* stories since Troylus in *Perceforest*. And he was based on the real Prince Phillip who denounced his title of Prince of Greece and Denmark and became a naturalized citizen of Britain before the official engagement announcement to Queen Elizabeth II, taking on the last name of Montbatten. The last name of his maternal grandparents. Before the wedding, he was given new titles, Duke of Edinburgh being chief among them. With Troylus being a Scottish knight and Phillip being the Duke of Edinburgh, I decided Félip would be Scottish-like, even have the Gaelic form of Phillip. And come from the royal House of Batten *winks at reader*

Circling back to 14th century northern Europe . . .

The 1300's endured one major catastrophic event after another. Around 1290, the European Warm Period (EWP) came to a sudden end. The weathered cooled significantly, marked with heavy rains and winter-like conditions, earning the title Little Ice Age. This resulted in "blighted" crops. Btw, "blight" is a fancy word for destroyed or rotting. A common example is "leaf curl" in certain fruit trees. *winks again* But I digress . . .

Thus began the Great Famine in 1315. Not only did crops rot, but a parasitic worm infested sheep that resulted in a seventy percent loss of sheep livestock across a good portion of northern Europe. *Seventy percent!* Hunger is a horrible way to die and often leads to madness. And in medieval Europe, this is exactly what happened. The people went mad, and the rate of crime (including rape), cannibalism, infanticide, and mass deaths increased at alarming rates. Parents left their children on the side of the road or in forests to die or sold them into slave labor for immediate pay. Puts a lot of faerie tales into perspective, doesn't it?

With population decline, there were fewer hands to work the farms, fewer soldiers for the church's Crusades (which were still going strong), or the church's cathedral raising. Don't even get me started on classism issues during this period. Needless to say, the combination of many terrible social, economic, and political factors put pressure on women to rebuild populations—naturally. It was their "duty" to restore the land to its former glory.

The Great Famine ended around 1317 (though some speculate around 1322), but smaller famines happened in the 20's, 30's, creating perfect conditions for the Black Death (aka Black Plague), which swept across northern Europe in the late 1340's—one of the most devastating pandemics of human history. The Black Death officially ended around 1360, but the damage was great. And the rate of crime, cannibalism, infanticide, and mass deaths increased to horrific rates once again.

Interestingly, scientists are not convinced the Black Death was caused by the bubonic plague after pathology studies, as most commonly believed. Many mass grave sites from the 14th century in the UK reveal high amounts of pulmonary anthrax, also known as Wool Sorter's Sickness / Wool Sorter's Disease. Grass-grazing animals, like sheep, are easily infected by the anthrax spores in the soil. But the bacteria (which can lie dormant for decades) is believed to have sprung to life with the weather changes. Millions of spores just floating in the air for people and livestock to breathe in. The common symptoms are extremely high fevers (aka the sweats), shortness of breath, coughing, bruising, and boils. Most people died within twenty-four hours. Sorting and preparing wool for spinning was a common job for children too.

Other mini famines continued through the end of the 1300's until the weather became *slightly* more favorable (though, not by much). But after a 100 years of misery, where Europe died (aka slept), the 1400's saw the end of the medieval era and ushered in the renaissance.

Perceforest was composed in the French countryside sometime between 1330-1345 . . . which puts some of the rapey, women are saved through childbirth themes into light. But it wasn't until the The *Tales of Mother Goose* that a maiden who slept for 100 years was introduced. The maiden, in my opinion, being metaphoric for northern Europe who saw all kinds of horrors and reigned triumphant in the end after bearing children (growing her population).

So, that's my . . . ahem, *spin* on *Sleeping Beauty*'s deeper metaphors. I haven't read this elsewhere. If you do, PLEASE share with me!

The Victorian Industrial Revolution and more blight

The medieval era introduced the spinning machine and the Victorian Industrial Revolution saw the end to homespun cloth as the norm. There are stories (even fictional stories of that era) of women who were thrust into deeper poverty when tailors no longer purchased their spun yarns, woven cloth, and tatted lace. Industrial machines were able to produce more and faster. And, thus, more cheaply. Similar to the famines and lung diseases of the 14th century, the Dickens era of industry carried many of the same problems. Except, this time from coal furnaces in factories and income loss when assembly line production shadowed the small business owner.

Also during this time was the Great Potato Famine in Ireland because of . . . blight. Potato Blight to be exact. This is partially why I made Rothlín an Irish-Scottish-like region. But also because Celtic faerie lore held that if a heavy frost came right after Samhain (Halloween) and destroyed unharvested crops, it was because faeries had "blighted" their crops. The Kingdom of Ealdspell is on a leaf and Rothlín is in eternal autumn . . .

The parallels between 14th century northern Europe, Celtic faerie lore, and the Victorian Industrial Revolution were too rich for me to ignore. And I thought they created a strange and beautiful dystopian backdrop for my textile realm, Rothlín.

Cyberpunk and, yet again, more blight

Just like the Victorian Industrial Revolution, the age of high-tech machines has taken over production. Robots are replacing human hands, and quickly. Small business is shadowed by mega corps, run by AI algorithms. Modern production takes assembly lines out of the factories and oozes the idea into white collar offices. Cubicle lands are essentially new factories. The Age of Machines is sometimes referred to as a "blight" to humanity's socio-economic future as well. It's a common enough reference in spec fiction.

I liked the idea of high technology linked to my medieval, Victorian Industrial Revolution inspired, dystopian world. Not only as a system of magic, but also to highlight the familiar. This is a world we know. A world we interact with on the daily. To me, it makes the faerie aesthetics of years past more poignant.

Spindle Trees

They are real! This is not a faerie tale tree. *Euonymus*, is a small shrub or tree (depending on region) named after Euonyme, the mother of the Greek Furies (aka Erinyes). And who were they? Three goddesses who were appointed to punish humankind for their crimes.

"The wrath of the Erinyes manifested itself in a number of ways. The most severe of these was the tormenting madness inflicted upon a patricide or matricide. Murderers might suffer illness or disease; *and a nation harbouring such a criminal, could suffer death, and with it hunger and disease. The wrath of the Erinyes could only be placated with the rite ritual purification and the completion of some task assigned for atonement,*" (https://www.theoi.com/Khthonios/Erinyes.html). Notice what I italicized? A rather Rothlín-esque problem, no?

Spindle trees are poisonous, hence the connection to Euronyme. And because the blossoms, leaves, and berries are poisonous (and well known to be so, even in the Medieval era), they were tied to "sleeping maiden" tales through the spinning tool of the same namesake. The fiery leaves and blossoms? Gorgeous. Truly beautiful. Google images so you can see for yourself.

But the real question: were meieval spindles actually made from spindle trees? Yes! Though this tree is slight in appearance, the wood is remarkably strong. So much so, the Norse (aka Vikings) carved spindles from a tree they named spindlebaum. The Irish Celts called the tree Oir, which is one of their ogham runes and a sacred druidic tree.

Later, spindle trees were used to make the first skewers and toothpicks, which were known as prickwood. Sometimes skewerwood too. Oxen yokes as well as the first matches were also made from this hardy deciduous tree. Spindle trees were even used in Medieval herbal medicine to treat cows and horses with mange.

Aaaaaand, that's it. Now onto writing book two of *The Ealdspell Cycle*, "Eirwen" . . . aka, *Snow White.* And yes, I'll have a weird world and genre mash-up there too!

To be continued . . .

Jesikah Sundin

GLOSSARY

Check out the Historical Notes at the
end of *ÆROREH* for more information.

Aroreh Rosen	(A-roar-uh) Queen of Rothlín, Eirwen's younger sister, queen consort of King Félip Batten McKinley of Dúnælven
Aisling	(Ash-ling) An artificial intelligence created by Queen Líeh to control the realm of Rothlín through a form of goddess religion. [Irish for "dream"]
Aye	(Eye) Yes in Irish and Scottish
Bampot	(Bam-pot) an idiot/fool in Scottish Gaelic
Blight	(Bl-eye-t) A child who was damaged by the Cold Winds with a telling frostbite scar. It is believed they can cause others to rot from the inside out with skin-to-skin contact.
Brandu	(Brawn-dew) A raven, Gedlen Fate Maker's familia -- Welsh for "black raven."
Cerwyn	(Sir-win) Faerie warrior
Charaid	(Caw-radge) friend in Scottish Gaelic

Clifstán	(Cliff-stahn) A realm in the Kingdom of Eald-spell.
Dalbréath	(Dahl-brey-ith) Elven faerie, Rune Whisperer
Dalbrenna	(Dahl-bren-nuh) Elven faerie, Huntress
Dream Weaver	Someone who can weave new realities while dreaming. What they do in their dreamscape affects the real.
Dúnælven	(Dune-al-ven) A realm in the Kingdom of Eald-spell, Milfae Faeries.
Ealdspell	(Awld-spell) A kingdom upon a leaf, an interdimensional realm of Éireanna and Earth. Ealdspell contains eight different realms (Dúnælven, Rothlín, Clifstán, Merenna, Avenbury, Dreglind, Aurelienne, Glenashlen).
Eejit	(Ee-jit) Idiot in Irish and Scottish
Éireanna	(Air-ran-nuh) Ireland; faerie dimension on Earth
Eirwen	(Air-wen) Lost princess—Welsh for "white as snow"
Faither	(Fay-ther) Father in Scottish Gaelic
Félip Batten MacKinley	(Fay-lip) King of Dúnælven, king consort of Queen Aroreh of Rothlín, nephew of Gedlen and Gellynor Faerondarl
Fer	For in Irish and Scottish
Gedlen Fate Maker	([g]ed-lin) Unseelie Prince, General of Dúnælven, the Fate Maker, older twin

Gellynor Death Talker	([g]ell-in-ore) Unseelie Princess, Master Spell Weaver, the Death Talker, younger twin
Korrigan	(Core-i-gun) A fairy or dwarf-like spirit. A creature in Breton folklore that often lived around rivers and wells and usually had long hair. They are known for behaving similarly to a siren and/or telling the future, like a Seer.
Líeh Rosen	(Lee-uh) Queen of Rothlín, royal House of Rosen
Mælfallyn	(Male-fall-in) Queen of the Malfae, Queen of the Sluagh
Malfae	(Mal-fay) Bad faeries
Milfae	(Mill-fay) Good faeries
Mither	(Mih-ther) Mother in Scottish Gaelic
Nae	(Nay) No / Not -- Scottish Gaelic, including the following variances: anaether, cannae, couldnae, dinnae, didnae, was nae, could nae, naebody, naething
Rònan Ó Conell Macbeatha	(Row-nun) High Druid and prince of Éireanna
Rothlín	(Roth-leen) A realm in the Kingdom of Ealdspell
Rune Walker	A faerie who can "walk" through various planes (like the In-Between, Otherworld, Underworld) as well as a faerie who can "walk" through another's glamoured mind to steal or rewrite spells.

Rune Whisperer	A faerie who can control another's bioelectric signal and nanotechnology with runic verbal commands. A form of faerie glamouring.
Runic Technology	The Earthen computer technology system the High Druid blended with elemental magic in Ealdspell.
Shadow Walker	A faerie who uses a rare enchanted cloak woven in Éireanna to blend into light and shadow and attack or sneak away unseen. A lesser Runic / Elemental magic in Ealdspell because of cloak material resource scarcity.
Spell Weaver	A faerie who can program and hack runic technology (for spell coding or weapon making)
The Dream	The program (glamour) that controls mortal minds through nanotechnology, created by Aisling, an artificial intelligence.
Tylluan (Tyllie)	(Till-shwan / Till-ee) A spotted owl, Gellynor Death Talker's familiar —Welsh for "owel"
Wool Sorter's Sickness	The medieval term for anthrax.
Ye/Yer/Ye're	(Yey / Yeyr) You, Your, You're in Irish and Scottish

MORE BOOKS

By Jesikah Sundin

THE BIODOME CHRONICLES

ECO-DYSOTOPIAN FAERIE TALE

She is locked inside an experimental world.
He has never met the girl who haunts his dreams.
A chilling secret forever binds their lives together.

LEGACY
ELEMENTS
TRANSITIONS
GAMEMASTER

THE EALDSPELL CYCLE

DYSTOPIAN FAERIE TALES WITH A HISTORICAL FANTASY TWIST

Dreams are dangerous . . .
Unless she unlocks the powers of her mind.
He fights his Otherworld shadow self.
And with only fae magic to re-spin their tales.

OF DREAMS AND SHADOWS
OF HEART AND STONE

THE KNIGHTS OF CAERLEON

AN ARTHURIAN LEGEND REVERSE HAREM FANTASY
Under J. Sundin

Four cursed knights. One warrior princess.
A faerie sword that binds their lives together.

THE FIFTH KNIGHT
THE THIRD CURSE
THE FIRST GWENEVERE

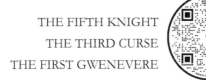

A HARTWOOD FALLS ROMANCE

CONTEMPORARY ROMANCES

Under Jae Dawson

MOONLIGHT AND BELLADONNA

HEARTBEATS AND ROSES

SNOWFLAKES AND HOLLY

THANK YOU
Happy Reading!

ETSY SHOP

A dash of moon magic. A pinch of tree laughter. Stories whispered on the wind.

Hello Etsy wayfarers! Welcome to my bookish shop. When not slouched behind a computer, cursing the keyboard gods, you can find me frolicking through the woods with a camera around my neck or on the Comic Con circuit as MoonTree Books. Have fun poking around at my wares.

BOOKISH WARES FOR SALE

- Signed Paperbacks
- Limited Edition hardbacks
- Book Swag
- Book Boxes
- Custom Character Candles

Scan the QR code to visit my store.

Have questions? Message me on Etsy and we'll figure out your next fantasy adventure together.

JESIKAH SUNDIN is a multi-award winning Dystopian Punk Lit, Fairy Tale, and Historical Fantasy writer, a mom of three nerdlets, a faeriecore and elfpunk geek, tree hugger, nature photographer, and a helpless romantic who married her insta-love high school sweetheart. In addition to her family, she shares her home in Seattle, Washington with a rambunctious husky-chi, a red-footed tortoise, and a collection of Doc Martens boots. She is addicted to coffee, GIFs, memes, potatoes, cheese, mossy forests, eyeliner on men, and artsy indie alt rock.

www.jesikahsundin.com
www.jesikahsundin.com/moontreebooks

Printed in Great Britain
by Amazon

15787605R00146